JUNIPER ROAD

Hal Duvall

ISBN: 1-4392-1333-X
ISBN-13: 9781439213339

Visit www.booksurge.com to order additional copies.

DISCLAIMER

DEDICATION

This book is gratefully dedicated to Anne Watson, whose unfailing encouragement kept the author at work.

ABOUT THE AUTHOR

Hal Duvall is a retired merchant who has spent his entire life in Cheraw, SC, where he lives with his wife. They have two children and four grandchildren.

Hal was a fourth-generation operator of a hundred year-old family hardware business. He was a member of the local school board during integration of South Carolina public schools. He has served people of both races, absorbing their speech patterns and attitudes, their hopes and fears, their strengths and weaknesses.

JUNIPER ROAD is his first novel.

TABLE OF CONTENTS

CHAPTER

CHAPTER ONE

Truro, South Carolina
June 1935

SUMMER JOB

He was wide awake, but he just lay there, waiting for Jake. That old rooster had waked him at the crack of dawn as far back as he could remember. This morning, he was as excited as he had been the morning he would go to the first grade for the first time. He didn't need Jake for the waking; just to verify the time.

He, Woodrow Wilson Jones, was fourteen years old. He was already the man of the house, and today, God willing, he would become the wage earner. He had talked about it with his mother the night before.

"But Wils," she had protested, "you are just a boy. Do you really think you can stand a full day swinging an ax out in the hot sun, alongside a bunch of grown men?"

"Yes'm, I think I can. Daddy has worked the pure-tee tar out of me plenty of times when it was hot as blue blazes! And now, Daddy's not here, and we've got no money coming 'n."

It was true. Jefferson Davis Jones, always ailing, had been diagnosed with tuberculosis. He was now in Columbia in the state's sanatorium for tuberculosis treatment. He had never been a good provider, but now he was not even present.

"Well, tell me again what you heard about that gov'ment project."

"Mama, I told you. They're hiring axmen for a dollar a day! You have to furnish your own ax, but that's no problem. That's five dollars a week! You know we need that money, with Daddy gone—and you know I can swing an ax, 'cause Daddy's given me plenty of practice."

Mary Jones, already showing signs of middle age, though she was only thirty-three, considered her son. He was a typical gawky teenager, all arms and legs, feet and hands and knees. There was not a visible muscle anywhere. There was, however, a promise of strong sinews, encouraged by hard exercise and a Spartan diet. "There is no fat on that young'un," she concluded.

"You think you can do it, Wils?" she asked. "You're not full grown—and you might get hurt."

"I can do it, Mama. If they take me, I can do it. We need the money, and the ax is already sharp as a razor."

"Well, all right then, you can try to get on. But don't take any notion of working after school starts, Your daddy made that mistake. He quit school so we could get married. I'm glad we got married, but his lack of schooling hindered him from getting a good paying job."

The next morning, as she lay in her bed waiting for the sounds of Wilson rising, dressing and leaving for what he hoped would be his first day as a wage earner, she thought, "I'm real proud of Wilson's get-up-and-go. He's exactly right—we're in pitiful shape when nobody in the family is working for wages. If he gets this ax job, five dollars a week will help, but it won't take care of the two of us. I'm going to have to stir my stumps and get me a job, too. What kind of job could I get, with no experience or training? I don't know, but I've got to try for it."

Her mind began going around, thinking of possibilities. Retail clerk? Waitress? Cook? Machine operator in a cotton mill? She decided to make a list, with the least disagreeable possibilities at the top. She would go into Truro and see what she could find.

Wilson, meanwhile, had gotten out of bed and dressed in his bib overalls, shirt and shoes.

He picked up a sweet potato from the fireplace ashes, went to the chopping block out back, picked up his ax and was on his way.

Mary stood in the doorway, watching him disappear down the road. "Good-bye, Wils. Good luck!" she called. Then, to herself, she added ,"Be careful." But he didn't hear her, for he didn't turn around.

* * *

The sky overhead was a clear light blue, with a few scattered clouds. The air smelled fresh and clean as he walked along the sandy road away from the house. The harsh glare that accompanies a hot day was not yet apparent. "Nice little breeze," he thought. "Bet it won't last through the morning. It's bound to be hot in those woods where we'll be working."

June is always hot in South Carolina, and humid.

"Hey, Wilson! Wait up!"

Wilson looked behind him and saw someone approaching, also bearing an ax on his shoulder. Wilson waited, and recognized the muscular figure of Simeon Bates. Sim was an older colored boy who lived not too far from the Jones house. He had numerous brothers and sisters. Relations had always been good between the two boys, and Wils was glad to see him.

"You fixin' to sign up with the gum'ment, Wilson?"

"Hope so—if they'll take me. They might think I'm too little, or too young, or somethin'. I'm a little worried about that."

"I'm worried 'bout me, too. Hope it'll work out. My problem might be 'cause I'm colored. I heard they already hired some niggers. If that's so, it may not be a problem this time".

"If they ask me how old I am, I'll just have to fudge a little. Need that money with my daddy gone", said the determined Woodrow Wilson Jones.

They walked in silence, saving their strength for the long day ahead.

"Hey, wait, fellows!" They had come to a side road, and trudging toward them, also with an ax on his shoulder, was Jim Lane.

Lane was a blustery, aggressive boy who always seemed to be throwing his weight around. He usually chose his targets from those he considered inferior in size or strength or experience. He was a few years older, a few pounds heavier than Wilson who was obviously his physical inferior. Sim was colored, Jim was white, so there was no argument, in Jim's mind, as to which was inferior.

"Where y'all headed? From the looks of those axes you must be hopin' to sign up with the gov'ment crew, but I 'speck you're wasting your time."

"Why is that?" Wilson wanted to know.

"Well, Wilson, you ain't much bigger than that ax. They're looking for men, not kids.'

Wilson kept walking, said nothing.

"And you, Sim. You're wasting your time, for sure. I heard down town they ain't hirin' no niggers."

Sim said nothing, kept walking.

No more attempts at conversation were forthcoming, and the three boys trudged on in silence for another hour until they came to a long line of men, each with an ax. The boys took their places at the end of the line, which snaked its way forward through the shade, terminating at a table where a man sat in a wooden straight chair.

As the boys followed the line forward, Jim Lane managed to get in front of the others, so that he would be the first to be interviewed. "Just watch me, boys, and do what I do. I'll show you how to act."

As they neared the man at the table, Wilson felt his chest begin to constrict and his heart beat faster. His breath came in little pants, as if he'd been running. "Lord, help me get this job. We need it."

Wilson studied the man at the table. To Wilson, he seemed pretty old, at least twenty or twenty-five. He was dressed in a white shirt with a tie, his sleeves rolled back on his forearms against the heat that was sure to come. He seemed all business, serious, but sometimes Wilson could see a smile. His manner was calm and mild, and he didn't seem impatient or hurried.

Jim Lane, next in line, was beckoned to the table, and as he approached, he swaggered confidently. The man looked up, took in the swagger, and asked "Your name"? Jim answered.

"You know how to use that ax"?

Jim replied confidently, "Yep."

The man said, "We'll see. Report to Elijah over there. He'll be your foreman. He'll tell you what to do." He indicated a broad-shouldered white man with a three-day stubble of beard.

As Jim walked away from the table, he half turned toward the other two boys and gave a confident thumbs up.

Sim was next. He walked quietly to the table. The man followed the same line of questioning, sending Sim to Elijah also.

Wilson was next. The interviewer took in the scrawny frame, the beardless cheeks, the lack of muscular development. Without preamble, he said, "Kid, this is hard work, dangerous work. I'm afraid you won't be able to stand up to a full day of this kind of work. You'd better go on back home."

The beardless cheeks paled, then reddened, as Wilson "talked back" to an adult for maybe the first time in his young life.

"Mister, I can handle this ax. I can do this job. Give me a chance and I'll show you and Mister Elijah what I can do!"

Admiring the boy's spunk, the man continued in a kindly tone, "Look, son. The rules say you have to be a certain age before I can hire you. How old are you?"

Wilson swallowed, and lied, "I'll be sixteen in two weeks."

"Not old enough." He shook his head regretfully. The minimum age was eighteen.

Wilson persisted. "Please, mister. My daddy's in the hospital with consumption. I'm responsible for my mama, and I need a job. I tell you, I know how to swing an ax. Please give me a chance. You can fire me if it don't work out."

Impressed with his gumption, the interviewer said, "Can you be eighteen by Monday?"

"Yessir!" the boy responded.

"Then come back Monday."

Wilson shouldered his ax and began the walk back home. He was disappointed not to be hired immediately, like the other boys. At the same time, he was relieved that the door was not slammed in his face. He still had the prospect of a job.

* * *

Mary Jones was sweating. Perspiration ran into her eyes, stinging. Her shirt was soaked, and she could feel the moisture running down between her thin breasts, sweating as befits anyone wielding a hoe in the broiling hot sun of a June morning. She was working to get the Johnson grass out of the garden. That wiry "joint grass" could swallow the green beans, and anything else within its reach. Johnson grass ("Dern that Johnson grass!") and hot weather had already done away with the English peas, and she was be-derned if that dern grass was going to take the green beans and squash! "My boy and I are sick and tired of eating last winter's sweet potatoes every day!" We need variety, and if we don't get it in the summer, when are we going to get it?"

She was rather tall and angular, thin, her hair caught in a bun at the back of her head. Her costume was a faded, well-worn cotton dress, of which she owned three. Wrinkles, from squinting in the sun, were becoming permanent around her eyes. Her hands were rough and red from hard work, constantly washing clothes, tending chickens, hoeing.

Just then she caught some movement out of the corner of her eye, and looked up to see a figure approaching the house and garden at a rapid clip. It was Wilson! She knew her fears had been realized. "If he is back home this early in the day they must not have hired him. He will be so disappointed—and we need that money".

Mama!" he shouted. "Jim Lane got hired, and Sim Bates got hired! And—

"And you didn't?" Wilson would be so disappointed, she knew.

"No, Mama! I'm trying to tell you! The man—a really nice man—who was doing the hiring told me to come back Monday, and be eighteen—and he would put me on! I've got a job! We'll have money!"

Mary gave a great sigh of relief, for two reasons. One was that her son had been granted the chance to be the "man of the family"; and the other was thanksgiving for the prospect of having a few dollars come in each week. Those dollars would ease their burden, a little.

"Wils, that is wonderful news! Great news!" She smiled brightly in praise.

"Now", she said briskly, "if you don't have to go back to the woods until Monday, what about helping me with this garden? We need to get this dern grass out of here, then we need to water the corn. It's about to tassel."

Mother and son spent the rest of the morning hoeing grass, then she went inside to fix their dinner. "Dinner" was the midday meal, and was usually the heavy meal of the day.

While she was preparing food, Wilson took a pail and a dipper to the pitcher pump, pumped the pail full of water, then proceeded down the corn rows, putting a dipperful of water on each stalk. This was repeated over and over until he had watered the entire corn patch.

Dinner consisted of a steaming bowl of dried pea soup with side meat (thick bacon), and cornbread.

"Mighty good, Mama!" he pronounced.

"I have to keep my working man happy", she said.

* * *

When Wilson left the table and she began to clean up the kitchen, her mind went back in time. Spurred by her conversation with Wilson the night before, she began to think of her youth, and of Jefferson Davis Jones. She and Dave had known each other all their lives, it seemed. Their parents were neighbors, they attended the same church.

One Sunday when the members of Bethel church had gathered for a homecoming service and picnic, the two of them had slipped away for an hour after lunch. They found a secluded spot beside a stream, plopped down on the bank and had a long conversation. The leisurely conversation eventually led to the sharing of private thoughts and dreams that they had never voiced before. It was the first of many meetings and conversations. The heady, giddy feeling that comes with first love filled their waking moments. Soon, each began to think of the other as "my" Mary, "my" Dave. One thing led to another, and the question of whether they should marry changed to "How soon can we marry?"

Woodrow Wilson Jones was the result.

Dave tried a number of different lines of work in an effort to support his family. He plowed a mule for his uncle, following the north end of a southbound animal day after day in the hot, dusty Carolina sun. The next year he tried being a barn foreman for the same uncle, taking care of the livestock and their feed. The year after that he worked in a dry goods store, selling shirts and socks. He reported for work punctually and regularly, but just didn't seem to take much interest in it, regardless of the job, often staring into space.

The list of former occupations grew with each year. "Dave Jones means well", people said, "but he doesn't seem to be able to "plow to the end of the row." He was a very likeable fellow, unfailingly good to Mary and young Wilson—never laid a hand on either one—but his record as a breadwinner was not good.

The family lived in a four-room house belonging to Dave's uncle. It had been a sharecropper's house until the uncle, knowing Dave's need, had allowed the family to move in, rent-free. The house had plenty of cross-ventilation from doors and windows and cracks, particularly noticeable in winter. It lacked electricity and running water, normal for a tenant house. The roof did not leak, and the house provided shelter from the sun and the rain. Furniture was minimal; a bed for the couple, a smaller one for Wilson. A couple of tables and a few straight chairs completed the ensemble.

The house was located only a mile or so from the small town of Truro, a dusty crossroad in the sand hills region of the state. The family walked into town for groceries, or to school.

Mary gazed into space, wondering what their life might have been like if Dave had found a job he liked and was good at.

"Enough of that, woman," she sternly told herself. "You love Dave, he loves you, and we have a fine son. Pay attention to making that combination work out for Wilson, and quit feeling sorry for yourself!"

* * *

Wilson was chopping wood for the cook stove and for the upcoming laundry day when he looked up and saw Sim coming down the road.

"Hey, Sim, come on in! I want to hear about your day!"

Sim turned in to the Jones' road, his ax on his shoulder. He was still moving at the same gait as in the morning, but Wilson could see that he had put in a full day. He sat down on the stump that served as a chopping block, took off his cap, and just sat. His shirt was wet around the collar, down his back and under his arms. His odor was musty and coppery.

Without a word, Wilson brought him a bucket of water fresh from the well, along with a dipper. Sim drank, rinsing his mouth with the first mouthful, then taking the second and third straight to the place it would do the most good. He sat there a minute or two more, then smiled his thanks.

"Mighty good water! Thank ya, Wilson. Hey, what happen' today. Why you not stay? What they say?"

"The man at the table told me to come back Monday, and be eighteen! I think that meant he knew I was too young, but if I said the right word he would give me a try anyhow. I thought that was mighty white of him." Then Wilson thought, "oh, oh!"

"Sorry, Sim, I wasn't thinkin'."

"'S all right. I'm used to it. That ain't nothin'. You don't mean no harm. You give me your water out of your dipper, I know you don't mean no harm. You ain't like Jim Lane.

"What did Jim do, or say? How did it go today?"

"Well", Sim began, "he try to butter up Elijah, the foreman. Tol' him how many ax jobs he'd done had before... tol' him he knowed how to pace hisself so he can go all day without monkeyin' in the heat... next time I heard Jim Lane was asking for a water break 'cause there was no air moving in those woods!"

"What did Elijah say?"

"Nothin'. But he didn't call for no water break".

"Anything else happen?"

"Then Jim he started talking about colored folks, niggers, he called us, taking jobs belongin' to white folks. Jobs like this. Jim claimed to know plenty of white folks would be glad to have the job given to a no-good like me—if they'd only known about it".

"What did Elijah say?"

"He said, "Shut up and work 'stead of talking".

"What did you say?"

"I didn't say nothin' . . . just kept swingin' that ax. I don't talk much on the job. Uses up energy."

"Pretty hard work, Sim?"

"Pretty hard."

"Do you think I can handle it?"

"You want the job, and the money, you got to handle it."

* * *

When Monday arrived, Wilson and Sim walked together to the job. They did not encounter Jim Lane on the way, which suited them just fine.

As soon as they arrived, Wilson anxiously sought out the man at the table, and was relieved to see that it was the same man he had talked to the first time. As before, he was greeted with a kindly smile.

"How old are you, young fella?"

"Eighteen, sir."

"That's good, because I can't hire you unless you're eighteen. Do you know how to handle that ax?"

"Yessir."

"Then you can report to the foreman, Elijah, over there. He will show you where to work. He'll be your boss. Good luck, young man,"

"Thank you, sir."

Wilson walked over to where Elijah was gathering his crew. He introduced himself and said he had been told to report to this crew. Elijah grunted to himself as he surveyed the whiskerless cheeks and scrawny build of this new arrival.

"How old are you, Boy?"

"Eighteen, sir."

"Can you handle that ax?"

"Yessir."

"Well, we'll see how you work out." Then he called out "Let's go, men. The sun is high in the heavens. Time to get started."

* * *

Elijah led them to a valley between two rises of ground. "I told you before we're cutting these trees because there's going to be a lake here. Another crew is building a dam, down yonder way. Maybe someday you'll catch fish where you're standing today.

Now, cut these trees no more than a foot above ground. Be careful how you fell them. We don't want trees falling on anybody. Spread out, and keep your eyes open. Okay, get started."

The trees were mostly pine, but mixed with some scrub oak. They were not terribly large, but they were numerous. Wilson began work on the first one, setting a deliberate pace that he thought he would be able to maintain. Elijah had stationed himself where he could observe the new man's work, and after a half hour Wilson looked up to find that Elijah had transferred his attention to another group of workmen who had been chattering away as they worked. Wilson remembered Sim's comment about talk on the job being a waste of energy.

After a couple of hours a break was declared, and the men lined up for some water which had been brought by the water boy. Wilson was experienced enough to drink sparingly, rinsing his mouth before taking only a few swallows. Soon they were back at work. When the noon break came along, all the men sank gratefully to the ground where they stood, thankful for the chance to stretch out, relax, and eat the lunch each had brought from home.

The afternoon was very like the morning, with the men more tired and the weather hotter. Gnats and mosquitoes buzzed around their heads, but thankfully there were no deerflies. Wilson's hands were already callused from the work he was doing around the house, but as the afternoon wore on he became conscious of their swelling and growing sensitivity. His forearms, too, were very tired from gripping the ax handle, and sweat had long since soaked his shirt. "There will be sore muscles tomorrow", he thought as he doggedly fought the heat and his fatigue. When the big bell sounded signaling the end of the workday, it was as welcome a sound as he could remember. Wilson was surprised by the stillness, following the ring of many axes striking trees.

After a few minutes rest, he and Sim began their journey toward home. They were accompanied by Jim Lane, who had worked in another section of the woods. He, too, was very tired, and the walk home was accomplished in near silence.

When he arrived home, Mary was solicitous of his obvious fatigue. She allowed him to rest awhile before helping her with feeding the chickens and other daily chores.

While they were having supper, Mary told him about her day, and her efforts to find a job. "I made a list of places I might try, and went to the retail stores first. Visited three dry goods stores, two five-and-ten cent stores, three grocery stores, both drug stores and the hardware. All the people were nice to me, but none of them needed more help.

Then I tried the eating places, and struck gold! Mr. Frank Zervos, you know, has the Sanitary Café. He had just fired this waitress, he said, for being more interested in flirting than she was in working. He asked me if I am a flirt. I told him right off that I am a happily married woman with a grown son, and that's enough men for me, thank you very much!

Anyhow, he hired me to work lunchtime, Monday through Friday, for a dollar a day plus tips. May have to work some evenings, if I work out. Start tomorrow. Not bad, eh?"

"That's great Mama!"

Wilson slept soundly that night.

* * *

The next morning Wilson rose from his bed, stiff and sore from his exertions of the previous day. Clamping his mouth tightly to avoid groaning and waking his mother (who, in the way of mothers, was awake and listening for him), he dressed and found some breakfast. He selected a sweet potato and a cold biscuit for his lunch, picked up his ax and was on his way.

The walk to the job site loosened his back and leg muscles so they did not ache so fiercely, His hands and forearms still let him know they were tender. Because of this, the second day was more difficult than the first. Fortunately, however, a hard shower came up in the mid-afternoon, causing Elijah to call a halt to the day's work.

As Wilson and Sim were preparing to depart for their walk home, Elijah called them over. "I want to tell you boys that you're off to a good start. You swing a good sharp ax, you work steady and you keep your mouths shut. That's all I ask of my crew. Keep on working like you started and you can work for me as long as you want."

Jim Lane joined them after they'd walked a little way. "I saw Elijah talkin' to you two. I bet he gave you Hell like he did me. Pulled me over to one side and reminded me that *he* is the boss of this crew. Said if I wanted to stay with him I need to keep my mouth shut and work! He must be a little crazy, 'cause I've been workin' harder than anybody else, the whole time. What did he say to you?"

"Oh, about the same thing. Said we needed to keep working and keep our mouths shut."

"Ain't that somethin'? The only talkin' I've been doing is to tell the other men which trees to cut next."

"Maybe he wants to be the one to do that. He's the boss."

* * *

As the summer wore on, frequent rain showers doused the countryside. Mary's garden matured, and the family began to eat fresh vegetables again. Green beans, squash, okra, sweet corn and cucumbers graced their table in great quantity. Mary was able to do some canning of the surplus to save for another, less fruitful season. There were table scraps for the chickens and forage for the hog pen.

Wilson, too, was benefiting from the improved diet, as well as the physical activity. His hands were no longer sore. The blisters were gone, replaced by callouses. His hands were beginning to outstrip the rest of his fame in size. His forearms and shoulders, once bony and slender took on muscle and shape. His voice had already begun to deepen. He began to look and sound like a gangly, half-grown man rather than a tall skinny boy.

A hard day's work in the woods with Elijah's crew no longer took all his energy. He and Sim often talked and laughed on their way back home in the afternoons. Often Jim Lane was with them.

One sultry day Jim was reprimanded by Elijah, who had seen him shove a fellow worker out of the water line and take his place. The other worker was a colored man. Elijah had sent Jim to the tail end of the line.

On the way home, Jim was bristling with anger. He began to make belittling remarks about "niggers" to Sim, who remained silent. As the remarks became more explicit and offensive, Wilson spoke up.

"Jim, be quiet."

"Mind your own business, Wilson. I ain't talking to you."

"But you're talking to my friend. Sim hasn't done anything to you. Leave him alone."

"Lord's sake, Wilson. Niggers don't have any right working with white people—they don't have any feelings, neither! What's the matter with you? Are you a nigger lover?"

"Sim is my friend, like I told you. If you can't speak to him like he's a human being you can find somebody else to walk with."

Jim looked at Wilson like he'd lost his mind, shook his head in disbelief, and walked on in silence. When the group reached Jim's road he turned for home, muttering to himself, "A nigger and a nigger lover! Ungh!"

The boys walked on in silence for a few minutes.

Then Sim said, "Thank ya, Wilson. For sayin' I'm your friend. You don't have to protect me. Can take care of myself. Jim Lane don't scare me none."

"But Jim didn't have any reason to take out his whatever on you. You haven't done anything to make him mad."

"'Cept be colored—and that's the whole thing, right there. Jim and a lot of other people don't like us, and wish we'd get out of their way—'cept when they need some help with some hard work. Anyway, thank ya."

They continued on their way until they reached the Jones' house. Wilson invited Sim to stop for some water. The two boys sprawled in the yard in the shade of a chinaberry tree. They were surrounded by the sweetish odor that pervades a chicken yard. Most of the chickens were in shade, also, but one or two were stalking around the chicken yard, looking for stray bits of food. It was a hot, still afternoon, and even the birds were quiet.

"You know", said Wilson, "this ax job is the first job I've ever had, outside working here at home. Have you had jobs before?"

"Law, yes. I been workin', tryin' to make money, ever since I was a little tad."

"What did you do?"

"First job I had was shinin' shoes down street in town. Made me a shine box, got three or four cans of polish—different colors, you know—a soft brush and a pop rag, and I was ready for business."

"What's a pop rag? Never heard tell of that."

"It's a piece of cloth you stretch tight between your hands, then you work it back and forth across the tops of the man's shoes. You do it right, you can make it POP, and they like that. A couple of good pops can turn a 10 cent shine into a quarter shine quick as you can say "Jack Robinson". I was careful not to get polish on their socks, and real particular when I shined Doctor Bull's light two-tone shoes. On summer days, when it was OK outside but their offices were still too hot, those white men would stand outside on the sidewalk and talk. If one of the men in the group wanted a shine, it usually worked out that all of them got one, so they wouldn't be left behind. White men like their shoes to be shined, 'specially on the weekend. So, I generally spent Friday afternoon and Saturday downtown. Did all right, some days."

"Have you had other jobs too?"

"Well, shoe shining was good in summer, but when the weather turns cold and wet and the ground gets muddy, the men just seem to not worry about shined shoes. So, I found myself something else to do when the weather turned. I lit fires for white people on my way to school."

"How did that work?" Wilson inquired.

"Well, I get up good and early, which ain't hard for me to do. I wake up, dress, get me a biscuit and head to my first house. I have to get there before they get stirring, you see. I go in and build a fire in every fireplace or heater that ain't in a bedroom—and leave. Then I go the next house. Can usually take care of three houses and not be too late for school. They don't care if you come late, no how.

Then, when school is out, I go back by my three houses and fill up their wood boxes for the evenin'—and do anything else they want me to do. Sometimes they give me some food for my dinner. I've been doing the fire lighting thing for a couple of years. Ma says it helps out."

"I'm thinking about trying to get me an afternoon job when school starts. We need to keep some money coming in," said Wilson.

Sim got up and headed for home, while Wilson prepared to begin his chores.

"See you tomorrow", he called.

Sim said nothing, but held up his hand in reply.

* * *

Sim walked down the road toward home. He had eaten little that day, and was very interested in what might be there for supper. Since his stomach was making noises, he thought maybe it might be rubbing against his backbone as he walked. It sure did feel empty!

Rounding a bend in the dusty dirt road he could see smoke rising from a crooked chimney atop a dilapidated unpainted shack. The roof was of tin, turned rusty over the years. The wooden walls consisted of planks of no particular width or length. Where the fit was bad, creating cracks or gaps, pieces of old metal signs had been tacked over, in a vain attempt to keep out the rain and cold. The whole effect was shabby and caterwampus.

Soon Sim was spotted by the children playing in the yard around the shack. Great shouts went up, several ragged figures running to meet him.

"Sim! Sim! Sim is home!"

The cluster of children moved slowly back down the road, toward the house, chattering and jumping in excitement around their eldest brother. As they reached the yard, the perspiring face of their mother appeared in the doorway and waved.

"It'll be ready in a few minutes, Sim. Have a seat and rest yourself."

Sim went to the pitcher pump, worked the handle. When the water began to flow he stuck his head beneath the spout and let the clean cool water refresh him. Drying himself with the family towel hanging nearby, he sat down with his brothers and sisters in the yard.

The yard was salt-and-pepper colored sand, swept clean of any grass "to keep the snakes away". It was littered with stools, boxes, broken chairs, and seat cushions from absent autos. During the summer months the yard served as the sitting room, much cooler than the interior of the house, heated as it was by the combination of the woodburning cook stove and the sun.

The younger children gathered around Sim.

"What you do today, Shad?" he asked his 14 year old brother.

"Took your old shine box into town", he replied.

"Do any good?"

"Not much. Fifty cents."

"Half to Ma?"

"She's already got it. But I don't see why I have to give her half. I'm the one on my knees down town. I'm the one did the shining. I'm the one they called 'Boy", "*Boy*, do this. *Boy*, be careful of my white pants. Are you finished yet, *Boy*?" I don't like it, and I don't wanta share the money."

"You ever ask Ma if she liked cleaning up after you when you been sick? You think she likes cooking in that hot house when you out here in the cool yard? I'm the oldest, and I'm telling you—all of you—what we make, we share with Ma, half and half. You don't like that, you deal with me. You don't like dealin' with me, you move out to your own place where you don't have to share."

"How was your day, Frank-o?"

"Took ol' man Renfro's cows to the pasture this morning. Went back this afternoon and brought 'em back to his barn."

"He pay you for that?"

"Not money. Gave me a dozen eggs. Ma's got 'em"

"Good. Dorothy?"

"Took care of Mrs. Simpson's little girls this morning. This afternoon I took them down the street to Mrs. Abbot's to play with her children. Gracie was nursing them, and we and the children had a good time. They were real good today."

"You work for Mrs. Simpson most every day. How much she pay you?"

"A dollar a week. And Gracie gets the same. And they feed us."

"And Ma gets half?" Nods of assent. "Good going. I'm proud of all of you."

Just then Daisy, Sim's mother, stuck her head out the door again. "Supper's ready! Come inside and get a plate!"

The children all trooped noisily inside and lined up at the kitchen table. Each took a plate and a fork or spoon, then passing by the stove, helped themselves to crisp brown fried fatback, field peas, boiled squash and cornbread, all steaming hot. As soon as their plates were filled, they quickly filed back into the cooler yard. Each took an available seat and began to eat. The chatter vanished as they satisfied their hunger.

Daisy came out with her own plate and joined them. She was a large woman, having borne five children and subsisted on the diet she could afford. Her stomach and hips were round and wide, her thighs prodigious. Her upper arms had lots of loose flesh that quivered when she moved. Her face was unlined and smiling, most of the time. She was amazingly strong. Could separate four or five children who were quarreling, or two dogs who were fighting, and when she had been saddled with a husband who had drunk too much, she could handle him too.

She was dripping perspiration from every pore. Her hair was wet, her bare arms glistening, covered with tiny beads of moisture. Her dress was soaked in back, all the way down below her waist. "That house is sho' hot today!" she declared, all the while smiling at her children, enjoying watching them eat their fill. "There's more on the stove if anybody want more", she said; whereupon Sim immediately got up from his seat and went inside, emerging with another full plate.

"Mighty good, Ma!"

"Well, with all you children working, it's easier to have plenty of food, like we did when your Daddy was home. Now that he's up North, it's been harder. We all have to pitch in, and that makes it better for all of us."

Sim exchanged a look with Shad.

* * *

"Ma, why did Daddy have to go up North? Why can't he live here with us?" Gracie wanted to know.

"Well, Gracie, Daddy used to work at Mister George's cotton gin. When your daddy was a little boy he used to hang around the gin. Loved to watch the mules and wagons, loved to listen to the drivers talking about their crop, and the other things men talk about.

Mister George noticed your daddy, being there almost every day and not getting in the way. He began to send him on errands, began to let him sweep out the office, things like that. Your daddy did what he was told, was always polite to the white men, and was always there.

When he got big and strong, Mister George offered him a real job, with wages instead of tips. Even paid him in the off season, when there wasn't any cotton to gin. But there was usually something going on down there, repairs and stuff. We got along pretty good on those wages, and the money came in real steady, not like these sharecroppers' money around here. We got along pretty good."

"What happened, Ma? Why ain't Daddy still at the gin?"

"Well, honey, one night that gin caught on fire. You know how men love to strut around smoking cigarettes and cigars? Lord, I sho hope none of you ever takes up that habit! Well, somebody musta left a cigarette or a cigar that wasn't out, and it came up against some loose cotton lying around. You know how much cotton flies around a cotton gin—that hot cigar got the cotton hot, and a few hours later—it was pitch black night—the whole place was flaming! You ever see a cotton gin burn? You talk about hot? Great God A'mighty, that is *HOT*!"

"Did they put the gin back again?"

"Lord, I wish they had! It turned out that Mister George didn't have no insurance, and he didn't have enough money to build the gin again. He couldn't borrow no money from the bank. Banks were in trouble, 'cause farmers were in trouble, lost their land, and weren't goin' to plant no more cotton—so who needs a cotton gin? They call it a Depression."

"So what happened to Daddy's job?"

"When the gin was gone, the job was gone. He tried to get on with a farmer or two. Hhe tried to get on with a sawmill. He tried to get on with the cotton mill and the box mill, and the railroad—but nobody was hiring.

So, he did what a lot of colored folks had to do, he got on the bus and went North to find a job. He's been gone a year—he's working in Dee-troit in a car factory. He and another man from down here are sharing a room. He sends some money home every two weeks, but we haven't seen him, not once. He says he'll get a vacation next year and can come home. I sho hope so!

We hope so, too, Ma! We liked it when he was home!"

When Daisy went to bed that night, tired as she was, her mind was still on the fire. "That's the same story I've told the chillun since that day. Ain't never said a word against Mister George or about what he tried to do to me. Never said a word about him firing Pete. How long can I tell my children that story before they hear the <u>whole</u> truth from somebody? Oh, Pete! I wish you were here to help me like you did the afternoon of the fire!"

* * *

One day, Wilson's mother received a letter:

> June 25, 1935
>
> Dear Mary,
>
> How are you and Wilson getting along? I guess you're having a harder time getting by. Wish I was there to help you, such help as I am. I've been here now for 8 weeks, I think. About that. It's a real nice place. They keep the windows open and the sun comes in, and the breeze. The nurses are good to us. They're always asking us how we're feeling and can they get us anything. The doctors come by every day and check our throats and lungs. They say I'll be OK as soon as my lungs get clear. Then I can come home and start helping you take care of our boy. I really want to be home with you and Wilson. That's where I belong, not stuck off up here in the sand hills where nobody ever heard of Truro.
>
> Your loving husband,
>
> Dave

When Mary received this, the first letter she had ever received from Dave, she wept. He was all by himself in that big hospital, no one to take care of him. He sounded so pitiful! And she couldn't do anything to help—that's what a wife is supposed to do for her husband—help!

When Wilson came home that afternoon she shared Dave's letter with him, as well as her frustration at not being able to improve the situation. "I feel so helpless! He's all alone!"

Wilson listened, thought a minute, then said, gently, "Mama, when he was here and he was sick, we couldn't help him. Now, he's in a place where they know how to help him. Let's turn it over to the doctors and nurses at the TB place. They can handle his problem better than we can."

* * *

In late August, Elijah called his ax crew together at the end of the workday.

"While we've been cutting out these young trees, that other crew has been working a half mile from here, hauling in rock and dirt to make a big dam. A concrete spillway in that dam will be able to control the water level in the lake that's going to be right where we're standing. Like I told you, in a few years you'll be able to catch fish in this lake.

The point of this meeting is to tell you that we've come to the end of the job. Tomorrow is the last workday. When you finish tomorrow afternoon, the paymaster will be here, and he'll pay you off.

I want to tell all of you that you've worked hard. My crew always does. Most of you have done a good job. If I'm ever where I can give you another job, I'll do what I can. That's all. See you tomorrow."

* * *

The three boys fell into step as they started home after Elijah's speech. Now hardened by a summer of hard ax work, they had plenty of breath to talk, and the talk flowed.

"What are you going to do now?" Jim Lane wanted to know. "I guess I'll be going back to school when it starts next month, though I sho' ain't interested in going. My old daddy would wale the daylights out of me if I mentioned quitting school".

"Sure enough", Wilson agreed. That's what I'll do. Mama has already been talking about it. She says I got to get that education'. "What about you, Sim?"

"Well, I don't know. . . Schools for colored people ain't much. Not much different for white chllun, in the country, either. Don't have classes 'bout half a year. Close up for cotton chopping time and close up for cotton picking time. The teachers try, but they ain't had too much schooling, neither. I'll talk to Ma, but I'll prob'ly see if I can get me a regular full-time job, or some part-time jobs. Need to bring in some money. Them chillun can eat!

"When does school start, anyhow?"

"I think it's the Thursday after Labor Day"

"'Bout two weeks off."

When Wilson arrived at his house he found his mother bringing in the clean clothes from the line. After washing up a little, he helped her fold them and put them away

"Well, we got the word today, Mama. Tomorrow is the last day with the ax crew. We'll get paid for the last time tomorrow afternoon."

"So that's it? I was wondering if the job would end before the start of school, or if you would have to quit the job to go to school. Pretty good timing. We need to look at your clothes, too. You've grown taller this summer, and filled out a good bit. Last year's school clothes might not do this time. I'll give you a haircut, too."

* * *

Mary made good use of Wilson's time before the beginning of school. He cleaned up the remains of the summer garden, burning off the grass, weeds, vines and stalks. Then he tilled the soil, freeing it of old roots, clods of hard earth, raking and hoeing until the soil was loose and friable. He broadcast guano over the area, tilling it in thoroughly. He used the "push" Planet Jr. garden plow, laying off the rows in parallel lines They went to Mr. Stokes' hardware store in town and bought seed for planting turnips, rutabaga, collards and mustard. "Let's get some pumpkin seed", Mary suggested.

They carefully examined Wilson's clothes. Some were too small, and were set aside to be given to Sim's brothers. Some needed mending, and some just needed freshening up. They decided to buy another pair of jeans to accommodate his longer legs, the next trip down town. Wilson's shoes, brogans that he had worked in all summer, were given a treatment of neatsfoot oil to soften the leather and make them look a little better.

Mary had always cut her son's hair, so she sat him down and snipped away at his unruly sun-bleached locks which had hardly seen a comb over the summer. When she finished, she looked at him, amazed to see how much he looked like his father.

"I declare, Wils, you've grown so, and filled out so—you look like a young man! I am real proud of the way you have handled yourself this summer—like a man, instead of a boy. Your wages have been a wonderful help taking care of us with your daddy gone. And I never heard you complain about being hot, or sore, or tired. I'm proud, real proud!"

"Thanks, Mama.... I was thinking, the other day, when we were in Mr. Stokes' hardware store... I'm going to try to get me an after-school job. That way I can still bring some money home like this summer."

"OK, Son, that's OK. But remember, schoolwork comes first. If you get a job and your grades fall down, the job is over. School comes first."

CHAPTER TWO

HIGH SCHOOL

After the "dog days" of late summer, Labor Day arrived. As usual, the weather was hot and dry. Ominous looking clouds gathered in the afternoons, a premonition of thunderstorms that so often brought wind and rain, along with streaks of lightning and loud rolls of thunder. Of course, those afternoon storms also brought relief from the oppressive heat of the day, and the promise of a cooler evening.

Three days later, the Thursday after Labor Day signaled the beginning of school. Bored with lazy days of summer, some young folks were eager to get back to the familiar routine of school. Others found it more difficult to drag themselves out of bed for such an uninteresting prospect.

Wilson's attitude fit somewhere in between. On the one hand, he was somewhat excited. This was to be a new experience—high school! Instead of being the oldest students in a school that included little children, his class would be the youngest class. They would mingle with older students who were almost "grown"! On the other hand, he was apprehensive. He had heard wild tales of "initiating" the freshmen, tales of belt lines and other forms of hazing.

Spending the summer in the woods with the ax crew, he had practically no contact with his peers, and was curious about how they had spent the summer.

After a special breakfast of pancakes and molasses, he left the house looking as clean and neat as he and his mother could manage. After a 20 minute walk, he found himself on the school ground.The campus was dominated by a two-story brick building with a double row of windows, open to catch the breeze. An American flag flew from a tall pole in front. He climbed the steps and entered the unfamiliar building.

The faint scent of dry chalk dust mingled with the odor of soap and furniture polish as he walked inside. Not knowing where to go, Wilson walked through the halls, looking for familiar faces of his classmates. Climbing the stairs at the opposite end of the building, he surveyed the second floor, and soon spotted familiar faces through an open classroom door.

"Hey, Wilson! Here we are! Come on in!"

There were some unfamiliar faces in the room, belonging to bus students who were transferring in to town from their much smaller country schools. Most, however, were familiar faces from his class last year, yet they looked different. Many of the boys were taller and more muscular. The girls were a different shape, too, in a very pleasing way. Their hair was neatly combed and curled. Some were even wearing lipstick.

After a few minutes for chatting, a bell rang. The teacher who had been sitting quietly at her desk asked everyone to find a seat. She introduced herself as Miss Austin, the homeroom teacher for the class. She seemed young for a teacher, and right pretty, too. A lot different from the average run of teachers, who tended to be older and stouter. Miss Austin made a list of names for the class roll. She instructed the class to report to her room, first thing each morning.

After a few minutes another bell rang, and Miss Austin marched the class in a line into the school auditorium, where the rest of the students were already gathered.

A man dressed in a suit and tie stood up and introduced himself as Professor Scott, the principal of the school. He proceeded to talk to the assembled students for fifteen minutes. He told them they could choose from three courses of study: college preparatory, for those planning to go to college, commercial courses for those interested in working in an office, or the general course.

Wilson, as well as most of his friends, had no notion of being able to go to college. Truro was a poor, rural community. They knew lots of people who were struggling to keep food on the table, and they didn't need to read the newspapers to learn about the Great Depression. Most of them opted for classes in the commercial subjects, or the general subjects. They visited classrooms where these subjects were to be taught, were issued textbooks, and then were released from school a little early. School would begin in earnest the next day.

No one invited Wilson to participate in a belt line, and he didn't bring up the subject. Instead, he headed for the hardware store in town. Truro Hardware was a fixture of long standing in the community. Matt Stokes was the son of the founder, and he had worked in the store all his life. Inheriting the business from his father, he didn't change a thing, but continued to serve his customers with supplies for the farm and home. Thoroughly honest, he could be counted on to give good measure at a fair price.

Wilson entered the store and waited until Mr. Stokes had finished with his customer.

"Afternoon, Mr. Stokes. I'm Wilson Jones. Mary Jones is my mother."

"Yes, I know you, boy. Your mother, too. What can I do for you?"

"Well, sir, I'm looking for a part-time job. I'll be getting out of school about this time every afternoon, and I'll be free all day on Saturday. Maybe you need some hard-working boy help to do the sweeping, run errands, haul freight from the depot, get the mail, things like that."

"Well, I don't know. Have you ever worked anywhere—away from your home?

"Yessir. This summer I worked as an axman in that government project building a lake and a dam. Mr. Elijah Turner was my boss. You can check with him to find out what kind of worker I am."

"Well, if you can please Elijah Turner you can probably please me. I'm going to see him tonight at a meeting. Why don't you check by here tomorrow afternoon after school, and we'll see what we see."

"I'll be here, Mr. Stokes. Thank you, sir."

* * *

That night at home, Wilson was full of talk about the first day of school, and especially about his talk with Matt Stokes. "I hope Elijah will give me a good rating. He said he would."

"Wils, tell me some more about high school. What was the biggest change from your old school last year?"

"This year we will change classrooms after each class. The teachers stay in the same room, and we go to them. And...the girls are prettier."

* * *

The next day Wilson made a beeline for the hardware store as soon as school was over. He didn't exactly run, but he didn't waste any time, either. He waited quietly until Mr. Stokes was free, then presented himself to him.

"Afternoon, Mr. Stokes. I came back, like you said. Did you get a chance to ask Elijah about me?"

"Sure did, Wilson. He remembered you. Said you are a good worker, never gave him any trouble. I think maybe my helper Sam and I are both getting a little slower, and we get more tired these days. We could probably use a pair of young legs around here in the afternoons to help us out. Tell you what....why don't we try you out for two weeks and see how we get along. If you can show me you're not afraid of work, if you can come to work on time, if you can treat my customers with respect, if you can learn something new every day...well, then, we'll make this a long-term arrangement. To start off, I'll pay you 50 cents an afternoon and a dollar for all day Saturday. How does that sound to you?"

"That sounds great, Mr. Stokes! I'll work real hard for you and try to learn everything I can. Do you want me to start today?"

"Well, I don't see why not! Put your books down back there where the bathroom is, then come back here. I'll introduce you to Sam and show you around."

Wilson deposited his books in the back and returned. Mr. Stokes introduced him to a balding middle-aged, wiry little man, wearing wide suspenders and a large leather belt, from which dangled a key ring with an assortment of keys that would choke a hippopotamus.

"Sam, this is Wilson Jones. I think you know his mother Mary. He is going to be helping us after school and on Saturday. Wilson, meet Sam Jernigan. If you keep your ears peeled you can learn a lot from Sam. We go back a long way."

"Howdy, Mr. Sam," said Wilson.

"Just plain Sam will do, young fella."

"OK, Wilson, come with me, and I'll show you around the store." Matt proceeded to walk Wilson around the store, pointing out the hardware section, the tools, the plumbing, the electrical section, the paints, the repair parts for mule-drawn plows.

"There's one thing that is the most important thing for you to learn, and that's the right way to count change. Suppose a customer owes you $1.69, and he gives you a five dollar bill. Lots of people try to subtract 1.69 from 5.00, but it's easy to make mistakes, even if you're a good "subtracter".

This is the way I want you to do it, and I *insist* you do it my way: You begin by saying, out loud, "$1.69 out of five dollars".—put a penny in the customer's hand and say "this makes 1.70", put a nickel and say "1.75, put a quarter and say "two dollars", add three ones and say "three, four. five dollars". Then you look him in the eye, smile, and say, "Thank you!"

There's a lot to be learned here, young man. Some of it you may already know, but a lot you don't. Don't be ashamed to ask questions. God didn't put any of us here already knowing. We all have to learn, and a hardware store is a good place to start."

"Now, every afternoon, about 30 minutes before closing time, I want you to get a broom and sweep all the aisles. We scatter dustdown—that's this sawdust with oil sprinkled in it—at one end of each aisle. Using the broom we sweep the dirt and trash and dustdown to the back of the store. Then we take it up with a dustpan and put it in the trash. Next we go back and sweep the other aisles. That's one of your regular jobs. I don't have to tell you to do it—you just do it. Now when you use that broom, I don't want to see you flipping end of the bristles. That throws trash on the bottom shelves. Brush the floor with the broom—don't flip it. Got that?"

"Yessir. Got that."

"Another thing, now. I don't want to hear you say, "Will that be cash or charge?" If you say that, you're offering the customer a charge account, and you aren't the Credit Manager—I am."

Mr. Stokes spent the better part of an hour with Wilson that first afternoon, showing him how he wanted things done. Sam took care of the customers, several times having to call on Matt for some help. Wilson helped several customers carry cumbersome purchases to their wagon or car.

"Always give full measure, Wilson. Always be polite, to colored or white. Always give the correct change. When a customer enters the store, stop whatever you're doing and see if you can help. The customer pays the bills.

One more thing, Wilson. When someone comes in the store, always greet them. Say Hello. If he's a customer, he'll know we're friendly. If he's a shoplifter, he'll know he's been seen."

As the afternoon drew to a close, Wilson swept the store, being careful to do a thorough job, not flipping the bristles. He thanked Mr. Stokes for letting him work and started out the door for home.

"Wilson, don't you live out Juniper Road?" Sam asked. "I drive right past your house. Would you like a ride?"

"Yessir, Sam!"

* * *

When Wilson arrived home that night he was full of talk about school, and was very excited about the job. "Fifty cents an afternoon, and a whole dollar for Saturdays! That's almost as much as this summer's job—no way it can be as hard work!"

Mary just smiled at her enthusiastic son. "We'll see," she thought.

The next day was Saturday. As soon as Wilson reported to work, Mr, Stokes handed him a broom and directed that his first job each morning would be to sweep the sidewalk. Then he washed the large plate glass show windows so that they shone.

Wilson had assumed that store hours would be the same as on other days of the week, and that the store would be open until about suppertime. Matt Stokes explained the peculiar nature of Saturday's retail hours in the rural South.

"Most of our customers live in the country, just like you do, but you live pretty close to town. Most people can't get to town except on Saturday—so Saturday becomes pretty special. Not only is it the only day country people can get supplies for the coming week. It's also the only day they get to visit with their friends and neighbors. They're too busy the rest of the time, farming or logging or washing clothes or whatever. On Saturday they come to town to stay, all day and into the evening. Lots of times they don't even begin shopping until dark! So, we merchants stay here with them—or give up their business."

Truro Hardware's floors were wood which had been treated with oil to preserve them and make them shine.. In some places the floor creaked when anyone walked on it. The high ceilings, too, were of wood. Wooden shelves reached from floor to ceiling on both walls. The store had ladders in both outside aisles. The ladders had a wheeled trolley on the upper end which rolled along a track suspended from the ceiling. The ladder's lower end had wheels which rolled on the floor, enabling the workers to retrieve items from the upper shelves. The shelves were neatly lined with merchandise, such as oil lamps and lanterns, kerosene cans, pots and pans, dishpans and wash basins. Like most other hardware stores, this one had a distinctive odor—a mixture of leather, insecticides, fertilizer, oil, paint and dust.

After the sidewalk and the show windows had been cleaned for the day, Mr. Stokes put his new helper to work on dusting the shelves and the merchandise on the shelves. "Begin at the top shelf.

First you bring the merchandise down, one shelf at a time; then clean and dust the shelf, then clean and dust the merchandise and take it back up the ladder. After you have cleaned the top shelf, then work on the one next to the top."

While he was busy on the ladder, into the store walked Jim Lane, Wilson's not-so-favorite cohort from the ax crew.

"Well! Will you look at the monkey on the monkey ladder! Wrap your tail around that ladder, boy, so you won't fall! Where did you find this monkey, Mr. Stokes? Hey, Mr. Stokes, better check your insurance—I worked with him all summer, and he was the clumsiest guy on the crew. He'll fall and hurt himself, for sure."

Knowing Jim Lane, Wilson was sure he was not receiving good-natured teasing. He made no reply, and continued what he was doing.

"Hey, Wilson! They sent me down here to borrow a set of shelf-stretchers, if you ain't usin' them. What about it?"

Mr. Stokes intervened. "Wilson is working. He doesn't have time for your foolishness, Lane. Anything I can do for you?"

"Nope. I was just coming in, looking for a job. Do you need a good man?"

"I don't think so, Lane. I've hired Wilson, and he's working out just fine."

"Well, You hired the wrong one, I'm afraid. You should fire him and hire me. I'm older and stronger and smarter."

"Wilson is OK with me. Thanks for coming by"

As Jim Lane left the store Mr. Stokes turned to Sam and muttered "That boy is all brass and no sense. He'd be bossing me around in ten minutes, 'til I fired him!"

* * *

When Wilson got off from work that first Saturday he was mighty glad to accept Sam's offer of a ride home. "I might not have swung an ax all day, but I sure did climb a ladder and run errands and stand around waiting on customers!" he told his mother.

The next day was Sunday. It required no attendance at school or job. Wilson enjoyed staying in bed a little longer, relaxing, but when he arose he found his mother stirring around, busy, just like any other day.

"There's no rest for the weary, young man. You've been going off every day at the crack of dawn and coming back after dark. That leaves me with the house and the animals and the laundry, and the garden. There's a few things I've been saving for you to do, so go ahead and eat your breakfast, then you belong to me for a while."

Later, when he had finished some of his tasks and was watering the garden they had planted the week before school began, he saw Simeon Bates passing by on the road.

"Hey, Sim! Come in for a minute! Haven't seen you for a couple of weeks! What you been doing?"

"Nothin' much, Wilson. Helped Mama a few days, then found a man who's going to sell firewood this winter. Working with him now. It's a pretty easy job after being in the woods with Elijah this summer."

Is the pay all right?"

"Not too bad. The man furnishes all the tools. Teached me how to use the crosscut saw. He pays me every Friday, and I'm off all weekend, just like before. With Elijah, we didn't have any stand-around time; but now I get several breaks in a day's work. It's not bad.

How about you, Wilson? How is school?"

"School is Ok. I'm just about the youngest one there. Classes are not too hard, yet, and nobody is giving me any trouble. But speaking of trouble, I saw Jim Lane yesterday. He came by the store where I'm working after school. Applied for a job, and told the boss he should fire me and hire him, 'cause he's so much smarter and harder working!"

"No stuff! Ain't that just like Jim? He ain't changed a bit in the two weeks since I last saw him! So you're working at a store? What store?"

"Truro Hardware. Working for Mr. Matt Stokes. He knows exactly how he wants the job done. He believes in getting his dollar's worth out of me, but he's treating me pretty decent so far. There's a fellow named Sam works there, too, and he gives me a ride home every afternoon."

"That's nice. I've been in that store. They treat colored people pretty decent there. And my daddy used to have to go in there a lot, to get things for Mister George at the gin. Hey, Wilson—I'm fixing to go fishing in a little while. You want to go?"

"Like to, Sim, but I've got a couple more things I promised to do for Mama. Will it be all right if we wait an hour?"

"Nothing wrong with that. It'll give me a chance to dig some worms. Come on down to my house when you get through, and then we'll walk down to the millpond and drown some of those worms. Maybe even catch a br'im or a crappie at the same time."

* * *

The next Saturday Mr. Stokes was teaching Wilson how to approach customers as they enter the store, when a man walked in the front door.

"Go ahead, Wilson. Go meet him", he instructed.

"Good morning, sir. How are you this morning? How may we help you today?"

The customer, a nicely dressed man, answered Wilson, smiling, "I'm fine, thank you." Then, curious, "You look familiar. Where have I seen you before?"

Wilson, too, was trying to make the connection, when the answer hit him. "Well, sir, you are the man who hired me for my last job, out in the woods. You had me report to Elijah Turner. When that job ended I came here and began to work for Mr. Stokes."

"Are you—yes, you are! You're the fellow who had to come back when he was old enough!! What is your name? And how did you make out with Elijah?"

"My name is Wilson Jones. Elijah and I got along fine. I sure do appreciate you giving me the chance to get on that ax crew."

The man extended his hand, took Wilson's hand, and shook it. "I'm Tom Stone. Glad to meet you, Wilson. But I'm curious about something. How old are you, really?"

Wilson grinned. "I'm fourteen. But I'll be fifteen soon, around Christmastime"

Stone, laughing, said "I didn't realize we were cheating the rules that much. You had to say you were eighteen before I could legally hire you, and you came through with the right words when you came back the second time. Say, my hat's off to you. I don't think I could have stood up to that work in that heat when I was fourteen."

Matt Stokes, curious about the happy conversation his young clerk was carrying on, walked up and joined the group. "Hello Tom. I thought you were back at school."

"I am back at school—for my last year at law school," he explained to Wilson. "I needed to take some things back so I won't freeze when the weather turns cool."

"Boy, I wish it would start doing that pretty soon. It's been a hot summer. But they're all hot."

Stone said to Mr. Stokes, "I think you've got a good man here. I met him early this summer, right after his birthday," with a wink to Wilson. "He's a determined fellow. Now, Wilson, help me. My mother needs a butter mold, and I also need some faucet washers."

"Nice to see you, Tom," said Matt Stokes. "Drop in any time you're in town."

"Oh, I will. Have to check on my young friend, here."

After Tom made his purchase and left, Mr. Stokes complimented Wilson. "That's what I call making customers feel at home!"

* * *

As he became more accustomed to being in high school, Wilson began to understand what the teachers expected from him. He felt that he could do the work, and he was enjoying the heady feeling of walking the halls with the older, more mature students.

He watched them, learning how they acted in different situations, so he could do likewise. He noticed that most of the boys walked around very casually, looking bored, poker-faced... Were they as bored as they looked? Wilson decided that was a possibility. But, he thought, they might only be unsure, like he was, not knowing exactly what to do. Their hair might have been brushed when they left home, but after several hours at school it was definitely disheveled, and the boys were oblivious of that fact, nor did they seem to care.

The girls, on the other hand, were very different. They walked around in groups, chattering animatedly among themselves. Frequently they broke out in smiles, or even giggles, following something that was said. Their faces were happy, and they were constantly looking around, interested in everything that was going on. They dressed more neatly than the boys, lipstick applied, hair neatly brushed. Wilson noticed that some of the girls came to school with a kerchief covering their hair. Immediately on arriving at school they disappeared into the girls' restroom, and soon emerged with curls shining. Wilson later learned they rolled their hair using socks as curlers.

He watched both the boys and the girls, but the girls were fascinating to him. He was an only child, and all his friends were boys, so he had been around the other sex very little. He noticed them more this year than in previous years, had confided to his mother that "the girls are prettier this year". He wished he felt comfortable around them. They seemed to enjoy life a lot more than the boys did.

After a week or so of walking to the store downtown after school in the afternoons, he noticed that one of his classmates, Betsy Jordan, was walking in the same direction. He had admired her as one of the prettiest girls in the class, and decided he would try to speak to her, and maybe walk alongside her. That way they might become friends.

For several days he watched, waiting for an opportunity to say hello and walk alongside, but she always seemed to have a friend with her. Finally, he saw that she was alone leaving the building, so he hurried to catch up, and, with his heart in his throat, croaked out "Hello, Betsy".

She looked around, saw who was speaking to her and smiled at him. " Oh, hi, Wilson".

"Mind if I walk with you a little ways?", he bravely asked.

I certainly don't mind, but I'm only going a little ways. My house is in the next block."

"Well, I'll walk that far with you, then. I'm going to town. I have an afternoon job at Truro Hardware."

"I've never had a job, except helping my mother with the dishes. Is it fun?"

"I wouldn't call it fun, but I think it's interesting. I'm learning a lot, but Mr. Stokes says there's a lot to learn".

"Oh, you work for Mr. Stokes. He's my cousin."

He's a nice man—he's treated me well so far."

Betsy slowed, and turned in toward the next house. "This is where I live. Thanks for the company."

"Thanks for letting me walk with you. I enjoyed it".

"Me, too. Bye".

Betsy's house was a neat cottage set in a grassy yard, surrounded by shrubbery, with several large trees providing shade. There was a small front porch, with two chairs and a swing suspended by chains from the ceiling.

As Wilson walked on toward town, he thought "That was nice, and it wasn't so hard. Why was I afraid to try it?"

Wilson continued to think about Betsy, both at work and at school. He looked forward to the afternoon walks to her house, as he was on his way to work. Those walks didn't happen every day, though he would have liked that. Some days she left the school in the company of a group of girls, laughing and talking. If she saw Wilson, she waved gaily and smiled, but made no move to leave her group to join him. He was content to join her on the days she emerged from the building alone. She always seemed glad to see him, and the conversation never lagged on the way to her house.

Betsy wore her dark hair rather short, close to her head. She frequently wore a white blouse and a red sweater. Wilson often went to sleep at night thinking of that dark hair, white blouse, and red sweater. Being an inexperienced country boy, he probably had never heard of a "crush", but he definitely had a crush on Betsy.

Several times they were spotted by Jim Lane as they walked together. Being a couple of years older, Jim sized up the situation right away, and decided to have a little fun with Wilson and his "love affair". He thought over the possible ways he might attack the problem, then decided on his course of action.

One day as classes were changing, he managed to get close enough to Betsy to speak to her as they descended the stairs to the classrooms on the ground floor.

"Hi," he said.

"Hello."

"My name's Jim Lane. I've been watching you. You're cute. Too cute for that Jones boy I've seen hanging around you".

"How is that?"

"He's mighty friendly with those colored girls that live out his way. Did you know that?"

"What are you talking about?"

"He takes long walks with them, holding hands. I'd be careful of him, if I were you. You're a nice girl. Could ruin your reputation, easy".

Jim moved on off to his next class, smiling to himself at the burr he had inserted under Wilson's saddle. He left Betsy surprised and perplexed, her mind racing, heart beating wildly. She was almost in tears. "He seemed such a nice boy", she thought.

After school, Betsy and Wilson came out of the building at almost the same time. He said "Hi!", and walked to her side.

Betsy said nothing. She kept walking, looking neither to the right nor the left.

"Are you OK?" No answer. "Is anything wrong?" No answer. May I walk with you?"

"It's a free country," she said, but did not speak another word all the way to her house.

Wilson continued on to work at the store, wondering what he had done to change the situation.

* * *

The situation remained frosty for several weeks. Wilson doggedly tried to resume their little short walks to her house in the afternoon, but Betsy always managed to leave the school in the company of at least one girlfriend, thwarting his efforts to be alone with her.

Her best friend, Dot Hubbard, noticed the change in Betsy's routine, and asked her about it. "Has something happened between you and Wilson? You used to walk together pretty regularly. Now you don't, and he's hanging around looking like a lovesick puppy. What's going on?"

"Oh, Dot, I don't know…Somebody told me something about Wilson….It's… well, it's something I never would have expected….I don't know what to think….I really did like him, but….I don't know."

What were you told…and who told you?"

"Do you know a boy named Jim Lane? He's older than we are. He told me that Wilson has a girlfriend who is colored. They walk together, holding hands, he says. He says if I go with Wilson it could ruin my reputation."

"I don't know Jim Lane. I've seen him, but don't know him….. What does Wilson say about this?"

"I haven't said anything to him. I haven't spoken to him in weeks!"

"Well, goodness gracious! Are you going to abandon the boy you know and like, on the word of somebody you don't know from Adam, without even asking Wilson his side of the thing? There may be nothing to it!"

"Oh, Dot! I'm really afraid of what he'll say. Suppose it's true!"

"Well, Betsy, at least you'll know the truth instead of wondering!"

* * *

"Wilson, would you walk home with me today?" Betsy had approached him between classes.

"You bet I will!"

He was waiting for her as she descended the steps from the school. He was excited. They had not exchanged a normal word for two weeks. Betsy was nervous as a cat. She didn't know what to say or how to begin. Then, taking a deep breath, she said,

"I've been very upset. Upset with you. And I don't know if what I heard is true or false. I guess the only way to know is to ask you, and when you answer I want the truth. Will you tell me the truth?"

"Betsy, I've never told you anything but the truth. You'll get it today. What in the world do you want to ask me?

She took another deep breath. Then, her voice trembling, she said, "We've walked after school, like this, a good many times. I have enjoyed it. In fact, you were getting to be my favorite friend among the boys....but....oh, Wilson, somebody told me that you also walk with a colored girl, holding hands! Is that true?"

Wilson was incredulous. "Of course it's not true! Who in the world could have told you that? I know some colored people… know one boy pretty well…but no girls….Who told you that?"

"A boy named Jim Lane talked to me one day. Said he didn't want me to ruin my reputation by walking with a boy who holds hands with…you know".

That sorry son of a gun! I know Jim Lane. He's a troublemaker from the word 'go'". He loves to pick on me. Don't pay any attention to anything he says. Especially about me."

"Oh, I'm so relieved. Dot was right. I went to her for advice, and she said I should talk it over with you."

"I'm going to thank Dot the next time I see her. Tomorrow. Now…let's go back a bit. Did you say I was getting to be your favorite friend among the boys? If you believe what I said, can I still be your favorite? You certainly are my favorite friend, boy or girl!"

"Yes, Wilson, I believe you, and I'm so relieved. You are my favorite."

* * *

Wilson whistled all the way to work. His mind was a-whirl. He felt like running and jumping, like a kid! He was so relieved that Betsy was no longer giving him the chill, so pleased that she said he was her favorite. What a great day!

Mr. Stokes put him to work assembling joints of stovepipe. "Cold weather is on the way, Wilson. We'll have to be ready for the change in seasons. And when you finish that, use this yardstick and measure off some of this cotton rope in 12-yard lengths. Cut it and coil it neatly. We always sell a lot of plow lines, whatever the season."

When Wilson returned home that evening he found his mother in a somber mood.

"What's the matter, Mama?

"Oh, nothing, Wilson".

"Yes there is, Mama. You're worried up about something".

"Yes, I am worried. Wils, we got a letter today, from the hospital. Your Dad is not doing so good. They say his condition is worse than it was when he got there. They say I should come to Columbia and see him. Maybe that will cheer him up, help him get better".

"That's what you must do, Mama. It will do Daddy so much good. How much will it cost to ride the bus over there and back?"

"About five dollars, I think. But I'm not sure we can spare the five dollars."

"Of course we can do that for Daddy! Let' see. Today is Tuesday. Why don't you plan to go Thursday on the early bus. You can visit him for a few hours and come back late in the afternoon!! That will work out fine. Daddy will be so pleased to see you!"

Mary finally agreed to go. She was anxious to see her husband, It had been several months since he left for the hospital. She had really missed him....And now he is not doing well!.....Maybe her presence would help...but she can't stay...just a quick pop-in visit, then back here to Truro. Oh, Lord! What if he doesn't get well? What if he..."

The next day after work she shampooed her hair, scrubbed her face and hands, her knees and feet, washed and carefully ironed the dress, her best dress, that she planned to wear. All the while she was praying for a good visit, for Dave's recovery, for his return to Truro.

At work Wednesday afternoon Wilson had very little to say. Mr. Stokes noticed the difference in his demeanor and asked if there was something wrong. Wilson didn't need much urging, and he soon had told the whole story of his father's worsening condition and his mother's impending trip to see him the next day.

"Are you going to see your father, too, Wilson?" Mr. Stokes asked.

"No, sir."

"Do you want to go? Does she want you to go?"

"Oh, yes sir. I really want to go see my dad, and protect Mama...but we can't afford it".

"I'll be glad to buy your ticket, Wilson."

"You will?.... No, sir, I couldn't let you do that...How could I pay you back?"

"It's not necessary. We have a rule here at the hardware. Anybody who has family trouble gets a free bus ticket. Sam used his, once, but he's happily married now. No kidding. I want you to go."

Unused to such generosity on the part of any other than his parents, Wilson spent the rest of the afternoon alternating between exhilaration that he would be able to accompany his mother to Columbia, and a feeling of guilt that he was causing Matt Stokes to dole out money to his newest employee.

On the way home that evening, Wilson and Sam talked about Mr. Stokes. "Let me tell you how I see Matt Stokes. He knows exactly how he wants us to do certain things, and he *demands* that we do it that way, *his* way," Sam opined. "But underneath that insistence on his way of doing business, he is a kind man. Been good to me."

Wilson hopped out of Sam's car that evening and raced into the house.

"Mama! I'm going with you! Mr. Stokes says I must go with you! He says the store has a policy that gives a free bus ticket to any employee who has family trouble! He has given me the day off, and he has bought my ticket! Isn't that wonderful? Now I can see Daddy, and help you".

Mary didn't say anything for a minute.

"Mama! Did you hear what I said? I can go, too!.... Do you want me to go?"

"Oh, Wils! I'm so thankful! I was deathly afraid to go off by myself to a strange city where I've never been before. I didn't know what I would run into in Columbia. But .I knew your daddy needed me, and I want to do anything I can to help him...but I was afraid....Not afraid any more, if my strong son is going with me....

Wasn't that good of Mr. Stokes to buy your ticket? We'll have to do something nice for him, soon. Now, let's see what you're going to wear....school clothes I think. That's the best we've got, and they're clean.... What will we do about lunch?"

* * *

They were awake at first light, and mother and son hopped out of bed quickly. They donned the clothes they had laid out the night before. They ate their breakfast, and, taking the box lunch Mary had prepared, were soon on their way. They covered the mile into town in record time and were waiting when the Trailways bus arrived.

It was Wilson's first ride on a bus, and he was intrigued with watching the speed as they roared out of town. He soon tired of watching the monotony of cotton fields, separated by patches of woods and ditches, and relaxed back into his seat. He glanced at his mother, and saw that she was lost in thought and apprehension. He patted her hand.

"Daddy is really going to be so surprised to see us! He will be so happy!"

"Yes, he will," she assured him, patting him back. Then they both fell silent, looking out the window, each lost in thought. The rest of the hour-long ride passed without conversation.

As the bus pulled into the large station in Columbia, Mary and Wilson climbed down the steps and looked around. They went over to a window marked "Information" and asked of the person inside, "We want to go to the TB Hospital. Can we take a city bus from here?"

"Yes Ma'am. You sure can. Take the bus labeled "Southside". It will come to the corner outside in about ten minutes. It will take you to the front door of the Hospital."

"Which bus do we take to come back here to catch the 4:30 bus to Truro?"

"That same Southside bus, but you'll catch it on the other side of the street, because it will be returning."

"How much does it cost to ride the bus?"

"Ten cents apiece, each way."

"Thank you."

"You're more than welcome."

They located the Southside bus, paid their dimes, and took their seats. Wilson noticed that his mother's hands were clenched so tightly to the strap of her purse that the knuckles were white. "It'll be all right, Mama. In just a few minutes we'll see Daddy."

After about a ten minute ride the bus stopped in front of a large brick building with rows and rows of windows, all of which were open. White curtains were flapping in the open windows as the breeze worked its way through the building.

Mary and Wilson climbed the stone steps that led up to the front door and went inside. They approached a desk which advertised "Visitors".

"May I help you?" The smiling lady across the desk greeted them.

"Yes, Ma'am. We're the Joneses from Truro. We've come to see my husband, Jefferson Davis Jones."

"Is he expecting you?" the lady asked.

"No, Ma'am. We just decided to come, and here we are."

"All right. Just a minute while I see where his bed is located. Ah, here we are. Mr. Jones is in Ward C. Take this Visitor's Pass, go up those stairs and to the right. You'll see a sign that says "Ward C". Show your Pass to the Nurse in charge, and she will take care of you from there."

They climbed the stairs, full of uncertainty and apprehension. How will he look? How bad is he? Will he know us? Thoughts and fears swirled around in their heads. They were afraid to hope, afraid of crushing disappointment.

They approached the open door over which hung a sign that proclaimed it to be "Ward C". They stood in the door and looked inside at a large room. All the windows were open. Many white metal beds were grouped in that portion of the room that was flooded with sunlight. The beds had large wheels at the base of each bedpost. There was a patient in each bed, some sitting up and conversing with each other, others lying inert beneath the sheets.

After a few minutes a nurse noticed them standing there and came over to meet them. "Hello", she said. "May I help you?"

Mary handed her the Visitor's Pass and said, "I'm Mary Jones, and this is my son Wilson. We've come over today to see my husband, Dave Jones. We got a letter from the hospital saying he is not doing so well. Can we see him?"

"Yes, Mrs. Jones. I'll take you to him. We would rather you not stay too long. He is pretty weak. After you've had a little visit, we three can talk about Dave, and you can see the doctor, too. He will be making rounds later this morning. Follow me, please, right this way."

Mary and Wilson followed the nurse to one end of the sunlit area where they found Dave, lying motionless on his bed, eyes closed. His skin was pale, almost colorless. His face was very thin, as were his hands, clasped across his chest.

"Mr. Jones," the nurse said, "Wake up. You have a nice surprise."

Dave opened his eyes and turned his head in their direction. His eyes lit up in surprise and an expression of pleasure came into his face. "Mary!... Wilson! How did you get here? How long can you stay? I have missed you two something awful!"

With Mary on one side of the bed and Wilson on the other, they each held one of Dave's hands which trembled in weakness. He looked from one face to the other, basking in the pleasure of seeing them and being with them.

He tried to ask them questions, but soon had to stop because talking led to coughing. His visitors took up the conversation, relating details about the house and garden, Wilson's summer employment, his job at the hardware store, and high school. They kept their comments light and happy, omitting any reference to hardships they may have faced without him.

After twenty or thirty minutes, the nurse approached Dave's bed and crooked her finger at the visitors, signaling them to follow her. "He's getting tired," she said.

She led the way to an unoccupied corner of the ward and pulled up three chairs. "My name is Clara Melton. I work on this ward every day and have taken care of your man since he got here. He's not doing so well, Mrs. Jones. We're concerned. He has lost some weight, and you can see his color is not good. He complains of chest pain, and he coughs."

Mary and Wilson exchanged worried looks. "Do you think you can help him?" Mary asked.

"You probably should ask that question of the doctor," the nurse replied. "Dr. Shipley will be making rounds any minute now. You can talk with him after he has seen the patients on the ward".

Very soon after this conversation Nurse Melton excused herself and went to join a middle-aged man in a white coat. Dr. Shipley was an energetic looking man of medium height, almost completely bald except for a fringe of sandy hair. He wore horn rimmed glasses which he used for reading the charts, then he pushed them up above his eyebrows when he talked. A stethoscope hung around his neck, and was constantly in use as he visited each patient's bedside. He listened intently to the comments of nurse and patients, and spoke to the patients in a calm, reassuring tone.

After he had visited all the patients, Nurse Melton spoke with him for a minute or two, indicating Mary and Wilson where they sat in the distant corner. The doctor nodded, and walked over to where they waited.

He took the seat that had been used by the nurse and introduced himself. "Good morning. I am Sidney Shipley. Glad to meet Dave's family. You received my letter about Dave, I suppose. Decided to come over and see for yourself, did you? That's good. I'm glad you're here. He has felt pretty lonesome."

"Oh, Doctor. He looks so weak! Tell us about his condition. Do you think you can help him? Will he be able to come home? Will he get well?"

"Mrs. Jones, tuberculosis is a tough disease to beat .We believe it is caused by a bacillus, a germ, that can be passed from person to person. We don't have a medicine that stops the bacillus in its tracks, nor do we have a medicine to repair the damage to lungs that have been affected by this disease. Sometimes we are able to slow and control the effects of tuberculosis by exposing the patient to lots of fresh air and sunshine. We even go so far as to have the patients face the sun and open their mouths, hoping the benefits of sun will reach their inner parts. That's why these windows are all open, and the patients' beds are grouped on the sunny part of the ward.

Your husband has not responded to our fresh-air-and-sunshine treatment, so far. We want to give that more time. It may yet work. If his situation does not improve within a few more months, we will consider the next step, and will discuss it with you fully at that time.

In the meantime, may I suggest that you write to him regularly, and, if possible, come over for a visit from time to time. Love and loved ones are very helpful in treating serious illness. Now, do you have any questions?"

"Doctor, we don't know enough to ask many questions. We just want Dave back home with us, where he belongs. We need him so bad!"

"You can be sure we will do our best for him, Mrs. Jones, Mrs. Melton and the other nurses are very kind and very capable. He will have the best care we can give him."

"Thank you, Doctor. The nurse said we can visit some more after Dave rests, so if it's all right we'll just sit right here and eat the lunch we brought from home. Then when he's awake again we'll talk some more before we head back to Truro."

An hour later Dave was awake again, and Nurse Melton escorted them back to his bedside, where the three of them enjoyed patting, holding hands, and smiling at each other. When

Dave again exhibited fatigue, Mary and Wilson gave him hugs and kisses, along with promises of more visits.

As mother and son walked out of the hospital they clasped each other's hands, each seeking strength from the other.

They were very quiet until they were once again on the bus bound for Truro. Mary broke the silence. "Wils, your dad looks so sick! White as a sheet! Weak as water! It is such a shock to see him like this!"

Wilson patted her hand. "Yes, Ma'am. I feel the same way. Didn't expect it to be this bad. I hope and pray he'll get better."

"Well, for sure I've got to write him and come see him—do anything we can to cheer him up."

She was quiet again for a long time. Then, she said firmly, "Wils, there is a good chance it will be a long time before your daddy can get back home; even longer before he will be strong enough to hold down a job. And we have to face it—as bad as I hate to even think about it, he may not get out of that hospital at all."

"Yes'm," Wilson replied. "After seeing him today, it appears you may be right."

Then, hesitantly, his mother went on. "That means everything is up to us. We can't count on your daddy to add anything to our earnings for the family. Everything is up to us. This is a heavy burden to put on a high school boy, but there's no way around it. I'm going to need your help, Wilson."

"You can count on me, Mama."

They rode the rest of the way to Truro in silence.

CHAPTER THREE

BETSY

The next day Wilson and Betsy walked together to her house after school. He was preoccupied, unusually quiet.

Betsy queried, "Is something the matter? You're mighty quiet."

With that, his emotional gates were opened, and the entire story of his father's illness poured out. He recounted the bus trip of the day before, the fragile appearance of his father, the doctor's comments,—everything.

She put her hand on his arm. "Wilson, I'm so sorry. Is there anything I can do?" Her facial expression showed her empathy for his situation.

"Thanks, Betsy, but I don't know of anything anybody can do, except the doctors. I do appreciate your friendship, and count on seeing you like this, when we leave school. But, say, this is always such a short walk. Would you let me come see you, like on Sunday afternoon when I don't have to work? We could swing in your porch swing, and walk around the block…things like that."

"I'd like that. Let me ask my folks, though."

* * *

"Mother. I think I've told you about my school friend, Wilson."

"Is he the boy who walks home with you on his way to the hardware store?"

"That's the one. He's an awfully nice boy, and I like him. He has asked if he can come see me some Sunday afternoon when he's not working. We could swing in the porch swing, walk around the block...things like that. We wouldn't bother you and Daddy."

"I don't know, Betsy. You're awful young to be having dates..."

"Oh, Mother! This is not a date! It's just a Sunday afternoon visit, in the broad open daylight, for Heaven's sake! Not a date at all!"

"Well, okay. I'll talk to your father about it, but I'll tell you right now, he is not going to allow you to have a date when you're this young. It's just too soon!"

"It won't be a date, Mother. And you can watch us through the window if it worries you all that much. He's a nice boy, I tell you."

"I'll ask him. But don't get your hopes up."

* * *

The day after the visit the hospital, Mary Jones was serving lunch customers at the Sanitary Café. "Meat loaf, ham, pork chops or chicken, and choice of three vegetables, fifty cents." That was the Monday menu, and the other days didn't vary too far from it. Though, on Fridays, like today, Frank always offered fish. There were powerful few Catholics in town, but he thought it was the thing to do. "One of those mackerel-snappers might come in, some day, and if we didn't offer it, where would we be?," he thought. Frank didn't have anything against Catholics, he just liked to call them "mackerel-snappers". It sounded colorful, and the way he figured it, if a man didn't speak English real well, colorful was a good way to be.

As the lunch trade slackened, then disappeared, Mary sidled up to Frank as she was bringing clean crockery from the dishwashing sink to the shelves where it is kept. "Mr. Zervos, when you have a minute..."

"I ain't no Mister, Mary Jones. My name is Frank."

"Well, Mr. Frank....Frank... when we have a minute I'd like to talk with you."

"Whatsamatter, Mary? You not happy? Thinking of quitting? Don't talk to me about that. You doing good job. Best job any waitress in coupla years. Don't quit."

"No, Mister...No, Frank. I don't want to quit. I want to know if you can give me some night work, maybe on the weekends. Frank, we need some more money. My husband is sick."

"You want more work? You want to work Saturday night? And you don't flirt with the customers! I'll be son of a camel driver, if the great God is not on my side today! Yes Ma'am, you can get more work. You can start Sat'day, tomorrow, four o'clock til eleven, two dollars, plus tips! I warn you, though, some of them Sat'day customers a little rougher than the ones you see at lunch. Don't take nothin' off of them."

"I'll be careful. Thank you, Mis...Frank."

* * *

Saturday arrived, and Mary reported to work at 4 PM. She found the menu different from the fifty-cent plate she was accustomed to.

Hamburger steak, fried potatoes, and salad	65 cents
Ham steak, boiled potatoes, green beans	75 cents
Fried flounder, cole slaw, hush puppies	75 cents
Round steak, baked potato, salad	1.00
T-bone steak, mushrooms, onions, potato and salad	1.25
There was a notation at the bottom of the menu: set-ups	25 cents

Upon inquiring, Mary learned that a set-up includes a bucket of ice, a tablespoon in lieu of ice tongs, a 7-up, or ginger ale, coke or water. It was also possible to get a wedge of lemon if that was desired. It was explained to Mary that many customers brought their own liquor, in a brown paper bag, and placed it on the table, or on the floor at their feet. The set-up was to help make the drink palatable. This was, after all, soon after the repeal of Prohibition, and Truro was in the Bible Belt. State law made it illegal to sell liquor by the drink, but anyway, no self-respecting Christian would dream of ordering a drink in a public place. It was far more respectable and proper to bring your potable from home in a paper bag.

Mary was one of two waitresses on duty that night, the other being a slip of a girl named Bonnie who was obviously the one whom Frank had complained about. Bonnie spent a fair amount of time posturing herself in what she deemed her most attractive pose. Her walk from the dining room to the kitchen was less a businesslike, purposeful striding than a languorous stroll complete with hip motion and smiles, right and left. It was an impressive performance, but Mary noted that her customers looked annoyed as they waited for their meal, or for their check.

That first night Mary's tables were occupied primarily by couples, groups of two or four. She had an easy time serving them, and ran into nothing unpleasant. There was a table composed of nothing but men, with several brown bags in evidence. That gave her the opportunity to sell a few set-ups, and she noticed that the volume of the conversation increased as the men downed a few drinks. They treated her well, however, and she gave them attentive service while keeping her distance.

By the time the tables finally emptied and had been re-set for the breakfast meal the next morning, Mary had three dollars in tips in the pocket of her dress, and she was very tired. She told Frank and Bonnie "Good night" and went outside to begin her walk home. She found Wilson waiting.

"Wils! What are you doing here?" She asked, surprised.

"Thought you might like some company. That's a lonely road after dark."

"What a thoughtful thing to do", she thought. "Just like his daddy."

She said, "That's very kind of you, sir. I'd love to walk with you", and they walked home, arm in arm, while she related the experiences of the evening.

"Frank Zervos is a nice man", she reported. "He does most of the cooking, but manages to keep an eye on the dining room, and the cash register. He knows what goes on out there where we are.

"Zervos is a strange name around here", Wilson observed. "Did he grow up in Truro?"

"Oh, no. He was born "across the water"', a place called Armenia. Have you ever heard of the "starving Armenians"? Frank was one of them. But he was able to get a job on a steamship, a freighter, and he worked his way across the ocean. He landed in New Jersey, got a job in a restaurant kitchen, and after a couple of years of saving money and learning the food business, he decided to come South. He says the towns are smaller and the people don't hurry around so. At least, that's the way he describes it."

"And you got tips? How much is a tip?"

"A tip is whatever your customer wants to give you, to thank you for good service. Some people don't give you any tips. They probably don't realize waitresses don't get a regular salary, but it's salary plus tips. At that big table of men tonight, the check came to ten dollars. They gave a whole dollar, as much as you got for working in the woods all day! But most of the time, my tip is a dime or a quarter. It depends on the size of the check, and how well you served them. Ten cents on the dollar is the usual amount for a tipper—though, maybe a flirty waitress like Bonnie can do better. But that's not for me. I'm a married woman, and not interested."

They talked companionably all the way home.

* * *

That same evening, as soon as Betsy was asleep for the night, her mother got Mr. Jordan's attention by saying, "John, we've got to talk."

He put aside his newspaper and said, "What is it, Alice?"

"It's Betsy. She wants to have a date."

"A date? At her age? What is she, fourteen, or fifteen? That's pretty young."

"All right, I'll tell her. Even if it's on our front porch. I don't like the idea."

"Wait a minute, Alice. Let's start over. What did she ask to do?"

"The boy who walks home with her from school most days—Wilson Jones is his name—asked her if he could come by on a Sunday afternoon when he's not working. He suggested they could sit in the porch swing and talk. My first reaction was "No", but she protested—said it would be daylight, we could watch through the window, all that."

"Who is this boy, what kind of job? Where does he live? Who are his parents?"

"His father, Dave Jones, is in the TB hospital, I think. His mother's name is Mary, and I think she may work at the Sanitary Café. The boy works at Truro Hardware after school and on Saturdays. That's about all I know about them, except that Betsy thinks he's very nice."

"Well, give me a day to check around. The mother may be that new waitress at the Café, and I'll ask Frank about her— I'll ask Matt about the boy—what's his name again? Wilson Jones?" That should give us a little bit to go on."

"John, I don't know about his family situation. They live out in the country somewhere. I've never seen him wear anything but jeans. How can a boy today make anything of himself with a start like that?"

"Don't forget about Abraham Lincoln and Horatio Alger, Alice. And, besides, he hasn't proposed, as far as we know, so we don't have to cross those bridges yet. Just give me a day to check him out."

* * *

The next evening after the supper dishes were put away and the house got quiet, John asked, "Has she gone to sleep?" He got an affirmative nod.

"Well, let me tell you what I found out. Mrs. Jones has only been working at the Café for a month or so, but Frank is high on her. Says she is personally neat and clean, has a good manner toward the customers, good relationship with the colored help in the kitchen. Hard worker. Frank said the boy, Wilson, waits for her on Saturday nights, and walks her home.

Matt Stokes knows something about the family. Says the daddy is OK, but not a good provider. They live in a tenant house on Juniper Road that belongs to an uncle. The daddy does have TB, and has been in the hospital for several months, doing no better than 'fair'. The mama is a hardworking, good woman. She apparently knows the right way to do things, because Matt says Wilson has been raised right. He's working hard, and learning, Matt says."

"I'm still worried about their financial condition. What will people say if she starts out dating a boy who is a redneck?"

"Gosh, Alice. You haven't even met the boy yet. Why don't you tell Betsy she can invite him to sit on the porch with her some Sunday afternoon soon? We'll have a chance to meet him, see what he's like. We can put a stop to it if that seems to be the right thing to do. But let me say this: I'd rather she date, or see, a boy who has the gumption to get and keep a job and be somewhat independent, than some sissybritches Lord Fauntleroy who doesn't have enough sense to come in out of a shower of rain!"

* * *

October with its clear dry air and blue skies was the prettiest month of the year in Truro, unless you like April and May. Wilson and Betsy were walking home from school, and she said, "Would you like to come to my house Sunday afternoon? Mother said it would be all right. We can sit on the porch swing and talk, as you suggested."

"Would I like to come? You bet I would! Mama is planning to take the bus to Columbia for a day with Daddy—and I'll look forward to seeing you for more than just a few minutes at a time. What time? Around three o'clock?"

"That should be all right. I'll look forward to it."

"Me, too!"

On Sunday Wilson appeared at the Jordan home, promptly at three. He was scrubbed until he shone. His hair was neatly combed. His clothes were clean and his shoes brushed. He was nervous. He rapped tentatively on the door. Apparently the knock was sufficient for Betsy waiting just inside, for she opened the door immediately.

"Hi, Wilson. Glad to see you".

"Glad to see you, too", he replied.

Let's have a seat on the swing", she suggested. "Mother and Daddy are taking their Sunday afternoon naps right now, but they want to come out to meet you after they get up."

"Oh, good," he said, repressing a gulp.

It was an Indian Summer day, sunny and mild. There was a slight breeze, and the sky was that special October blue. The air was clean and dry, but it carried the acrid smell of smoke from the leaves that had been burned the day before. They swung in silence for a few minutes, then each turned to the other, at the very same time, and said. "I—" They giggled a little, then Wilson said "You first."

"Well, I was just going to say that this is nice. What were you going to say?"

He grinned sheepishly. "The very same thing." They both giggled again, and smiled at each other.

Soon the conversation began to flow naturally, and there were few gaps, none of them awkward. She told him about having gone to a college football game with her father, about her friendship with Dot Hubbard, and about enjoying reading novels, especially Nancy Drew mysteries. He related the story of meeting Tom Stone, and how he had been hired for his summer job, four years before he was old enough to be legal.

As he was winding up that story, the door opened, and out walked Betsy's mother and father. Wilson's mother had given him training in manners, so he stood up as they joined the group.

"Hello, Wilson, I'm John Jordan, Betsy's father, and this is her mother, Alice. Please take your seat. We're glad to have the opportunity to make your acquaintance."

"Thank you, sir. Hello, Mrs. Jordan. Thank you for letting me come to see Betsy this afternoon."

"Wilson, as we were coming out to join you, you were finishing a story about your summer job. Would you mind sharing it with us?"

"Well, sir, my daddy is sick in the hospital, and both Mama—Mother and me –I—Mother and I had to find jobs to keep the family going." He related the entire story from beginning to end, emphasizing the role Tom Stone had played. He told of his pleasure that they are now friends, through the hardware store.

"My goodness! All that, and you're still fourteen?" Mrs. Jordan asked.

"Yes'm. Until the 19th of December."

"Do you like the hardware store?"

"Oh, yes'm. There's a lot to learn there". I've really enjoyed it. Mr. Matt has taught me a lot."

Betsy, impatient with the niceties of getting acquainted, interrupted with, "Mother, is it all right if we walk around the block?"

Mrs. Jordan glanced at her husband, received a nod, and replied, "That will be all right. Don't be gone long, and let us know when you are back."

Wilson stood up, extended his hand to Mr. Jordan, and said, "Nice to meet you both. Thank you again for letting me come."

The Jordans returned to the interior of the house as Betsy and Wilson walked down the steps to go around the block. They walked slowly, glancing around at their surroundings while stealing sidelong glances at each other.

As soon as they had turned the corner, out of sight of her house, Wilson ventured, "Betsy…?" "Yes', she answered. "I know you're not a colored girl…" Her head swung around quickly to look at him, a puzzled look on her face.

"I know you're not colored, but do you think I could hold your hand, anyhow?" He grinned. Her shocked expression turned to amusement as she realized he was playing with her, teasing.

"It's all right with me, if you don't think it will ruin your reputation!" she replied. And they each happily clasped the hand of the other. They proceeded on down the sidewalk, talking and holding hands. They covered three blocks before returning to Betsy's house.

She opened the front door and called "We're home" to her parents before settling back down in the swing with Wilson.

Mrs. Jordan appeared a few minutes later with a pitcher of iced tea and some cookies. After partaking of the refreshments, Wilson said his goodbyes and departed for home.

"You're right, Betsy. He is a nice boy", her mother declared.

* * *

Simeon Bates grinned with pleasure as he drove the pickup truck along the road that wound through the pines. He was careful to keep an even speed, and to steer where the sand was most packed and rutted, away from the steep sides of the track where the sand was loose, and deep.

The Boss had taught him to drive the truck. He recognized Sim's native intelligence, and realized he had hired a person who could learn. He immediately began to teach him those things that would benefit the Boss in his business. He taught him the best way to use a two-man crosscut saw. He taught Sim how to use the one-man saw, and how to choose between them. Sim learned how to split pine, or oak. He learned how to load, how unload, how to stack wood in a customer's yard so the customer was pleased, etc. The boss also taught him to change the oil in the truck.

Sim soaked it up. He was already good with the ax. He became proficient with the other tools, the saws, the splitters, the truck, the customer-pleasing ways. He began to see that he, Sim Bates, could be the boss of his own crew, once he learned the business—and saved some money.

The truck climbed the last hill, rattled to a comfortable stop, and Sim surveyed the view afforded him. He saw a wooden house, much like Wilson's— a typical tenant house, but with chinaberry trees, a swept yard, and a few outbuildings. All were in pretty good condition. There was a porch attached to the front of the house, with rocking chairs. A pump nearby was housed in a pump house. "Now, that's nice," thought Sim.

He drove on up into the yard. As he drew nearer, he could see an old man sitting on the porch, watching the truck. He stopped, cut the ignition, and got out.

"How do, sir", he said. "You Mr. Harrington?"

"Mose Harrington is my name," the old man said gravely.

"I'm Sim Bates, Mr. Harrington. My Boss is Malachi Rogers. Sent me out here. Said you had some timber you would sell for firewood."

"Dinah! Come out here!" the old man bellowed. "Them people are here about the firewood!"

In a minute a young woman appeared on the porch. "Yes, Granddaddy, you want me to show him the trees?"

"Yeah. Take 'im down there and let him look 'em over. When you come back…is it Sim?…you can tell me what your boss will pay. And it better be a good price, Sim, or we won't do no business! I don't have to sell to you!"

The girl got in the truck with Sim and directed him to drive behind the house about 300 yards, where she indicated a small grove of trees. "Granddaddy wants these trees cleared off. If they're gone, he says, the fields around this grove will be easier to work."

Sim dismounted the truck and walked around the grove, surveying the situation. He had already decided how much to offer, but was in no hurry. He wanted to sneak a few looks at the girl while he looked at the trees. He hoped to have a conversation with her.

"Your granddaddy got a nice place here. You live here all the time?

"Most of my life. I go to school in Truro, to Coleman Institute. You know it?"

"Yeah. How you get there? It a long way from out here."

I board there, five days a week. Live in a dormitory. Study hard, 'cause it's important. Then I come here most weekends, to help my Granddaddy."

"He live by hisself? How he plow these fields?"

"He has helpers. Pays them by the day to tend the animals, plow, and everything else."

"He so old. How he manage them?"

Granddaddy's tough. He's had this place a long time. His daddy had it before him. Got it after the War, from the Yankees. Had to be tough to keep it all this time, through those rough times.

"You right. Well, we better go back up to the house and see the old man. He waiting to hear the price..."

As they drove back, Sim watched Dinah out of the corner of his eye. "Never saw anybody look that good, smell that good, talk that good", he thought.

Mose Harrington was still sitting where they had left him. "Well, did you see it? How much you offer?"

"Mr. Harrington, it's a nice grove, but..."

"Don't "but" me, boy! Tell me your price, and be ready to crank that truck and go back to town!"

"A hundred dollars, and we'll leave the stumps no more'n a foot out of the ground..."

"Good enough. It's a done deal. You can start sawing when you hand me the money in U S greenbacks."

"I'll bring the money, and we'll start work in a day or two."

* * *

Sim came back to the Harrington place a week later, armed with a helper and a hundred dollars which he conveyed to Mose Harrington. "All right," Mose said, "you can cut now."

Sim did not get a glimpse of Dinah during the business transaction, but it was not because he didn't look for her. He paid little attention to Mose, for he was occupied in surveying the porch and the windows. Mose Harrington was an alert old man, and realizing how attractive his young granddaughter might be to a young man near her age, he smiled to himself.

Accompanied by his helper, Sim drove his pickup truck around the house and down to the grove of trees. They unloaded their tools and began work on the first trees. As they felled a tree they lopped off the branches, piling the twigs and other small material into a pile to be burned. The larger limbs and the trunk they cut into lengths that were convenient for them to handle, then stacked them neatly to be loaded onto a larger truck when all the trees had been cut.

They worked steadily for about two hours, then dropped their saws and plopped down on the ground for a break. At about the same time Dinah appeared, carrying a pail.

"Morning", she said cheerily. "Thought you-all might like some cool water fresh from the well."

"'Deed we would," Sim answered, getting to his feet. He relieved her of the pail of water and invited her to sit on one of the newly created stumps. She took a seat, carefully smoothing her skirt over her knees.

"No school today?" Sim wanted to know.

"None this week", she replied. "So many of the students needed to help with late cotton picking that the school decided to take a little holiday. So, I'm home with Granddaddy. And we're both enjoying it."

"I'm mighty glad, too", said Sim, "and not just for the water. It's nice to have somebody like you to talk to."

The woodcutters worked at the Harrington place all week. Dinah brought them water every day, and usually sat with them on their breaks.

* * *

In late October, Frank began thinking about what he would offer the patrons of the Sanitary Café as a holiday treat for Thanksgiving. After much fruitless pondering, the answer came to him in a flash.

The people in New Jersey were crazy about roast goose as a Thanksgiving or Christmas feast. He thought, "I'll order some goose, and many new customers will come to the Café because of them!"

He knew the geese would arrive in Truro very much alive and he would need some time, after chopping off their heads, to prepare them for his customers. Two and a half weeks before Thanksgiving he wrote the poultry broker in New Jersey: "Please send six goose to Sanitary Café, Truro, SC., by Railway Express."

In the 1930's. Railway Express was *fast*! As soon as the train arrived with freight marked for you, Railway Express would bring the freight to your door before the train that brought it had hardly left the station. It was *fast*! So, Frank was confident he would have the geese by Thanksgiving.

Friday before Thanksgiving arrived, and Frank had heard nothing from Railway Express. "I give them the weekend," he thought, "then call on Monday. Need time to clean the goose!"

When Monday arrived, and the southbound train blasted its triumphant whistle as it pulled into Truro station, Frank could stand it no longer. He grabbed his telephone, barked to the Operator, "Central, get me Railway Express!" She responded with her usual efficiency, and in a minute or so Humphrey Diggs answered, "Hello. Railway Express."

Frank took no time to identify himself. "Humphrey," he demanded. "You got dem goose?"

Humphrey mistook the urgency in Frank's voice for something else. "What did you say?"

"You got dem goose?"

"You goddam goose yourself!" was the indignant reply.

The geese arrived the next day. Frank and his helpers went furiously to work, cleaning the big birds so they could be cooked. Great was the pile of feathers!

* * *

Thanksgiving arrived and Mary was scheduled to work at the Café. Frank invited Wilson to come to town and eat Thanksgiving Dinner with his mother after the customers departed. Wilson took full advantage of the opportunity to satisfy his teen-age appetite with goose, sweet potatoes, rice and gravy, cranberry sauce, hot rolls and butter. He was plumb full when he finished, but thought it would seem ungrateful if he failed to take a big slice of that pound cake topped with ice cream.

* * *

Quail season always opens on Thanksgiving Day, and Opening Day brings much excitement to hunters and their dogs. Many had been in the fields several times already, without guns, getting themselves and the dogs in tip-top physical shape. Opening Day was looked forward to by the avid hunter as much as was Christmas Day by his children.

Many hunters were in the field on Opening Day, but an equal number were family men. They did not feel it right to go hunting on a family holiday like Thanksgiving. So, when Wilson opened the store on the Day After, he found a cluster of men waiting at the front door. Before he could begin sweeping the sidewalk, they were gathered at the ammunition counter, money in hand, pleading to be served so they could get into the field.

Some received their shells, paid the bill, and ran out the front door to the train depot, where they boarded the train baggage car (with their dogs). They rode the train to a scheduled stop four or five miles away called Kimball. When the train stopped for Kimball, they disembarked with their dogs. Then, having already secured permission from the landowners, they spent the rest of the day hunting bobwhite quail in the previously harvested fields between Kimball and Truro. They arrived back home as daylight was fading, tired and happy. If the hunt had been successful, there would be birds yet to clean; but often the birds were taken to a nearby retainer who would take care of the messy task of removing the feathers and dressing the birds for consumption.

After the first flood of gun shell business subsided, Wilson busied himself with his regular morning duties, sweeping and straightening, filling empty shelves from the reserve stock in the back room. The weather was turning cooler as November progressed, and he had been instructed by Mr. Stokes to keep a good supply of combinets on the shelf in cold weather.

"What is a combinet?" he asked Sam.

"Well, Wilson, you ever hear of a chamber pot? A slop jar? A night glass? A thunder mug? A combinet is the correct name for all of those. And on a cold night the thought of going outside to the privy to relieve yourself is plumb unattractive if you have a combinet under your bed. We always sell more when it's cold."

"Makes sense to me," Wilson replied.

About that time the front door opened, and in strode a familiar figure. "Happy Thanksgiving, everybody! Hi, Matt, Sam, and I'm glad to see Wilson is still here."

"Tom Stone! Welcome home! You still in Law School?"

"Yep. They haven't kicked me out yet—it's close, though." He grinned at Wilson.

"Wilson, you get so old so quick, I stopped by to see if you're married yet."

Wilson blushed a little at being the subject of adult banter. "Not married yet. I'm about as close as you are to getting kicked out of Law School, maybe."

"Good answer, my friend. You show promise. May make a good lawyer."

"How is your mother, Tom? Heard at church she was poorly," said Matt.

"She's not as well as when I left, Matt, but hopefully that will change, and she'll be better. She's a little confused sometimes. I probably need to find someone to check in on her and give her a little help when she needs it. You know, she's all alone in that big old house."

When Wilson reached home that night he told his mother about the conversation with Tom Stone, and about Tom's mother.

"I don't know if you feel you can take on anything else, but looking in on Mrs. Stone could be nothing more than checking on her on your way to work at the Café."

"You're right, Wils. This seems like a good way to repay Tom for letting you be hired for that summer job, and if they want to pay me for my time, every little bit helps. How do you think we should go about it?"

"Suppose I ask off long enough to go by Tom's house and ask him for an appointment for you. Then when you come to work you can come by the Store and I can report."

"OK. I'll check with you late morning."

* * *

Tom's mother's house was a big old Victorian with gables and porches galore. It was set back a little ways from High Street, shaded by huge elm trees. Tom's grandfather had built the house shortly after the Civil War. Tom's father, who had been a Circuit Court Judge, had occupied the family home all his life. Since his death, five years earlier, Mrs. Stone had lived there alone, except for the infrequent times when Tom was at home between school terms.

Wilson walked up on the front porch and twisted the bell handle that was set into the massive front door. In a few seconds he heard footsteps approaching. The door was thrown open, and Tom Stone looked at him in surprise, followed by a grin of welcome.

"Morning, Wilson! Did Matt Stokes fire you because of "advancing age"? Is that why you're not at the store on a Saturday morning?"

"No, he's still stuck with me, but he gave me a few minutes away from the store to ask you a question."

"Ask away."

"Yesterday at the store you said you are getting concerned about your mother, and are considering asking someone to look in on her every day, to make sure she's all right. My mother works at the Sanitary Café six days a week. She would be glad to do that daily check for you, if you haven't found somebody else."

"That is very thoughtful of you and your mother, Wilson. Do you think she could come by here to meet Mother, say, tomorrow, Sunday afternoon? I'll be going back to Columbia to school in the late afternoon, so if you two could come soon after dinner that would be fine. I look forward to meeting your mother. You come, too, if you'd like, and you can both meet my mother."

"Good, Tom. We'll see you then."

The next day Mary and Wilson presented themselves at the big house on High Street, as Tom had requested. Tom greeted them warmly at the door, and ushered them into the front room on the right, the parlor. The room was furnished with a horsehair sofa, three rocking hairs, and an upright piano. A colored shawl was draped over the top surface of the piano, and there was a wool rug on the floor. A small coal fire burned in the fireplace grate near the chair where the lady of the house was seated. The heavy drapes were partially closed to keep out the sun and its glare, so the light in the room was dim.

"Mother, I'd like you to meet two friends of mine. This pretty lady is Mrs. Mary Jones, and the young man is Wilson Jones, her son."

"How do you do? I'm very glad to see you. Please have a seat. Can Tom get you something to drink?" Irene Stone was a gracious hostess.

Tom brought four glasses of cold lemonade, and a small plate of ginger cookies, which he offered first to the ladies, then to Wilson.

"These cookies are delicious!" thought Wilson. "And I've never seen a room like this in my whole life!" Actually, Wilson had entered very few houses that were not tenant houses, like his own.

Mrs. Stone was small, a trifle bent. Her hair was quite white, coiled into a bun at the back of her neck. She wore a gold brooch pinned to the front of her dress over her heart. On the other side was a round button-like thing from which dangled pince-nez glasses. Her eyes were bright and penetrating. She had a small tremor in her hands.

"Mrs. Jones, do you live in Truro?"

"Not exactly, Mrs. Stone. We live just outside town, on Juniper Road. I work in Truro, and Wilson goes to high school here."

"Oh, what grade are you in, Wilson?"

"I'm in the eighth, ma'am."

"Law, I remember when Tom was in the eighth grade. That's when he got his first long pants—isn't that right, Tom? You were really pleased with yourself, as I remember." She gave a little chuckle, remembering a happy time.

"Mrs. Jones, if I may inquire, what kind of work do you do in Truro?"

"Well, Mrs. Stone, let me begin by saying that my husband is ill with tuberculosis. He has not been able to work for months, and it may be a while before he can work again. So, my wonderful son and I have the task of supporting ourselves. I am at the Sanitary Café, where I wait tables. Frank Zervos is a good man to work for, and I enjoy serving good food to hungry people."

"I'm sure that is satisfying. And what is your job, Wilson?"

"Well, ma'am, I work for Mr. Matt Stokes at the hardware store in the afternoons, after school, and on Saturday.

Goodness, you two are certainly busy people! I'm afraid I don't have the energy to do all that, any more", she confided with a smile.

"I suppose Wilson and I should be getting along, Mrs. Stone. We certainly enjoyed meeting you. I hope you'll call on me if there's anything I can help you with. Oh, and thanks for the refreshments. Those ginger cookies were delicious! Did you make them?"

"No, child. I don't cook much anymore. A neighbor sent them in. Now, both of you, please come back to see me, any time. I love having company. It gets lonesome here in this big old house."

"Goodbye, Mrs. Stone."

Tom showed them out, and once on the porch, out of earshot, he said, "I'll speak with Mother about your checking by, Mrs. Jones. She will be reluctant to make any changes in her lifestyle, but she may agree. I'll drive by your house on Juniper Road on my way to Columbia. We can talk about it."

* * *

Irene Stone went to her room to enjoy her customary one-hour nap after the midday meal. Tom took advantage of the time to finish his packing for his return to school.

He heard her stirring around after she awakened, and he knocked on her door.

"Come in, Tom", she called, and he walked into her bedroom.

"The Joneses are nice, don't you think?" She nodded her assent.

"Mother, I've been doing some thinking. You have mentioned that you sometimes get confused these days. Do you think it would be helpful to you if we found somebody who could drop by, most days, and see if they could run an errand for you, or get some groceries, or help you with paying bills? What do you think?"

"I don't think I need that, Tom. Do you really think it's time to do that?"

"Maybe not, Mother. Maybe we should both think about this, and talk about it again when I come home for Christmas."

An hour later, Tom pulled his car into the road that led to the Jones' house. Not wanting him to see the unfinished nature of the interior, Mary and Wilson came out in the yard to meet him. "Hi, Tom! You on your way back to school?"

"Yep", he replied, "and I need to get there in time to look over a paper that is due tomorrow. I don't want to let up my efforts in my last year. This is crunch time.

Folks, I talked to Mother about getting her some help, but she doesn't feel that she needs it right yet. We agreed to talk about it again at Christmastime. I didn't mention any names. It was just a general discussion.

I really appreciate y'all coming by the house today to meet Mother. We both enjoyed it, Mrs. Jones."

"Just 'Mary' please, Tom. We enjoyed meeting your mother and visiting with her. She is a very nice lady. I would be glad to be of help to her, any way I can."

"Well, you know, if you could manage to drop by once or twice a month to pay a little visit, and see how she's doing, that would help her know you better, and you could maybe tell how she's getting along. That would be very helpful."

"I'll be glad to do that. We'll see you at Christmas, we hope."

"I'll bet you will, 'Bye."

CHAPTER FOUR

LIFE AND DEATH

A week later, Mary again took the bus to Columbia to see Dave. While she was gone, Wilson completed the list of chores his mother had asked him to do in her absence. He decided to clean up a little and drop by Betsy's house, though he had said nothing to her about the possibility of his coming. He arrived at the house and knocked on the front door. No answer. He knocked again, louder this time. Again, there was no answer.

Disappointed, he walked away in the direction of the high school, for he could hear shouts of glee from that direction. When he reached the school, the shouts were coming from behind the building, from the athletic field. There he saw a score of boys of high school age engaged in a game of touch football. As he rounded the corner of the building, he was spotted by one of the players.

"Hey, Wilson! Come play with us! We need one more to make the teams even!"

Wilson immediately trotted out onto the field, joined one of the teams. The game proceeded for twenty or thirty more minutes, until someone called "Time out!"

The boys were all breathless and in need of a rest period, so no one protested. They dropped to the ground where they stood, giving their lungs and hearts a much-needed respite.

Soon, however, the resilience of youth showed itself, and talk began again, about the game, about the week before and the week to come. Someone in the group noticed a milk cow, staked out at the twenty yard line at one end of the field, grazing.

"Look, boys. That's Mr. Cecil Burton's cow. "Fessor" lets him stake that old cow out on the field to keep the grass mowed. I tell you what; our principal is Scotch— tight with a penny! He's fertilizing the grass and getting it mowed at the same time!" The boys howled with laughter.

A moment of silence fell over the group, then a voice was heard. It was Jim Lane, his mind always up to some devilment. "Hey, guys. You suppose we could lead that cow inside the schoolhouse? Just lead her in, and leave her there? I'll betcha by Monday morning there would be so many cow droppings, there's no way we could have school—and we'd get a holiday!"

Shouts of approval greeted Jim's suggestion, and some boys were dispatched to see if any of the doors were open. Sure enough, one of the side doors had been left unlocked.

Jim Lane continued to take charge. "Wilson, go and pull up that stake. We'll lead the cow to the door, and inside."

Getting to the door was no problem, but climbing the steps was a puzzler. Jim said, "Wilson, don't you have a cow at your place?" How is the best way to go about this thing?"

Wilson thought for a minute, then said, "I think if we put two boys on each leg, and two in the back to push….we can guide the cow's feet onto the stair treads. I'll take her head."

They lined up the team as Wilson directed, and slowly the cow began to ascend the brick steps into the building. In a few minutes the climb was completed.They stood in the hall on the first floor, the cow looking curiously around.

Cheers erupted from the group, and were quickly shushed by Jim Lane. "Quiet, fellows! 'Fessor' doesn't live far from here, you know. Do you want him to hear you, and come to investigate?"

"Let's see if we can get the cow to the second floor", one of the boys suggested. The group quickly agreed to try it. The team was reassembled, and the ascent of twenty more steps, plus a landing, was begun. Soon the triumphant climbers were in the upper hall, as elated as if they had successfully scaled Mt. Everest.

"Now, let's leave "Old Bossie" here, and we'll all report to school tomorrow for a very short Monday. Old John will never be able to clean up this mess before noon!"

Each boy was sworn to secrecy as they filed out of the building. They went home with a surge of secret excitement bubbling through their beings, hoping they could keep a "straight face" through the evening meal and not give away their stunt.

* * *

Monday dawned cold and clear, and all students began to wend their way toward the schoolhouse. This particular day many of the boys who were normally reluctant to experience another week at school were excited, and anxious to enter the building, curious to see what they might see.

When Wilson arrived he noticed an unusual odor permeating the building. Having spent all his life around animals, he quickly identified the source of the odor. There was a hum of conversation throughout the school, most students being unaware of the Sunday afternoon trick.

He made his way upstairs toward his homeroom, and found the cow in the same area she had been left. She was surrounded by her waste and some pools of water.

Professor Scott and Old John, the janitor, were surveying the situation. Mr. Scott looked around, spotted several boys in the group of onlookers. He pointed to two of them. "You two boys! One of you take the upstairs rooms, the other the downstairs rooms. Tell each teacher to send all the boys up here. Now!

The boys hurried off, and soon the hall was filled with the boys, looking at the cow and the mess. They were chuckling a little under their breath while managing to retain their usual poker faces.

After a crowd has assembled, Professor Scott called for quiet. "I don't know how you boys got this cow up here, but you're going to have to get her down. I'm going to my office, and if this cow is not gone from here in thirty minutes we're going to have an investigation and those responsible will be punished. If you get her out in thirty minutes, I won't know who is responsible.... Now John, you get your mops and water, and..." and the two men walked off together.

As soon as 'Fessor' and Old John were out of sight, the Sunday afternoon crowd looked at each other. Without a word, Wilson picked up the cow chain, prepared to lead the cow down the steps. The other boys took their same positions as before, and they began the procession.

"Now remember, we can't let this cow stumble. She'll fall on those in front, and we'll all end up at the bottom—dead!" They very carefully placed each hoof on the proper stair tread, and worked their way down. The cow seemed very unconcerned, thinking, "I'm working with an experienced crew. Didn't they get me all the way up here yesterday?"

The onlooking students watched the proceedings, unable to believe their eyes. Never had anything this wild taken place in Truro High School! And look who is involved in this crazy stunt!

Betsy was late arriving at school that morning, and found her friend Dot Hubbard looking for her, "Betsy! Come quick, and see what's happening!" When Betsy saw Wilson in the strange procession, leading a cow down the steps while a well-drilled team of helpers assisted him, she was dumbfounded. She borrowed one of her grandmother's favorite expressions, "Great goodness, Miss Agnes!" she exclaimed. "What in the world?"

When they reached the ground outside the other boys scattered, but Wilson continued to lead the cow back home. He knocked at Cecil Burton's back door. "Morning, Mr. Burton. I'm returning the cow some of the boys borrowed yesterday. I'm afraid she needs water, and she hasn't been milked. Thought you'd like to know." The puzzled Mr. Burton took the chain from Wilson without a word, and watched as the boy made his way back to the school.

When he got back in the building, Wilson found that Old John had already cleaned up the mess in the upstairs hall, and that classes had begun, only thirty minutes behind schedule!

As he slipped into his seat in the classroom, somebody whispered, "Howdy, Cowboy!"

* * *

As he waited for Betsy to appear at the end of school that day, students passing by waved and spoke cheerfully to him. He heard the word "Cowboy" a couple of times, and was conscious of being pointed out. Without seeking it, he had achieved new status in the student body as "the boy who led the cow out of the building". Apparently it was an easy transition from "the boy who led the cow" to "the boy who led the daring group" of pranksters. High status, indeed!

When Betsy finally appeared, she greeted him with a smile and hooked her arm through his as they walked toward her house. "Wilson", she said, "tell me what happened! How did all this come about?"

He went through the entire sequence of events, beginning with his attempted visit to her house the afternoon before. ""The family went for a Sunday afternoon drive," she said. Wish I had stayed home and seen you…but then you would not have become a celebrity!"

"Celebrity?" he said, in amazement. "How am I a celebrity?"

"Everybody saw you lead the cow down the stairs and out the building. Girls kept coming up to me all day with admiring comments about my boyfriend. You're a marked man, Tex!"

After waving goodbye to Betsy, Wilson continued to town and his job at the hardware store. He was busy assembling red wagons to go on sale for Christmas when he looked up and saw several students, both boys and girls, watching him.

"Hello," he said.

"Hi, Cowboy," they replied, and burst into laughter. "That was some trick you and your boys pulled," they said with admiration.

"They aren't 'my boys' ", he said. "I was almost an innocent bystander."

"Maybe so," one of them replied", but it looks like they elected you Captain."

"Not really," Wilson said. "They just gave me the chain to hold."

"Yeah, right. So long, Cowboy." And they trooped out of the store.

"What was that all about, Wilson?" Matt Stokes wanted to know. So Wilson went through the whole thing for his amused benefit, then had to tell Sam the entire tale again.

"So 'Fessor' doesn't know who the rascals were, since he chose not to watch. You boys were lucky he decided to handle it that way," Matt remarked.

"He doesn't know right now, but everybody else in school knows. I expect he'll know all the names by suppertime," Wilson gave as his opinion.

"What will he do?"

"Just have to wait and see, I guess."

* * *

When Sam dropped him off at home that might, Wilson went inside to find his mother and relate the events of the day. She, too, was amused, but also concerned about the punishment Mr. Scott could choose for the group who caused such a stir.

"You realize, don't you, Son, that you boys caused the janitor a lot of extra work, upset the school with a distraction that made teaching and learning very difficult—and, school lost thirty minutes of valuable time. Mr. Scott could paddle you boys, he could keep you in after school, or, he could even expel you!"

"Yes'm, I guess you're right. It wasn't my idea, but I joined in the fun, and if we get punished I'm sure I'll get punished along with the rest. Have to take what comes. But, no sense in worrying about that tonight. We'll find out soon enough."

The next morning in school, he half expected a summons to Fessor's office, but received none. At recess he asked the other boys if anything had happened to them. No one had heard anything from Fessor so they relaxed a little bit, though they were all nervous, as if waiting for the other shoe to fall.

Wilson still felt he was the subject of conversation from both boys and girls for his part in the affair. He heard the word

"Cowboy" whispered several times, and when he walked Betsy home she called him "Tex" again, with a sly smile.

During recess the following day Wilson was confronted by Jim Bates. "Think you're hot stuff, don't you?" he demanded without preamble.

"What do you mean, Jim?" Wilson wanted to know.

"Claiming credit for our cow stunt. Everybody thinks you're the Big Hero, the Mastermind behind the whole thing, the Leader. Well, it ain't so! It was my idea, ask anybody! Then, before anybody can stop you, there you go to the front to lead the old cow down the stairs, in front of everybody like a drum major leading a parade! It ain't right! It was my idea in the first place! You got no right to take all the credit!"

"Jim, I'm not trying to take anything that belongs to you. The way I remember it, on Sunday you told me to get the cow and lead her over to the schoolhouse. We arranged the boys to guide her feet, and you told me to lead her up the steps into the building, then up the stairs to the second floor. On Monday, when Fessor told us to get her out of there, we all took the same positions we had the day before. Didn't you push from the rear, both days?"

"Yeah, that's right. And that's another thing I don't like about it. You had the nice clean spot, in the front. I was back by the cow's rear end. I was afraid of getting dumped on, and besides that, the air back there smelled bad. It was my idea, and nobody in the school knows "squat" about it. They think you're hot stuff, even call you 'Cowboy'!

"Well, Jim, I'm sorry. I've been telling people I'm just an innocent bystander. Why don't you tell them it was your idea?"

"Huh!!"

The remainder of the week passed without incident.

* * *

As November merged into December, the school calendar neared its Christmas break. Students' minds were wandering, diverted toward the holidays and the joys that come with "no school", the high good spirits that accompany the gathering of extended family, and the hustle and bustle and secrecy of holiday shopping. Even though the Depression hung like a wet blanket over the entire population, the optimism, happiness, and peace of the Holy Season managed to wedge its way through that cloud.

Wilson, too, was caught up in the expectation of Christmas, but his expectation was tempered by discouragement and frustration. "I want to give Betsy a present," he thought," but how can I do that when Mama and I are so strapped for money?" He finally decided his only recourse was to talk it over with his mother.

He began, "Mama, Betsy is a really good friend. We like each other a lot, and we laugh and talk together. Except for you, she's my best friend in the whole world. I want to give her a little gift for Christmas, but don't know if we can afford to take that money out of the family money."

"Well, Wils, I realize she is a good friend. You talk to me about her. It would be good to give her a gift. What price gift do you have in mind?"

I looked at the jewelry store window, and they have an identification bracelet for three dollars, and will engrave it with her name for another dollar. Do you think I could spend four dollars on Betsy's present?"

"Well, I certainly think her friendship is worth far more than that— but in our situation, four dollars is exactly the amount I would have suggested, if you had asked me first."

Wonderful, Mama!" I'll get it after my next payday!" He did go to the jewelry store and give instructions that he wanted that gold-colored bracelet that was marked "120 fine" to be engraved "BETSY" on the front and "WILSON" on the back.

Mary, too was in a quandary. "What can I give Wils that he really wants and needs, and is affordable?" She finally decided that clothing would be an important asset to a young man just turning fifteen who is beginning to be interested in girls. The next day, as she left for work in town, she left home an hour earlier than usual with a neatly folded shirt and a pair of jeans under her arm. She went straight to a dry goods store on the main street of Truro. The shop window proudly proclaimed

GUSTAVUS I. RAY
HABERDASHER

Once inside, she approached the proprietor. "Mr. Ray," she said, "my son will be fifteen in a few days, plus Christmas is coming. He is growing up, and he needs to look his best when he goes to school, or out with his friends. I want to buy him a nice shirt and a respectable pair of pants, *not jeans.* What do you suggest?"

They carefully compared sizes of the clothes she had brought in, then selected a nice pair of blue woolen trousers and a shirt that complemented the trousers. "I'd like to put these on layaway," Mary said. "I can give you two dollars now and the rest after I am paid on Saturday. Is that all right?"

Mr. Ray seemed to be delighted with the arrangement, and the deal was struck. Mary left the store feeling very pleased with the idea, and with the purchase.

Wilson had no idea what he might give his mother that would please her, and he decided a round-trip bus ticket to Columbia would be the best thing.

* * *

Mary said, "Wilson, what do you think about celebrating your birthday by going to see your father? It's been a month since you went with me, and I'm sure he is anxious to see his son, now he's fifteen. I'm having a hard time believing that you can be fifteen, no longer a boy but a man.!"

Of course Wilson could not refuse that kind of invitation, and he readily agreed to accompany his mother to Columbia again, to see his father. They rode over on the same bus, smoothly changed to the city bus for the ride out to the hospital. Wilson reminded his mother how nervous they had been on that first trip, unsure of how to get around in a big city. "We're experienced travelers now," he grinned.

At the hospital they picked up their Visitor's Pass and proceeded up the stairs to Ward C, where they found Dave lying inert. He was very pale. They spoke to him and he opened his eyes. He made an attempt at a smile of recognition, but did not raise his head from the pillow. Mother and son exchanged looks of alarm and consternation, then quickly put on forced smiles and greeted Dave warmly and affectionately.

"I've brought your fifteen-year-old son to see you," she proudly told him. "He is fifteen today!"

Dave looked at Wilson. Astonished, he said "Fifteen? Seems like he was just a little boy when I left home, and my, my! Look at him now! If we could measure, I bet he'd be taller'n me." He coughed weakly.

Mary and Wilson took up the conversation, bringing chitchat about their daily lives to Dave, who had been cut off from Truro for months. He listened attentively, his gaze shifting from one to the other, not commenting.

Mrs. Melton, the nurse on Ward C, walked past the bed in her crisp white nurse's uniform. She spoke to the two visitors with a welcoming smile. "We'll have a talk later," she said as she moved away to check on another patient.

They sat beside Dave's bed for nearly an hour, talking animatedly to the sick man. Noticing that his eyelids were beginning to droop, they suggested he take a nap, and promised to return when he awakened. They walked over to a quiet corner of the ward, found two chairs, and sat down.

"He doesn't seem to be any better than when we last saw him", Wilson commented. "Maybe even weaker." His mother agreed, a worried expression on her face.

In a little while Mrs. Melton came to where they were sitting, pulled up a chair for herself, and joined them. "I can tell by your expressions that you are worried," she said.

"Not only worried, but surprised," replied Mary. "There seems to be such a change in his condition since the last time I was here. Is he getting worse? What can you tell us? Can we see the doctor today?"

"Several days ago he began running a temperature," Mrs. Melton began, "he became nauseated and threw up. He still has the low-grade fever, but absolutely no appetite. I haven't heard him cough since you've been here today, but he is coughing more. That's about all I can tell you. Yes, you will be able to speak with the doctor when he comes in to make his rounds." She gave them a little pat as she got to her feet and moved away.

Mary and Wilson exchanged worried looks. She leaned over and patted him, and then the two of them sat tensely, waiting for Dr, Shipley to appear and make his rounds. In about fifteen minutes, which seemed like hours, they saw him walk briskly into the ward and begin looking at patients. One by one, he took their hand, felt their pulse, listened to their chests, and asked questions of patient and nurse. Before moving to the next bed, it was evident to Mary and Wilson, who could not hear a word that was said, that the doctor was giving Mrs. Melton instructions. She made notes, and nodded her understanding.

At Dave's bedside they could see Mrs. Melton gesturing to Dr. Shipley, indicating their presence. The medical team completed their examination of Dave, and then of the remaining patients on the ward, before turning toward the waiting visitors from Truro.

"Hello, Mrs. Jones. Hello, Son. It's nice to see you again," said the doctor in greeting.

"Hello, Dr. Shipley", they chorused.

Mary spoke up, "Please tell us about Dave. He looks *awful*—so much worse than the last time I was here!"

Dr. Shipley pushed his glasses up from his nose, so that they rested on his forehead above his eyebrows. "I'm sorry to say I agree with you, Mrs. Jones. Dave has not responded to our treatments in any positive way. We are very concerned about him, and we are having discussions about alternate methods that we might try in an effort to improve his condition."

"He is so pale—so weak—so thin."

"Mrs. Jones, you have just described the effect that tuberculosis has on people. They don't feel like eating, so they don't eat. They cough, because their lungs are less than healthy, and the coughing irritates the lining of the lungs and the throat. That induces bleeding, eventually hemorrhaging... Please forgive me for talking so bluntly to you about your husband, but he is gravely ill. You have seen it through the eyes of love, and I have seen the same things through the eyes of medicine.

"You said you are discussing alternate treatments—what are they?"

There is a new theory that deflating the lungs may be a good way to stem the advance of tuberculosis. It involves rather radical surgery, and, frankly, has not been proved to be helpful in the majority of cases. The verdict is still out on most new theories regarding tuberculosis, But, Mrs. Jones, I assure you we are doing everything we know to do to improve your husband's condition."

"Well, I sure hope you find that right answer, Doctor. He's the only husband I've got, and the only father Wilson's got, and we desperately want him back, and need him back!"

Doctor Shipley nodded his understanding, and he, too, gave her a sympathetic pat as he walked away.

Conversation was sparse on the bus ride home, as mother and son were each lost in anxious thought.

* * *

The week before Christmas was ahead of Wilson as he arose the next morning and prepared for the day ahead. There was no school, of course, but he was scheduled to report to Mr. Stokes' hardware store every day until Christmas Day. Wilson had been busy for several weeks previous, assembling tricycles and wagons for the Christmas business that was to come. A sample of each model was displayed on the sidewalk in front of the store, while the reserve stock was suspended from large hooks that had been screwed into the high wooden ceiling. Wilson was obliged to climb the rolling ladder to accomplish the temporary storage, which allowed salesmen and customers to see which items were available. The store did a big business in layaways, and those "sold" items were taken to the warehouse and arranged in alphabetical order for easy retrieval on Christmas Eve.

Christmas Week was an exciting time in a hardware store, with customer traffic greatly increased over normal. The customers were excited also, and many were in a cheerful mood, despite the pressure most of them felt.

A large potbellied stove sat in the center of the store, and was the only source of heat. Matt Stokes kept a coal bin outside the rear door, and from time to time Sam or Wilson went to the bin, filled a coal hod (also called a coal scuttle, or coal bucket), and brought it back inside to replenish the fire. On really nasty winter days when the wind and the cold drizzle were unrelenting, the space around the stove became crowded with the folks from the countryside who had come into town for the day. When it became too crowded for Sam to pass from one side to the other, he delighted in opening the door to the heater and throwing into the fire an entire bucket of coal. He them opened the draft all the way. Soon the stove became red hot, and the air was filled with the unmistakable odor of wet wool and unwashed bodies until the visitors became too warm, and they scattered.

It was a busy, tiring time, yet Wilson was young, and he managed occasionally to find the strength to decline Sam's offer of a ride home in order to drop by Betsy's house for a brief "Hello" on his way to Juniper Road. On one of those "drop-bys" he made a date to come see her on Christmas afternoon. "We're going to my grandmother's at four", Betsy said. "Can you come before then?"

"Sure can", was the prompt reply.

Mrs. Jordan invited Wilson to join them at their church, Central Baptist, on Christmas Eve, when a program was to be presented featuring the familiar Christmas music. Having been warned by Matt and Sam that the store stayed open late on Christmas Eve, whether it was Saturday or not, Wilson had to decline. He did so regretfully, for he liked music, and he knew he would enjoy sitting beside Betsy.

Much to his surprise and pleasure, Wilson received a little cash bonus from Matt as the store closed. "Merry Christmas, young fellow! You have been very satisfactory help this fall. You've been here every day, you've been on time, and you have been willing and able to learn. As I told you when you began, that's all I ask of my help. We always close two days for Christmas, paid holidays, so I'll look for you back the afternoon of the 27th We won't need quite so many hours from you as before Christmas. Just pretend school is in session, and come in the afternoon."

"Thanks, Mr. Stokes. Merry Christmas!"

Sam dropped Wilson off at his house a few minutes before midnight, and the tired young man entered to find his mother taking a pound cake out of the oven.

"Welcome home, Wils. Merry Christmas! This nice warm pound cake needs someone to sample it with a cold glass of milk, to see if it's good enough to serve on Christmas Day. Will you be a guinea pig?"

"You bet I will, Mama! You know how much I love warm pound cake!—Boy, did we have a busy day today! Bet I walked ten miles going back and forth to the warehouse for layaways! And guess what, Mama! Mr. Stokes gave me a five dollar bonus, for a Christmas present, and he said I had done a good job! Boy!"

Mary did not have to work on Christmas, so they agreed to stay in bed an hour later than usual before getting up for breakfast and exchanging gifts. Wilson went to bed with visions of—not sugar plums— but warm pound cake dancing in his head. And, of course, Betsy.

* * *

Christmas morning was cold and clear. Though they had agreed to sleep a little later because of their light schedule, neither Mary nor Wilson could get around that ingrained habit of waking at their usual early hour. It was nice, though, to realize that hopping out of bed immediately was not a "must" today, then burrowing into the blankets and quilts for few more minutes of toasty warmth. It was a rare pleasure for these hardworking people, which made it all the more precious.

As was the case every winter morning, the house was cold when they wakened. The floors, one layer of boards with no sub flooring and no insulation, seemed icy to bare feet. The remains of last night's fire were cold and lifeless. Wilson could see that what was needed was a fresh-laid fire, starting with paper, "lightwood kindling", and then some small pieces of light logs. A quick glance at the woodbox told him that all supplies were right there, and in "two shakes of a lamb's tail" he had a fire burning briskly. Then he could turn his attention to getting completely dressed for the day.

His mother was building a fire in the cook stove at the same time Wilson was working with the fireplace. Pretty soon she was boiling water for grits and making coffee. As a special salute to the holiday she fried some bacon and made scrambled eggs.

Mary reached for Wilson's hand and bowed her head. "Lord, bless this food that we are about to receive. Wilson and I thank you for sending Jesus into the world to teach us about your love for us, and to give us hope for better times. And we ask you, Lord, we beg you, to allow our man to return to health, and return to Truro, and stay with us who need him so bad. Hear our prayer, Lord. Amen.

When Wilson raised his bowed head, he saw that his mother's eyes were wet. "Good prayer, Mama. Wouldn't it be wonderful to have Daddy back"?

After devouring the breakfast, he said, "Boy, that was good!" Then he said briskly, "let's get on with our day. You worked extra hard on that good breakfast. I'll straighten up the table and wash the dishes while you sit down and be a lady. Then we'll get on with important matters, like opening gifts".

In a few minutes he had cleared away the table, washed the dishes and pans, and put them away. He turned to his mother. "Well'," he said with a grin, "what did Santa Claus bring me?"

Mary, who had been staring wistfully off into space, jumped out of her chair with a start and ran out to her bedroom, where she retrieved a package wrapped neatly in white tissue paper and tied with tobacco twine.

"Merry Christmas, Wils!"

He reached into his pocket and brought out an envelope, "Merry Christmas!" he said.

She watched eagerly as he carefully unwrapped his package, being sure he did not tear the paper, so it could be used again. He lifted the top off the box and surveyed the contents. ""Wow!"" he exclaimed. "What pretty blue britches! And a shirt too? They sure do look good together! This is exciting!"

"They're not jeans, Wilson. Santa thinks you are getting old enough need to dress like a man rather than a "country boy" all the time. You have a job, and a girlfriend, so we're going to try to improve your wardrobe a little bit."

"This is a really nice outfit, Mama. I'll save it for special times—like this afternoon, when I go to see Betsy—and keep on wearing jeans to school and things like that. These pants look warm. What are they?

"They're wool."

"Never had wool pants before. I sure do like them.... Now, you go ahead at look at your present and see what Santa brought you."

She opened the envelope. "Oh, Wilson! A bus ticket to Columbia! How sweet of you to think of something that would please me and your daddy, both. Thank you, Son. Very thoughtful of you... I sure do wish he could be here with us today. That would really make a *good* Christmas!"

* * *

Early that afternoon Wilson, bathed and shampooed and dressed in his blue wool pants and new shirt, departed his house. In his pocket was a small package, gift wrapped by the jeweler, containing his gift for Betsy. He stepped carefully as he traversed the dirt road that led into town. He avoided the grass that grew along the shoulders, wet from a recent rain; he also skirted the mud puddles and standing water along the way. His shoes had been carefully cleaned to match his new outfit, and he didn't want anything to mar the effect.

As he turned onto Kershaw Street he noted the holly or cedar wreaths on the doors of the houses on her block, and thought that next year, maybe he could arrange to get one for their house on Juniper Road and surprise his mother.

As he turned up the walk leading to Betsy's house his heart began to beat a little faster. He was conscious of being nervous as he knocked lightly on the front door. Fortunately he was not required to wait long before the door swung open and Mr. Jordan smilingly beckoned him in.

"Merry Christmas, Wilson! Come right in! HO! HO! HO!" in his best Santa imitation. Please excuse Betsy and her mother for not being here to greet you", and Wilson's face fell. "No, I didn't mean they're not here. They're in the kitchen serving the plates for dessert, and they have prepared one for you. Do you think you can handle a little fruit cake?"

Wilson allowed himself to be towed inside, where he stood awkwardly, not knowing exactly what to do or say. Thankfully, mother and daughter appeared in just a minute or two, bearing a fruit cake on a platter, plates and forks, and a coffeepot.

"Welcome, Wilson, and Merry Christmas!" Mrs. Jordan greeted him as she put down the coffeepot and extended her hand. He shook hands, gingerly, not sure how hard to grip hers.

He and Betsy exchanged smiles of greeting.

"We assumed that a young man like you would like to share our fruit cake. Would you like a piece?"

He nodded his thanks.

"And Wilson, will you have a cup of coffee? At Christmastime, as a special treat, we put whipped cream in our coffee instead of milk. Will you have some?"

"Thank you, ma'am, I'd like to try that."

Mrs. Jordan served the coffee while Betsy was cutting a slice of fruit cake for everyone.

While enjoying his coffee and cake, Wilson sneaked a glance around his surroundings. He thought the dining table was pretty, with a white tablecloth, and in the center an arrangement of greenery with two red candles. A Christmas tree, its electric colored lights glittering, was visible in the next room. To his eye, it was splendid.

Mrs. Jordan said she and her husband would clear the dessert dishes into the kitchen and perhaps take a little nap before going to her mother's home. "Betsy, why don't you and Wilson sit in the front room and have your visit?"

Wilson and Betsy gladly moved to the other room and sat down together on a sofa.

"Did you have a nice morning?" she asked.

"Oh, yes. It was very nice, but it would have been nicer if my daddy had been with us—but Mama and I get along very well. We had a good Christmas. How about you?"

"It was great! Very exciting! Unwrapping presents is a really fun thing to do, don't you think?"

"Yes I do. And speaking of presents, I have something right here in my pocket that has your name on it. Would you like to see it?"

You bet I would, Wilson."

He reached into his pocket and brought out the small package. He handed it to her, and said, "From me to you".

She carefully removed the paper, then lifted the cover off the box. Inside lay the gold-colored identification bracelet. She gasped with pleasure, then gasped again when she saw BETSY engraved across the top.

"Wilson! She breathed. "It's beautiful!"

"Do you like it?"

"Love it!"

Look on the back".

Betsy turned the bracelet over, and when she saw WILSON engraved on the reverse side, she let out a little squeal of pleasure, threw her arms around his neck—and before either one of them knew what was happening, she kissed him firmly, right smack on the lips!

It was the first kiss for either of them, and it left them stunned. Wilson stole a look over her shoulder in the direction of the dining room and kitchen. Finding those rooms apparently vacant, he promptly put both his arms around her and pulled her close, returning her kiss with vigor.

In a minute they both pulled back, and Wilson said, "Lordy! Lordy mercy! Talk about a wonderful Christmas!"

Betsy replied, "Wilson, you are so sweet to me. I did not know if you would give me a gift, and I certainly didn't expect anything as lovely and personal and dear as this bracelet. Thank you so much. ...Now", she continued, "I have a little something for you", and she handed him a small box. When he unwrapped it he found a bone handled pocketknife.

"Why, Betsy, this is wonderful! Would you believe it, Matt Stokes said to me the other day that good hardware man is never without his knife! It is needed several times a day, and now I have one, and won't have to borrow. Thank you so much", and taking another peek over her shoulder, he kissed her again

"Whoa, Cowboy!" she said. Then, teasing, "Hey, Tex, something just occurred to me. By giving me this bracelet with both our names on it, are you trying to brand me like the other cowboys do to their cows in the movies on Saturday afternoon?"

He grinned, "I hadn't thought of it, but it's not a bad idea. You're getting so pretty some boy, like Jim Lane, maybe, is bound to try to steal you away from me."

"Well, if Jim Lane is all you've got to worry about, you're in pretty high cotton. He doesn't appeal to me at all, but maybe you'd better worry about some of the other older boys," she said, returning to her teasing manner.

"I'm certainly not going to let on what a good kisser you are," he rejoined. I'd soon have trouble, for sure!"

You'd have trouble from me, Wilson Jones! And it would be long lasting trouble, too, if you can't keep this between the two of us! Are we clear about that?"

"I think you were teasing me, and I was just teasing you back, Betsy. The last fifteen minutes have been the best part of my best Christmas, ever, and it's all thanks to you. The kisses were unexpected, and so special, and of course it's between the two of us."

Hearing her parents moving around in another part of the house, Betsy walked him to the door. "We're off to my grandmother's, Wilson. You'd better go now. Thank you for my bracelet."

"And thank you for my knife—and the kiss. And I want to kiss you again." He said boldly.

"We'll see, Cowboy....We'll see....Bye".

As Wilson walked toward his house on Juniper Road, he could still smell the fragrance of Betsy's hair, that clean, fresh, faintly sweet, delicious aroma. His emotions were in turmoil. His heart was beating faster and faster, he was grinning from ear to ear; his lips...his lips had just been kissed, sweetly but thoroughly, by the girl he found to be the prettiest, the kindest—well, the most wonderful girl he had ever known!

"Merry Christmas, Mama!" he shouted happily as he entered the house.

"Merry Christmas, Son. Did you see Betsy? Did you have a good time?"

"Yes, ma'am. A nice time", he said as he walked on through the house and out the back door.

"Isn't that strange," Mary thought. "He usually is full of talk when he has seen Betsy. Hmmmm...."

* * *

It was two days after Christmas, and Mary was back at the Sanitary Café. She was clearing the buffet table where lunch had been served when the messenger boy from Western Union came in and walked up to her. He waited until she noticed him, and then he asked, "Aren't you Mrs. Jones? Mrs. Mary Jones?"

"Yes, I am".

"Message for you, Ma'am. Sign here"

Mary was astonished to receive a telegram, but dutifully signed where he indicated.

"I'm sorry, Ma'am", the messenger said, as he left.

The awful realization of what the telegram could tell her began to dawn on Mary, and with a sinking heart she left the serving line and made her way to the kitchen. She found a chair in the corner and fearfully tore open the envelope.

> We regret to inform you that Jefferson Davis Jones died in his sleep last night, December 26, 1935. Please have your undertaker give us instructions.
>
> Stanley Thredwell, Administrator

* * *

It was like a blow to her stomach. She caught her breath to keep her equilibrium as the room swam in a dizzying circle. Her mind raced as she hugged herself, and began to rock back and forth.

"What will we do?" she thought. "What will we do first? How can we get Dave back here to Truro so we can bury him here? Wilson! I've got to find Wilson, and tell him! Then the two of us can figure out what to do!"

The kitchen workers noticed her distress and called Frank. He was very sympathetic when she showed him the telegram. Frank volunteered to walk down to Truro Hardware, find Matt Stokes, and explain the situation.

As it turned out, Wilson had just arrived for work, and he accompanied Frank back to the Café where Mary still sat, hugging herself, and rocking. When she saw Wilson they embraced tenderly, and the tears began to flow.

Without a word, Frank brought another chair for Wilson, and the two sat close together, holding hands.

"Your father is over in Columbia all by himself", she sobbed. "How can we get him back here with the people who love him? Who can we ask for some advice?"

"One name jumps into my mind right away, Mama. My friend Tom Stone is about to graduate from law school, and giving advice is what lawyers do, I think. He's a nice man. Do you think we could ask him?"

"We sure do need some advice. Would he think it was awful of us to interrupt his Christmas holiday—intrude on his time at home?"

"I think he'd be glad to help. You sit right here in this kitchen, and I'll go find Tom and bring him here, if he'll come."

* * *

Wilson found Tom at home and explained the situation. Tom brought his car to the Café, picked up Mary, and transported her to his house, where they sat around a small fire in the fireplace. They showed Tom the telegram and explained they didn't have any idea how to proceed.

He explained their options of getting Dave's body to Truro. They decided to instruct the hospital to ship the body by rail. They called the local undertaker and made arrangements for transporting Dave to their house, where they would hold the "sitting up", the visitation.

"Tom, you are a true friend. You have accomplished so much in a short time, plus you have relieved our minds of so many problems. We can never thank you enough", Mary said.

* * *

It was two days before Dave's body arrived. The undertaker took it to the funeral home where they dressed him in the suit he had worn at his wedding years before. The 'sitting up" was scheduled for the following evening, when friends and family would call and chat and visit, some staying the entire night. Sitting up was considered a neighborly thing to do, and though the family appreciated the neighbors' concern, it added to their weariness.

As soon as she heard of Dave's death, Betsy was determined to see Wilson and tell him of her regret. Her parents brought her out to Juniper Road one afternoon to pay their respects. The condition of the house and its furnishings reinforced Alice Jordan's doubts about endorsing Betsy's interest in someone of Wilson's family's circumstances.

Simeon Bates, too, stopped by on his way home from work. He drove the pickup truck up to the Jones' house, and Wilson met him on the porch. "Heard your daddy has "passed", Wilson, and I sho' am sorry."

The sitting up, which lasted past midnight, was pretty grim. Kinsmen and neighbors called at the house, dressed in their clean work clothes. Some of them stayed for an hour, some stayed longer, and some were prepared to sit with the casket all night, which had been the custom years before. At midnight, Mary and Wilson thanked the guests for coming, and explained that they could be of more help to the family by going home than by staying longer. The guests reluctantly departed, enabling mother and son to go to bed.

The day of the funeral was windy and cold, with threatening clouds. Most of the congregation of Bethel Church had been members fifteen or so years earlier when Mary and Dave had been married, after growing up in the church. Today nearly all the pews held mourners. The casket, a plain pine box, rested on a wheeled cart belonging to the undertaker. The top had been removed, so that any who wished to do so could have a last look at Dave. Because of the season, there were no flowers.

Mary and Wilson sat on the front pew, downcast heads bowed in prayer and despair.

After "The Old Rugged Cross" the minister began to pray, recalling Dave's youth and his illness, and everything in between. It seemed interminable to Wilson and Mary.

Finally, the lid was returned to its place atop the box, and the pallbearers, following the minister, carried it out of the church, with the family directly behind. The procession led to a freshly-dug grave in the church cemetery nearby. The pallbearers lowered the box into the grave, using web straps.

When the minister finished talking and praying, he nodded to Wilson, who picked up a shovel and flung the first bit of earth into the grave. When the dirt landed on the pine box it seemed to Mary that the noise was deafening, like a mournful drum roll. She shivered and cringed. Wilson immediately gave the shovel to someone else, and led his mother away.

After speaking briefly with those in attendance, the grieving family went to their house on Juniper Road.

"A sad, sad day, Mama, but between us we can get through it," said Wilson, trying to comfort his mother as they entered their house.

CHAPTER FIVE

DINAH

After Sim and his helper had finished cutting Mose Harrington's grove of trees into firewood they transported it into town. Sim didn't see Dinah any more, but he found that she was still on his mind.

"Sho' is a pretty girl,' he thought. "Sho' would like to see her again."

He went about his work conscientiously, as before—but he discovered that his pickup truck seemed to want to drive by Coleman Institute in order to get to its destination, whatever the destination was. He scanned the schoolyard every time he passed, hoping for a glimpse of Dinah. To his disappointment, he never saw her.

One afternoon during the winter, his crew finished its job that had been assigned for that day in mid-afternoon. Malachi pronounced, "Boys, it's too late in the day to start something new....Why don't we just call it a day, and you can go home a little early."

Sim realized that he had been given what he had been wishing for—a chance to go to the Institute and look up Dinah Harrington. There was no time to go home, so he dusted his clothes in an effort to rid himself of sawdust, stuck his head under a pump's stream of water and washed as well as he could. Then he proceeded to Coleman Institute.

He had never been on the campus before, but it was a small place. A two-story classroom building, a two-story dormitory, and a gym. Sim marched up to the dormitory, knocked on the door, and walked inside. He found a little lobby with "tongue-and-groove" walls and ceiling that had once been painted. That had been fifty years before, when the school had been built by the Northern Presbyterian Church "to educate the former slaves". There was also a desk and chair, and a young girl sitting there.

Sim removed his cap and said, "Hey. I want to speak to Dinah Harrington. Is that all right?"

The girl at the desk, who was a student taking her turn as "duty person" replied, "Who are you? She expecting you?"

"She might be expecting me to come some day, but prob'ly not today. My name is Sim Bates."

"I see if she's here". She opened the door that led into the dorm and bellowed, "Di-nah! Man here to see you, name of Sim!"

There was an answering voice, unintelligible to Sim, and the "duty person" informed him, "She be down, directly", but she pronounced it "t'reckly".

There were no chairs or benches provided for visitors to wait for girls to be "down, directly", so Sim just leaned against the wall and waited.

"Directly" translated into about fifteen minutes, and Dinah appeared. She was wearing a dress and a sweater and had a pencil stuck in her hair. She obviously had been studying.

"Hello, Sim", she said. "What are you doing here? Are you coming to school here?"

"Nope. Just stopped by to see you. We finished a little early today, 'n the Boss gave us the rest of the day off."

"That's nice. Thanks for coming. It's mostly girls here. I get kinda tired of "girl talk" all the time, doesn't amount to much. What would you like to do?"

"Well, we could go outside and walk around, if you want to". Sim was plainly uncomfortable with the "duty person" present and obviously listening to every word.

"Sounds like a good idea. Let me go get a warmer jacket," she quickly replied.

Dinah returned in no time, and they went out. They walked around the campus slowly, conversation lagging at first, as they both felt a little ill at ease in the new situation. When Dinah had sat with Sim and his helper while they were on a water break from cutting her grandfather's wood, each had been comfortable in his role, and talk came easily. This was different, and they had to feel their way. Soon, however, they relaxed, and the talk began to flow with greater ease.

After about thirty minutes a bell began to ring.

"Oh, Sim. That's the supper bell, and I have to go in. I've enjoyed seeing you again."

"Me too. Can I come back when I have time, and we can do it again?"

"Sure enough. Please do. But I'm going to my granddaddy's this weekend, and come back Sunday afternoon."

Maybe I can come Sunday afternoon. About the same time?"

"That's good. 'Bye."

As she turned to go to supper, she thought "What a nice surprise."

Sim walked to his house out Juniper Road, thinking how easy she was to talk to. He hadn't found much to say to other girls he had known. "Nice girl. Pretty, too."

As he neared his family's house, no children came out to greet him. They were not aware he was approaching, for in winter they used the house as a central gathering place rather than the yard. They tussled, played, sat, or lay on the assorted cots and beds that comprised the majority of the family's furniture. Daisy oversaw their activities, listening for arguments, assigning tasks, picking up articles of clothing, cooking the next meal, Suggesting a new game, whatever it took to keep things on an even keel.

When he pushed open the door and entered the room, bedlam ensued. "Sim!", "Sim is home!" and they jumped up from whatever they were doing and gathered around their older brother, their surrogate father figure. He wasn't fully matured, fully grown, nor did he have the full authority of a father, However, right now he was the closest thing they had to that fount of knowledge and experience, and they acknowledged it.

"Hey! Hey, chillun! Calm down! One at a time! I'll listen to what you've got to say, but one at a time," he said. "This time we'll start with the youngest—Gracie, you need to talk?"

"No, Sim. I'm all right. Dorothy and I had a fight, but Ma got us straight, and we're good now."

"That right, Dorothy?"

"Yeah, I think so, but she better be careful."

"Sounds to me like you both better be careful. Ma don't like to get chillun straight on one argument, and then have to do the same thing again. How 'bout you, Frank-o?"

"I guess I'm OK...but I'm getting' big...too big for taking cows to the pasture in the mornings, and goin' back to get 'em in the afternoon. I don't see why I can't shine shoes down town like Shad and make some real money. I'm ready to move up!"

"What do you think, Shad? Could Frank-o make another shine box and join you on the street?"

"I don't know about that, Sim. Two of us on the street might just divide the business, and the money, and not be any better off. Can Frank-o have the shine box by himself, and find me something else for me to do? I'm ready to move up, too!"

"Not bad thinking, Shad. You got any idea what you'd like to move up to? Give us some ideas. If you can't think of anything, we'll all try to think. Is that OK?"

"Yeah! That's good!" they all chorused.

"How 'bout you, Ma? You get along all right today? What did you do?"

"Well, you know today was Wash Day. Three times a week is Wash Day, and sometimes it seems like you chilluns can dirty clothes faster than I can clean 'em. But it's not bad, except using that rubbing board make my back hurt. Sho' does." Daisy put her hand on her back and stretched, and smiled. She nearly always smiled when she looked at her children.

"What about you, Sim?" she inquired. "Anything different, or was it just cutting wood?"

"Yeah, it was different. First of all, we finished our work early and Malachi gave us the rest of the afternoon off. That don't happen much. The second thing, I paid a visit to Coleman Institute—not to go to school, now, but to see somebody who goes to school there....You remember about a month ago I told you about a job out in the sand hills at Mr. Mose Harrington's place...Mose is an old man who sold us some timber for firewood. He's got a granddaughter that lives out there with him, and she boards at Coleman Institute in town and goes to school there.

Well, she and I had some good talks in the sand hills, so I went to see her at Coleman. It wasn't hard to find her, and we had a nice time talking before she had to go to supper. Nice girl. I going back to see her again."

"Uh-huh! That sounds interesting!" Daisy commented.

"Sim's got a girlfriend!" the younger children were soon chanting.

Sim just grinned.

* * *

He went to see Dinah the next Sunday afternoon, and again they had a pleasant time. He found that she is studying to be a schoolteacher.

"Too many colored children growing up, not knowing how to read, or how to figure. They'll end up being as ignorant as their parents .I want to help my people get better jobs, get ahead".

Dinah's face became animated as she talked, as fervent and enthusiastic as anybody Sim had ever encountered.

He replied, "You mighty right. I can read a little bit. Can't write so you can read it, but I can read it. Prob'ly need to spell better. Sure wish I knew more 'bout figurin'. If I can get my own business I'll need to be good at that".

"Well, my goodness, Sim. Maybe I can practice my teaching on you. That would help both of us."

"Yeah. I like the sound of that, and I got another problem I'm working on. Maybe a smart schoolteacher can help me with it."

"I'll try. What's the problem?"

Sim proceeded to tell her about his family—where and how they live…how the children all contribute to the family finances by sharing the income from their mandatory tasks. He ended his description by talking about the need to allow Shad and Frank-o to graduate to more demanding and rewarding jobs.

"Shad needs something better to do, so Frank-o can shine shoes, Dinah. You got any ideas about what a half-grown kid could learn how to do that would help him and the family?"

Let me think on it, Sim. And I'll ask my granddaddy, too".

After this earnest conversation, Sim asked for another date the following Saturday. As she planned to remain in town and not go to her grandfather's, she agreed, and they parted.

* * *

Ý'know, Dinah, somethin' I saw during the week might be a way for Shad to get another job." Sim had just arrived at Coleman Institute a week later. They had left the campus and were strolling toward town.

"What did you think of?"

I had to stop by the gas station twice during the week to buy gas for the pickup, 'cause we were hauling more wood in from the country. Both times I noticed a young colored boy hanging around the station. He helped the boss man service the customers' cars, checking the oil, cleaning the windshield, sweeping out the floorboards with that little broom—do they call it a swish broom?"

"I think the name of it might be whisk broom."

"Okay, whisk broom. Anyway, Shad could do that, easy. And we've got more than ten gas stations in Truro.... seems like one on every corner. If he got a job like that, first thing you know he might learn how to change tires, even be a mechanic. I bet there are going to be more and more cars around here....What do you think?"

Sounds like a really good idea. I'll ask my granddaddy what he thinks when I go out there next weekend."

As they walked on down town, the crowd increased. The country people were in town, their mules and wagons parked in the back lots. Families were gathered in little knots, talking animatedly with neighbors they hadn't seen in a week or two. The men were dressed in clean bib overalls, jackets and caps or hats. The women had on dresses, most were down almost to their ankles, sweaters and coats, their heads tied up with scarves against the cold. The children were running around, chasing or being chased by their peers.

The smell of peanuts was everywhere. Peanut vendors lined the street on every block. They had gas-powered machines that kept the nuts hot, and they sold small bags of the fragrant "goobers" for five cents a bag. Usually the vendors were young boys, willing to stand on the street all day for a chance to earn a little money. The sidewalks and gutters were littered with peanut shells.

Several other couples walked the streets like Dinah and Sim. More often, however, the young people walked in groups, by gender. Four or five girls walked together, hoping to be noticed by the "right" group of boys. The boys, uncertain of how to proceed if they found the "right" group of girls, usually resorted to walking past, then turning around and walking past in the other direction, talking to each other about how they would approach the other group, next week.

When they returned to the Institute, Dinah produced an arithmetic textbook.

"Sim, you said you are interested in practicing your math. Would you like to spend some time on that the next time you come?"

"Sho' would."

Why don't you borrow this book and look over the first two chapters. You probably already know what's in those. We'll talk about those chapters the next time you come, and when you feel good about it, we'll move on. Is that OK with you?"

"Sho' right. What about next Sunday, week from tomorrow?"

"That suits me fine. See you then. 'Bye".

* * *

Dinah was intrigued by Sim. She had known a few boys her age, but none who were interested in talking, just plain talking! The boys she knew had observed the animals in the farmyard, had seen the couplings that were natural to those animals—and the boys were interested in trying out that male-female thing with a female—namely Dinah.

Her grandfather had seen that coming. He told her in graphic terms about the birds, bees, cows, puppy dogs, and men and women. He stressed to Dinah that she must not give in to the entreaties of her contemporaries, that she must remain pure, like the Virgin Mary in the Bible.

"Wait until the <u>right</u> man comes along" he said. "Don't lie down with these plow boys....They don't want nothin' but fifteen minutes with you. No future in that! What I want you to do is hold out for a man who wants you forever— right on, and on, and on; the right man will take care of you and see that you have whatever you need. You're not an animal in the barnyard!"

* * *

She asked Mose Harrington about future employment for Sim's brothers.

"Yeah. I think that's a good idea about learning car mechanics. There's bound to be more cars—and more people buying cars that don't know one thing about keeping them running. They'll need mechanics.

"You know what I heard in town the last time I went? You heard me talk about Mack Adams, that man that knows everything about mechanics... The big money people in town offered him part-ownership in a new car dealership, if he would service the cars.... Do you know what he told them?" He said "Thanks, but I don't think it's a good idea to try to sell cars. Everybody in Truro who can afford a car already has one!"

"I don't think he was right. I think Sim's brother should learn mechanics."

* * *

The next Sunday Sim appeared at the Institute in early afternoon. He found to his chagrin that Dinah had not yet arrived at the school. "Dadgummit!" he thought. "That's what I get for being so all-fired eager! Give the girl time tell her granddaddy goodbye and travel to town!"

He walked down toward the business section. When he reached Truro Hardware he stopped and looked in the store window. That made him think of Wilson, and he realized that he hadn't seen Wilson since he had stopped by Wilson's house when his daddy died.

The winter sun was warm as he leaned against the brick front of the store, so he propped himself against the warm wall, basked in the sunlight, and thought about the past summer's employment. "Me and Wilson walked to work every day, worked hard, walked home in the afternoon, and never had one cross word. He treated me just like I treated him—like we was the same color. That's comfortable. Now, I can't be comfortable with Jim Lane. Don't trust him as far as I can throw a blacksmith's anvil. <u>We</u> ain't the same color. I say it, and Jim Lane says it, louder. We <u>ain't</u> the same color."

As he stood there in the warm sun, his thoughts returned to the problem of his brothers, Shad and Frank-o. "I ain't their daddy—but Ma's got her hands full just being their mama, and I'm the oldest... What would Pa say, or do, if he was here..."

He mused on this for another few minutes, and decided to walk on back toward the school.

He went into the dormitory lobby to ask for Dinah, but the girl on duty recognized him. She said, "She just came in a few minutes ago. Want me to call her?"

When he nodded, she opened the inner door and bawled, "Di-nah! He's here again!" In a few minutes, Dinah appeared, a book in her hand and wearing a coat.

"Hey, Sim," she said. "How you?"

"Good", was his reply. "You wanna go to walk?"

"Sounds like a plan, and I've got my coat. Let's go".

Hand in hand, they walked away from the campus. He steered her through the business district, and toward the river. They found a clearing on the bank that was sunny, and sat down. She smiled and said, "This is nice. Not so many people."

He nodded. "Yep".

"I brought an arithmetic book like the one you took last time. Do you want to look at those two chapters together? Do you understand how to add?"

Adding is pretty easy, and so is subtracting. When I get to multiplying and dividing, that's where I have trouble."

Thus invited, Dinah began to talk about the multiplication tables, explaining how multiplying is similar to adding. She began teaching him the number facts, urging him to memorize them. "Sim, once you have memorized these tables, multiplying will be easy, and the answer will come quicker."

"Yeah?"

"Yeah. Now, if you're willing to do a little homework, why don't you try to memorize the tables, from two up to six? Are you willing to do that?"

"You think I can do that, before next Sunday?"

"Are you saying you want to come next Sunday?"

"That's what I mean. You mighty right."

"Okay by me. It's getting late. You think we ought to go back now?"

"Maybe so, but I don't want to." He scrambled to his feet, reaching down to help her up.

As she rose he moved closer to her so that when she was standing, they were practically touching at hips and chest.

Sim put his arms around her. "I sho' do like these times with you," he said, "It real nice".

"I like it too, Sim," she replied, hugging him lightly before disengaging.

"He's not your average plowboy!" she thought as they walked back to the school.

Later, "Sim, I asked Granddaddy about Shad learning how to be a mechanic. He thinks it's a good idea."

"Good, I'll talk to Shad about it."

* * *

"Shad, you thought any more 'bout what you can do 'stead of shining shoes?", Sim asked his brother the next time they were alone.

"Naw, I thought about it, but couldn't think of nothing".

What would you think about getting' a job at a filling station? You could help the men clean the cars out, wash windshields, pump gas…"

"Sim, you know I don't know nothin' 'bout pumping gas!"

"It ain't hard, and you can learn. If you learn to do that and be helpful, maybe you can learn how to change tires, and then you can learn how to be a mechanic. That's where the big money is. You done already dropped out of school, so you need to find some job you can learn to do that will pay you enough to live on—and maybe raise a family."

"Sure as shootin' can't do that shining shoes! What filling station you think I ought to try for? They all look pretty much the same to me."

"I don't rightly know, Shad. Why don't you walk into town tomorrow, and just look 'em over? Notice which ones already got colored people working there. Ask them boys what all they do—ask 'em where you should go to ask for a job—if they ain't busy they'll talk to you, but if they are busy you better leave 'em alone. The boss man won't like it if you take a man away from his work."

"Okay. I'll go check 'em out."

* * *

When Sim arrived back at his house after work the next afternoon, Shad was waiting for him. "Sim, there's fifteen gas stations in this town, and I hung around every single one today! I stayed long enough to get an idea what they do, and learn which ones already have colored help. I talked to some of the help. They said it's not really hard, hard work, but the hours are long and the hot weather and the cold weather make it tough sometimes.

Did any of them give you an idea where you could get a job?"

"They mostly said 'I don't know'. But while I was looking around I found a new Gulf station, just starting up. Mr. Watson has it, and he is working that station all by his self—sometimes while I was there he really had to hustle. If you think it's all right I think I'll ask him for a job. Do you know Mr. Watson?"

"Is he a little short white man with a good-size stomach, and his shirttail is always hanging out?"

Sounds like the one."

I think he a pretty good man. Hard worker. You won't have to wonder what he thinks, 'cause he's done already told you, plain as day. He'd be a good boss man, I think"

"Tell me what to say when I ask for the job. I don't know how to do that."

"Lemme see. First off, be sure your face is clean and your nose ain't running. Then walk up to him, when he's not busy, and say something like: 'Mornin', Mr. Watson. Can I speak with you for just a minute?'

Then if he says you can: 'My name is Shadrach Bates. I live with my mama out on Juniper Road. I'm looking for work, and I notice you don't have no help. Could you use a boy to help you here? I'll do whatever you tell me to. I'm a hard worker and I want to learn about cars.'

"What if he says he don't need no help"?

"Then you thank him, nice as you please, and tell him you'd like to work for him when he does need help".

"What if he asks me how much pay I want"?

"He won't. If he says you can hang around and help him, don't ask no questions. Just say. 'Thank ya, suh. When you want me to start?"

"You mean I might not even know how much he gonta pay?"

"Tha's right. You might have to wait til Sa'day comes and see what he gives you. 'Course, you might get tips from the customers."

"Great God, Sim, I didn't shine no shoes 'til the customer knew how much I was gonta get!"

"But you got to understand, Shad. You tryin' to hire yourself out to a white man, by the week, or day, or somethin'. Whatever he tells you, and you don't argue—not if you want the job. You can quit after the first payday, or any payday, if you not satisfied. That's the way it is, in Truro, or any other place around here that I know of."

"Humph! That don't make it right!" Shad muttered

The next evening when Sim got home, Shad was waiting for him with a grin on his face.

"Got the job, Sim! Mr. Watson say he been looking for a boy that wants to learn, 'stead of one who wants to get paid for doing as little as he can get by with! He let me start today, and he wants me to come to work at 8 every morning, 'cept Sunday, and get off at 6 in the winter and 7 in the summer. And you were right—ain't no trouble in pumping gas—you pump it up 'til the glass is full up top, then you let the gas feed down into the car's tank."

"He go' pay you?"

"He say he see how I do, 'n then he know how much to pay".

"Tha's what I thought. Tha's the way it work. If he be a good man, he treat you all right. If he ain't, then you can leave, 'less you desperate."

Several days later, Sim was sent by Malachi to pick up a dozen files at Truro Hardware. As he entered the store a familiar figure came forward to meet him. It was Wilson.

"Well, hey, Sim! I haven't seen you in a month of Sundays! How are you?"

"Getting' along pretty good, Wilson. How you 'n yo' mama doing?"

"We're making it. Mama's been kinda sad. I see her lookin' out the window a lot. She knows Daddy ain't coming down the road no more, but she still looks for him"

Changing the subject to business, Wilson inquired, "What can we do for you today, Sim?"

"Malachi wants a box of ten-inch mill bastard files, and a box of crosscut files. He wants 'em charged to his account."

We can do that. Here you go—sign this ticket and you can be on your way".

See you, Wilson. Tell yo' mama I said hey".

Later, Matt Stokes asked him, "You looked like you know that boy who works for Malachi. Who is he?"

"His name is Simeon Bates. He lives past me out Juniper Road. His daddy is Pete Bates, useta work for Mister George at the gin."

"Oh, yeah. I remember Pete. Haven't seen him in a while. Is he still around?"

"No sir. He went "up the road". Couldn't find any work down here after the gin burned. I think he's in Detroit."

"Detroit's not a good place to be right now. I read in the paper they're having trouble between the colored and the white. Race riots. Real violence."

"That's bad. I hope Sim's daddy is all right. Sim and I worked together last summer. He's a good fellow."

"I'm glad to find out who he is".

CHAPTER SIX

1939—four years later

CITY DWELLERS

Sim and Dinah had been 'keeping company' for nearly three years when she graduated from Coleman Institute in June, 1938. She was appointed to a teaching position at Sawmill School in the sand hills, about a mile from Mose Harrington's farm.

The school was typical of the rural schools that were provided for the use of the colored population in those days. It was a one-room frame building, furnished with a blackboard, a pot-bellied stove, a few desks, and a privy fifty feet to the rear of the structure. The privy serviced both sexes and all ages.

All the children in the vicinity who went to school attended that school. There were no buses provided, so each student was responsible for his own transportation, and it nearly always ended up as 'on shanks' mare'—that is, they walked. Of course, since there was only one room in the school, all the students were in that room, together, regardless of age or ability.

Dinah, a first-year teacher, learned to teach in that environment the same way she had learned to swim. She jumped in! Her own education and her enthusiasm for her goal was the rope around her waist that kept her from sinking. Being an idealistic, capable person, she was not daunted by the challenge, but rather was spurred on by the idea of improving the educational level of her pupils.

When Dinah stopped attending the Institute, she stopped coming to Truro, for she no longer was in school there. This put a complete stop to easy visits with Sim, and they both came to the realization of how much 'keeping company' had come to mean to them. Sim traveled to the Harrington farm nearly every weekend. Sometimes he borrowed Malachi's pickup, sometimes he walked.

He and Dinah began to speak of marriage, and when Mose Harrington became aware of it, he was pleased. He had grown to like Sim, and had always admired the way he went about his work. One day he said to Dinah, "If you two are thinking 'bout gettin' married, where do you think you would live?"

"We don't know, Granddaddy. That's one of the things we're talking about. Sim's work is mostly in town, and all of my attention is focused out here. Transportation is a problem."

"I'd be glad to have you two live out here," the old man said. "He could move in with us. You could cook for the three of us, and there wouldn't be any rent, 'cause you're family."

When Dinah told Sim about her grandfather's offer, he was elated. "Dinah! With both our incomes, and no rent, we might be able to afford a second-hand pickup truck. That would get me back and forth to town, and maybe I could go into the firewood business for myself!"

And so the young couple was married, in Sawmill Baptist Church, in the presence of their families. Dinah wore a white cotton dress and carried a bouquet of blue lupines which grow wild along the edge of the roads in the sand hills. Sim and the other men in his family wore white shirts, boiled in starch and so stiff they could could have stood without a person inside. Daisy alternated between tearful emotion and beaming with pride.

Sim moved in with the Harringtons, creating a little more room in Daisy's crowded shanty.

* * *

Christmas, 1938 was behind him now, but Tom Stone could not erase the memory of his mother's inability to cope with the holiday. Not only was she helpless in planning the holiday meal for the two of them and her widowed sister who lived nearby, she had not the slightest idea how to begin preparing it.

When Tom finally realized the state she was in, he suggested gently to her that he find someone to provide the traditional holiday treats. Contracting with Janie Mixon, a neighbor who made cakes and other goodies on order, they served appetizers of salted nuts and cheese straws, and spiced blackberry cordial. This was followed by turkey, cornbread dressing, rice and giblet gravy, and cranberry sauce,. There was a side dish of oyster dressing for Tom who had encountered that delicacy at a house party at Pawley's Island. The vegetables were whipped sweet potatoes served in hollowed out orange halves, asparagus, and green beans. Hot biscuits and butter accompanied the meal; and after the table was cleared, ambrosia and fruitcake followed. Hot coffee with whipped cream topped everything off.

Of course, that was far too much for the three of them to consume. But, after all, it was Christmas, and Tom wanted his mother to hark back to Christmases past, and feel that the holiday was well observed and well served.

He pondered the dilemma caused by his mother's confusion for the next several days, and finally came to the conclusion that they needed a housekeeper. Several years before he had seen this situation on the horizon, and had even mentioned the possibility of employment to Mary Jones, the mother of young Wilson Jones at the hardware store. His mother had not been ready to consider such a thing at the time, so the matter was laid to rest.

The day before New Year's he drove his little Ford runabout out Juniper Road and called on Mary Jones. He knocked jauntily on the door: *"shave and a haircut, two bits!"* and in a minute or two she opened the door.

"Well, Tom!" she exclaimed in surprise. "I was just getting ready to walk in to town to work at the Café. Will you come in?"

"Thank you, no, Mrs. Jones. I won't come in. But if you're headed into town, maybe you'll do me the favor of riding with me, and that will give us a chance to chat."

"Sounds like a good way to get to work. If you're ready, so am I, so let's go!"

After picking up a small parcel from inside the house, she came out and stepped into the car while he held open the door. "Thank you", she said.

After casual conversation about the observance of Christmas at each of their households. Tom took a deep breath and launched hesitantly into the reason for their meeting.

"Mrs. Jones", he began, "you and I have both observed that my mother is getting older… and less able to take care of herself.

"Yes, I've noticed that", she gravely replied.

"We had a difficult experience at Christmas that showed me that some changes need to be made, for Mother's sake. I don't want her to feel that she's not doing her part, the part she's always done. And I don't want her to feel pressure to do what she can no longer do." He blurted it out, as he had rehearsed it, then sat there behind the wheel, quiet.

"Yes, Tom", she said, "I understand what you're saying."

"Well, Mrs. Jones…"

"Mary", she interjected.

"Yes, thank you, Mrs.—Mary", he continued, "I think I'm looking for a woman—the right person—to be what you might call a live-in housekeeper. This person could move into the house with Mother and me, and have her own room, rent-free. I would like this person to buy the groceries for us, supervise the house—and eat with us, of course, and sometimes be a companion to Mother." He asked, "Would you consider that, Mary?"

"Well! My Lord! I'd have to think about it, of course. Wouldn't want to answer without thinking of everything! What about my son? What would he do, where would he live? Could I continue my job at the Café? What would you pay me? Does your mother know about this?" The questions poured forth.

"Mary, I understand that this idea is new to you, and you can probably think of many more questions as the day goes on. Why don't we continue this conversation the day after New Year's, starting an hour earlier? That will give us a chance to go over all your questions, and still get you to work on time. Is that OK?"

"That sounds OK to me, Tom. Thanks for thinking of me. Your mother is a sweet lady."

* * *

After the holiday, when Tom's car pulled into her yard, Mary was waiting on the porch. She got into the car, and they drove to his father's old office, now his. They walked inside. He showed her to a seat in front of his desk, and he took an identical chair beside hers.

As they sat down, another door opened and a middle-aged woman looked in.

"Virginia, this is Mary Jones, the lady I am hoping will agree to help me with Mother. Mary, this nice person is Virginia Grant.

She runs the office, and is trying to teach me a little bit about the law."

"Oh, heavenly days Tom! Nobody believes that, not even you! Glad to see you, Mary. I hope you will be able to help with Miss Irene. She's such a dear."

"I've seen her a number of times, and she is sweet. Tom and I have some things to work out, and I hope we can."

"Would you like coffee?" Virginia inquired. When they both declined, she left the room.

"What are your questions, Mary?" Tom asked.

"Well, to begin with, what about Wilson? What happens to him?"

"I took the time to look over our house last night, with that in mind. There are a number of rooms that haven't been occupied for awhile—two good-sized rooms, and a bath, that could be bedrooms for the two of you."

'That'll probably be all right. What about our groceries?"

"I thought all the household could eat together, out of the household groceries that you would order. You would plan meals and we would all eat together, schedules permitting. I would provide the money for the groceries, and the laundry, and the coal and wood, and for all the other household expenses."

"Do you mean Wilson and I would live there, free?"

"That's what I think I mean, unless there's something I haven't thought of. You'll be in charge of the house and of the cleaning woman, ordering and preparing the food, and I'd like you to spend some time with Mother every day. Wilson could keep the wood and coal bins filled, take out the trash and garbage. I'll teach him how to drive, if he doesn't already know."

"Can I keep my job at the Café?"

"We can talk about that. I'm not sure the lunchtime job would fit, but maybe so. The Friday and Saturday night jobs we can talk about. But you haven't yet asked a question about money. Of course I wouldn't expect you to undertake this responsibility for free room and board alone. Suppose I pay you twenty dollars a week. Would that be satisfactory?"

"Twenty dollars a week?" Mary seldom, if ever, made twenty dollars a week as a waitress, unless she happened to serve Joe Gibbes and Nick Miller when they were particularly happy. And then, as she knew very well, her expenses had to come out of that income.

"Would that be a satisfactory amount?" he asked again.

"Yes, I think it would," she replied, her heart beating furiously. Twenty dollars! And to live in town, with running water, and electricity! Lord have mercy!!

"Tom, I like what you have told me. It would be a pleasure to help you take care of your mother—but before I accept the job I must talk this over with my son. Wilson is almost a grown man now, and this affects him as much as it does me. I will have to have his approval before I agree to move into town, into your house. Do you understand?"

"Sure do. And with Wilson's help you might come up with some more questions."

"Well, here's one that just popped into my head. What does your mother think of all these changes in her house?"

"That's a bridge I haven't crossed yet. When you and I agree on the situation, then I'll figure out how to approach her so she'll like it—and then it will be up to the two of us to get her to *love* it."

"Well, all right, then. I'll talk to Wilson and get back to you."

After she left, Virginia came back to Tom's office. "She seems like a nice person", she said. "Any typing for me this morning?"

* * *

When Wilson got home from the hardware store that afternoon, his mother was waiting. She was sitting in the rocking chair, calmly rocking. There was nothing in her manner to show that she had been restlessly pacing, or, by turns, peering down the dirt road that led to their house. "I hope he's coming straight home tonight 'stead of going by Betsy's," she thought. He and Betsy were still devoted friends, a "steady" couple for these three years, and he frequently "curved by" her house on his way home.

Much to her relief, Mary soon spotted his form as he trudged up the lane in the gathering darkness. These winter days sure are short, she thought.

"Hey, Mama—you just sitting and rocking?"

"That's right, Wils. Just waiting for my wandering boy to come home. How was your day?"

"Not too bad, but High School is getting boring after being there these four long years. All of us are ready to be getting out. The store was pretty busy this afternoon. Matt had us counting the inventory and putting the Christmas stuff in the warehouse for next year. One or two customers, but January's not much in a hardware store. It was so dark I didn't stop by Betsy's—she told me she had a lot to do tonight, How about you? Anything new?"

"Yes, Wilson! — I've got plenty to tell you—and ask you! You know Tom Stone..."

"'Course I know Tom Stone. He's the lawyer, our friend—lives in that big old house on High Street."

Tom came to see me today morning, gave me a ride in to work…" And she related the whole sequence of their conversations—Mrs. Stone's condition, Tom's proposal that they move into town, their living arrangements, the salary—everything.

When she finished, she leaned back in her chair, her heart racing again with excitement, and said, "What do you think, Wils?"

"Great Goodness alive!—or as your Mama used to say, 'Saints preserve us'! If that don't change the game, I don't know what would! Let me see if I understand all this. He wants us to move to town, into his house, rent and groceries free, with two bedrooms and a bath for us, and all we have to do is help run the house, prepare the food, be nice to Mis' Irene, which ain't hard….and we have to put up with being close to school and the store, and Betsy. And be troubled with running water and electric lights? And then we'd have to find a way to use twenty dollars every single week?"

Wilson paused a minute, then said, "What do you think, Mama?"

"It seems almost too good to be true. I guess I'd like living in town—never tried it before. I don't know about living in another woman's house. We'd have to make some adjustments—no animals, no garden, different neighbors. Tom said I may be able to keep part of my job at the Café. But I've been thinking about that, and it probably wouldn't be fair to Mis' Irene to go running off all the time…"

"Mama, with twenty dollars coming in, free and clear, you don't really need the work, do you?"

"You're probably right, Son. But I will miss my friends, like Frank— and the regular customers. I've been there three years, you know. And, I'll miss this little tenant house your Uncle Ben has been good enough to let us use. It's not much, but it's Home.

"Do you think you want to do this, Mama?"

"If you're all right with it, I think we should do it. It looks like a good way to improve our situation."

Let's do it, then. I'll like living in town where everything goes on."

The next day, after a somewhat restless night, Mary went by Tom's office on her way to work. Virginia greeted her pleasantly, but said that Tom is tied up in court for the day, and wouldn't be able to see her. Seeing that Tom's calendar for the next day had no morning appointments, Virginia suggested that Mary come in around 10 AM. "I know he's anxious to see you," she said.

Mary agreed, and continued to the Café. She decided she would say nothing to Frank about the possibility of leaving his employ. "It will be better if I wait until it is definite," she thought. "We haven't 'shook' on it yet, and Mis' Irene has not agreed."

Her mind was awhirl as she went about her work at the Café that day. Frank noticed she seemed preoccupied, but said nothing. Women, he knew, could be different every day.

Wilson came home promptly from the store that afternoon. "Well, Mama, what did you and Tom decide? Are we going to town? When are we going? How will we get this furniture moved? Can I tell Betsy we're moving?"

"Slow down a little bit, Son. One question at a time. First of all, I didn't get to talk to Tom today because he was in court. I'll see him tomorrow morning. Virginia gave me an appointment for ten o'clock. Then we'll know some of the answers."

"Oh, shucks! I was hoping it would be all settled so I could tell Betsy tomorrow!"

"Be patient, boy. Be patient."

* * *

The next day Mary again called at Tom's law office. She was greeted warmly by Virginia as well as Tom. They discussed the proposed move at great length, realizing that it called for major changes in the lives of four people. They each had questions, and they worked out the answers, as far as they could see ahead.

Being a careful man as well as a lawyer, Tom called Virginia into the office and dictated the terms of the agreement. He asked for a copy for each of them. "This way," he said, there will be fewer questions about what was agreed."

The next step called for Tom to talk to his mother and get her approval for Mary and Wilson to move into her house. He began organizing his thoughts, just as if he were making a summation of his case before a jury, He and Mary agreed that she would wait for his signal that everything is OK before giving notice at the Café or preparing to move.

"Poor Wilson," she thought. He'll have to wait even longer before he can tell Betsy he's moving to town!"

* * *

Thoroughly prepared, as for a courtroom battle, Tom talked to his mother about the need to make some changes in their lifestyle. Much to his relief, he found that she was amenable.

"I can tell I'm not the woman I once was. I can tell I'm not able to do what I once did, and, if I can do it, I certainly can't do it as well as I once did, or as fast. What do you have in mind for taking care of this old woman and her lawyer son?

When Tom explained that he had found a live-in housekeeper who would move in and be in charge of the house—Mary Jones, whom his mother had talked to on several occasions. On hearing this, Mrs. Stone gave a great sigh of relief.

"I was so afraid," she said, "that you were going to want me to go to a smaller house, or some "old folks home", somewhere; and

I've lived here in this house on High Street ever since your daddy and I were young, and you were a baby! I do not want to leave my home!"

"No, Mother. I wouldn't suggest that".

"I imagine Mary Jones will be all right. She seemed like a nice person when we visited before".

Tom went over all the details of the agreement he and Mary had made, including the fact that Wilson would move in also, and told her where he suggested the Joneses would sleep.

"It sounds like a good arrangement, Tom. And you're right—I do need some help. Let's give it a try, and see how it works out. If the four of us don't get along, then we'll take another look at it.

With all parties in favor of the arrangement, Tom went by the Sanitary Café on his way home to lunch. He told Mary that his mother had n agreed to Mary taking over the management of the house, and moving into the spare rooms along with Wilson.

"It looks like it's OK to tell Frank you'll be leaving, and as soon as you have worked out your notice and packed up your things you two can move in. I'll have your rooms ready for you". He paused, then said, with a grin, "Oh, and don't forget to let Wilson know he can tell Betsy he'll be moving to town!"

"No danger he'll let me forget that important fact!" she responded.

* * *

Frank received Mary's announcement with disappointment, but not total surprise. "I knew there was something on your mind for the last week," he said. "You did good work, like always, but your mind was not on it. When do you want to stop?"

"Well, Frank, if I stay another week, will that give you enough time to find somebody else?"

"Sure, I can find somebody in a week. Of course, she ain't likely to be as good as you, 'cause I never had anybody before who was as good as you. Look, Mary, if this deal don't work out, all you got to do is let me know and you can have your old job back!"

"Thank you, Frank. I've enjoyed working here. You're a good boss."

She sat in her rocker, placed near the window so she could watch the road for Wilson's approach. She saw the headlights of Sam's car as he stopped to let Wilson out, then watched him walk toward the house. "Such a fine boy," she thought, "How did I ever get so lucky?"

As he came in the door she greeted him with a bright smile. "Well, Son, it's done. I've given Frank a one-week notice. After that week we can move into town. Do you think we can be ready in a week, or two?"

"Don't tease me, Mama! Is it true? Can we move to town—and can I tell Betsy we're coming? Can I be ready? I can be ready tomorrow!"

"Yes, I think you can tell Betsy now. But this is not going to be as easy as walking into town and sitting down at the supper table. We've got to get rid of our chickens and other animals. We've got to pack up everything in this house and leave it empty and clean. We've got to do something with our garden tools. Even though we don't have many things to take with us, we have to leave this place empty and clean, so we've got plenty to do!"

The next two weeks were awful, as anyone who has changed residences can attest. No stopping off at Betsy's house on the way home, while this cleaning was going on. Wilson made a beeline for home after work. There he found Mary knee deep in decisions. "Will we need this where we're going? If not, who can we give it to? How can we get this stuff to town?"

It developed that, when moving day arrived, Wilson had asked Sim to help them with his pickup truck which he had just purchased, second-hand, of course. Sim brought Frank-o along with him to help with loading and unloading.

On one of the trips between houses, Sim told Wilson that he and Dinah had gotten married a few months before. "We living out at her granddaddy's in the sand hills. Don't have to pay no rent. That the reason I can buy my own truck— no rent. Dinah, she teaching at Sawmill School, She can walk to school, but I ride her when I can. She is one fine woman, Wilson. I want you to meet her."

Wilson introduced Sim to the Stones, mother and son. "Sim Bates is a good man, and a good friend of mine. Anything you want done, he can do it."

The move was finally completed. Some of the excess, like garden tools, were stored in one side of the Stones' two car garage, once a carriage house.

After Sim and Frank-o left, Irene Stone, always a lady, welcomed the Joneses warmly into her home. "I hope you'll be as happy here as I have been," she said.

Mary took a quick look around the pantry and prepared a supper of grits and canned salmon, which was enjoyed by all.

Wilson excused himself, after helping his mother clear the table. "We've been so busy packing and cleaning and moving that I have neglected Betsy. Is it OK if I walk around there and visit?"

"Why don't you call her on the phone and let her know you're coming?" Tom asked.

"You mean you have a telephone, too?" Wilson couldn't believe his good fortune.

"Sure, the book is right there beside the phone. Go to it."

Wilson looked up the number and called the Operator. She connected him right away, and Betsy's father answered. "Hello?"

"Mr. Jordan, this is Wilson. May I speak with Betsy?"

"Sure, Wilson. Just a minute."

When Betsy spoke into the phone, Wilson said, "I'd love to walk the two blocks to your house and sit with you for a while. Are you free?"

"Wilson! Are you in town? How great! Yes, I'm free now—the last boy just left. I'd love for you to come, but give me ten minutes to freshen up."

"Give me his name and I'll take care of him," he said lightly. "I might mess up his face if he gets in my way."

"Well, Cowboy, it sounds like you've been out on the range too long. You need a little city living and female companionship?"

"You got that right," was his rejoinder.

"Ten minutes give you enough time?"

"Make it nine. I haven't seen you in a long time."

It was rather a chilly night, and Betsy's parents welcomed Wilson, then vacated the front room, giving the young couple a little privacy without their having to go out to the porch swing.

They sat together on the sofa, exchanging polite chatter for a few minutes. When Wilson judged the Jordans were in their room for the evening, he casually placed his arm on the backrest of the sofa, touching her shoulder.

"Now, tell me," he said, "who were those boys who were here earlier?'

"Wilson, you don't expect me to tell you, do you? After all, I need to protect my boyfriends from the jealous rage of the Wild Man of the hardware store," she teased.

"You're mighty right you'd better protect them. If I find out who they are, no telling what would happen, but it wouldn't be pretty!"

For a minute he held his tough expression, then said, in a different, milder tone, "Was there anybody here?"

"No, Wilson, I was just leading you on. Nobody was here."

Wilson put both his arms around her, her head on his shoulder. "I really wouldn't like it if you had other boyfriends."

"Wilson, you know I care about you—I have, since the eighth grade. There's not anyone else ."

With his free hand he tipped her face up to his and gave her an insistent kiss, which she returned. Her lips were soft, slightly parted. He put both arms around her and began to caress her back. The kiss continued, and she in turn caressed him. Then she pushed him away gently, both feeling the rush of emotion.

"Gosh, Betsy, that was nice!" and he gathered her into his arms again. Another kiss followed. Before either one of them realized it was happening, his free hand was cupping the soft roundness of her breast. Without breaking the kiss, she grasped his hand and placed it firmly on her back again.

"I don't think we ought to go there," she said softly. "But you can kiss me again."

CHAPTER SEVEN

"KEEP ON KEEPIN' ON"

Dinah and Sim had finished their supper of collards, potatoes and cornbread, and Mose Harrington had gone to bed. After they cleared the table and washed the dishes, they sat around the supper table again. Sim was tired, because of helping Wilson's family move. Dinah knew she was facing a full day at school the next day; they looked at each other and smiled.

"I'm so happy," she said.. "Living with my granddaddy and taking care of him was something I wanted to do and was glad to do—but it's not as nice as being here with you!"

Sim grinned shyly. "I like it too," he said

After a minute of silence, she asked, "Have you been by your mama's house to see how she's getting along"?

He shook his head. "Been in so much of a hurry to get out here where you are in the afternoons I haven't even thought about Ma and the others."

She smiled again, gratified, then said, "That's nice for me, Sim, but you mustn't forget you are responsible for her and your brothers and sisters, with your daddy gone. Maybe you should try to go by Juniper Road at least once or twice a week. What do you think?"

"I think you're right, and I'll go by there tomorrow."

The next afternoon after the day's work was finished, Sim cranked his pickup and headed it out Juniper Road. "Betcha I could walk this here road blindfolded all the way into Truro," he thought. "Wonder how many times I've walked it?"

He slowed and glanced over at the house Wilson had lived in for so long. "They've only been out of there for a day or so, and it already looks deserted."

He continued on the dirt track, rounded the last curve and saw the familiar unpainted, sagging wooden shack, complete with rusty metal roof and crooked chimney, from which smoke rose straight up, since the day was calm.

"Ma's cooking supper, I bet. She'll want to feed me, too—and so will Dinah. Maybe I can eat a little bit both places. Don't want to hurt the cooks' feelings!"

He got out of the pickup and slammed the door. In a second or two the door of the shack opened and a head peered out. It was Dorothy, now twelve. "Hey, y'all, it's Sim!" she called back inside, and before the words were out of her mouth a swarm of half-grown children erupted into the yard. No more jumping up and down, like in the old days when they were smaller, but broad grins were evident all around. He was loved and admired.

In a minute Daisy appeared, wiping her hands and grinning broadly at the sight of her firstborn. "Come on in, Sim, we're just getting' ready to have some biscuits and 'lasses. Plenty here for you. And I want to talk to you about sump'n."

They all went inside and helped their plates to several plump, hot biscuits, fresh out of the oven. The biscuits were soon covered with a generous serving of molasses, and the supper plate was then complete. The children made their way, with appreciative moans of pleasure, through several servings of this sweet, appetite satisfying family staple.

After the younger ones had finished and gone outside, Daisy moved her chair closer to Sim, and began talking a low, earnest voice, "I heard from your daddy today," she said. He talking about coming home—to stay, for good."

"Great day, Ma! That is good news!" Then, "But you ain't too excited about it! Why? What else you got to tell me?"

"I'm scared to death if he comes back the Klan will get him! You don't 'member much about it 'cause you were so little when it happen'—the other chillun don't 'member anything'cause I don't talk about it. Mister George blames your daddy for the fire at the gin, and the Klan was talkin' 'bout punishin' him for it, and that's why he had to go up to Dee-troit!"

"You think if he comes back they'll 'member the gin fire, and try again?"

"They might—and he feels like he has to leave Dee-troit "cause they're having those race riots up there; and it's so dangerous, he's scared to stay"!

"Well, Ma, you know, it's been four or five years since he left. You think Mister George and those Klan people go' remember and still be mad at Daddy? Wait, now—is Mister George still around here?"

"He sho' is. I see him every once in a while, and when I do I skedaddle outa his way"!

"What you go' tell Daddy to do?"

Would you and Dinah write him a letter and tell him Mister George is still around, and if he comes back here, he better be careful. You know I can't write good enough for anybody to read it, so I need some help. Can y'all do that?"

"Sure we can, Ma. I'll talk to Dinah, and we'll get a letter in tomorrow's mail."

As soon as Dinah, Sim and her granddaddy finished their supper and the old man went to bed, Sim told Dinah about the conversation with his mother. They talked over the situation for nearly an hour, in low tones as if a Klan member were in the same room trying to hear their conversation. Between them, they composed a letter urging caution if Pete decided to come home to Truro.

Sim went by the Post Office the next morning, purchased a 3-cent stamp, and carefully stuck it to the envelope before dropping the letter in the mail slot.

* * *

Sim kept to his promise and went by Daisy's shanty at least once a week for a visit. He and Dinah continued to help Daisy's family finances by regular gifts of money. She kept him up to date on the other children, and other news of his old neighborhood. He told what little he knew about Wilson and Mary, though he didn't see as much of Wilson since the Jones' move into town. Each time he came he asked if she'd heard anything more from Pete, and she shook her head.

"I jus' don't know what to hope for, Sim," she said, plainly worried. "I love that man, so I want him here, near us—but I sure don't want him to come back here and be picked up by the Klan! Lord knows what they'd do to him! I'd almost rather he stayed up in Dee-troit, 'cept those race riots are going on up there, and he might get killed and I'd never see him again! I don't know what to wish for…"

"Well, Ma, we ain't in charge of it, and we can't say how things are goin' to work out. Nothin' we can do to change it, neither.

Maybe the best thing we can do is 'keep on keepin' on'. We can be ready for Daddy if he comes, and help him lay low. And if he decides not to come, we can go along with that, too."

* * *

Two weeks later when Sim went by Daisy's to see how things were going, he found his father there. Daisy and the other children were there, too, and there were big grins all around. Pete was having a hard time adjusting to the size, and age, of the children he'd last seen several years before., but he was plainly delighted to be at home.

Sim was also having to adjust to his father's changed appearance. When Pete left Truro he had seemed a big, strapping strong man to his young son; now his hair was turning gray at the temples. His color was not healthy, and he seemed thinner. He was also jumpy and nervous.

When Sim, later, brought up his father's appearance, Pete explained, "Well, Sim, it's been rough up there. At first, they were glad to hire us. They needed workers and we needed jobs. We could find pretty good places to live—better than down here—and most of the colored lived in one part of the city. We worked, most of us were sending money home, just like me. That didn't leave us any money to raise Hell, so we didn't raise Hell.

Then, the white boys heard about the pay scale in the car factories, and they wanted to get some of that. They got some jobs. Then they started to need cheap places to live, just like us. That kinda crowded us all in a small section of the city, and first thing you know, there was some trouble between whites and colored. It got worse and worse., It got to the point I was scared to go out in the street, so I came home."

"But, Daddy, didn't you get our letter telling you about the Klan and Mister George?"

"I got it. But I decided I'd rather live here, and be scared of the Klan, than live up there and be scared of everybody."

Changing the subject, he said, " Don't know what I'll do to find a job. Couldn't find one when I left here. But spring plowing is right around the corner, and maybe somebody needs a hand. Maybe something else will turn up. We'll see. I'll find something."

* * *

A week of rest at home with Daisy's cooking worked wonders on Pete's color and his attitude. He looked like an entirely different person when Sim and Dinah stopped by for a visit. Dinah was glad to meet the man she'd heard so much about, and he was pleased and impressed with her.

"So your granddaddy is Mose Harrington," he said. "He was one of our customers at the gin. I 'member him."

"He remembers you, too. In fact, he wants you to come out to see him. He might know of a job for you. Anyway, he would enjoy a visit.

Both Daisy's and Pete's ears perked up at the mention of the word "job". "Tell Mose I'll be sure and come out to see him," he said.

Sim said he would arrange to get off work a little early the next day so he could give Pete a ride out into the sand hills for the visit.

The next day Sim's pickup truck stopped by the shack on Juniper Road, and his daddy got inside. The two rode in silence for a few minutes, then Pete began asking him questions about the other siblings.

"Shad and Frank-o both interested in working with cars, got regular jobs in service stations." Sim chuckled. "You made 'em, they keep 'em running. Now, the girls, they've always had jobs, mostly taking care of white folks' chillun. They're gettin' older now, and I'm tryin' to get 'em more interested in school. Dinah is a schoolteacher and she really like teachin' the children. She feels like she helping her race to get ahead. Since Dorothy and Gracie like children, and don't hate school, it seems like a nat'ral fit for them to be teachers. Sure would beat being somebody's cook or maid!"

"You thinkin' good, Sim," his father said.

About this time they pulled up at the Harrington place. Mose was sitting on the front porch, watching for them. He got out of his rocking chair and came out in the yard to greet them.

"Howdy, Pete! It's been a long time since I've seen you!"

"Well, Mose! It sho' has! And you ain't changed a bit! Lawdy me!"

"Looka here, Boy, you done gone off and lost your sight? When you left here I could still do—but now I'm a 'feared I'm getting' old. Can't do what I useta could, day or night."

"Unh hunh! I know what you mean! Yes, sir!"

"Come on in. We can sit on the porch and talk about the old days when you worked at Mist' George's gin and I was bringin' wagonloads of cotton to you."

"Those were good days, all right."

"What happened 'twixt you and Mister George, Pete? Why did you leave the gin? And why did you leave town?"

"Mister George and I, we had an argument," Pete said, cautiously, looking over toward Sim. "He got terrible mad at me, and fired me on the spot."

"Was that the same night the gin burned?" Mose asked.

"Yeah, same night."

"Well, why'd you leave town?"

"Two reasons. One reason is 'cause I couldn't find a job nowhere after that. Mister George mighta put out the word that I meant trouble."

"That's one reason. You said there was two?"

"Yeah. The other reason is the Klan."

"You mean the Ku Klux Klan? How did they figure in to it?"

"Mister George got to drinking, before and after the fire. He was already really mad with me, and the liquor helped him believe that I had set the fire, to get even with him for firing me from my job."

"How did the Klan get into it?"

Some of his drinkin' buddies are members of the Klan, and it didn't take much cussin' to get them mad at this little nigger boy."

I didn't hear nothin' about them burning a cross."

"No. They were drinkin' and talkin' loud, and one of my buddies heard 'em, and sent me word to get moving. Had to get a job, anyway, so I got out of town fast."

"What you going to do now?"

"I'm going to try to be careful. Ain't Mister George still around?"

He is. He's drinkin' more, and you know he's mean when he drinks. Better stay away from him."

"I'm gonna try. But I've got to find a job. Do you know of anything?"

"Not off the top of my head. You could plow for me, but that ain't much of a job."

"Yeah, you right. Any sawmills working? If I could get on with them I'd be working out in the woods, kinda out of sight."

"I'll think on it, Pete. Maybe betwixt us we can think of somethin.'

The two men continued their conversation, leisurely talking about bygone days. Sim listened, enjoying their reminiscing. After another thirty minutes, as Pete and Sim were getting up to return home, the older man said, "You know, Pete, I was at the gin the afternoon of the day it burned."

"That so?" Pete said. "I don't 'member seeing you. If I did, I forgot it."

"Guess you didn't see me, 'cause you and your wife were walking away from the office, with your back to me. Looked to me like she was upset."

"She sho' 'nuf was," Pete said. "I had just been fired."

* * *

As Sim and his father neared Truro on their return trip, they encountered a work crew busily digging holes on the shoulder of the road. Behind the crew a line of new utility poles stood straight and tall along the side of the road, showing where they'd been.

"Stop the truck, Sim," his father directed. "I want to talk to these people."

Sim applied the brakes, and his father stepped out. He approached the only white man in the group, obviously the one in charge. He took off his cap. "Excuse me, Mister,' he said. "I'm looking for work. Do you need another man on this crew?"

"Well, as a matter of fact I'm a man short right now. One of my new boys got tired, and he up and went home. I'm looking to replace him. What's your name?"

"Pete Bates, suh."

"You live around here?"

"In Truro, suh."

"You look strong. Do you have a strong back?"

"Yes, suh, I'm a good worker, suh."

"Well, I'll give you a try. Pay is two dollars a day. Meet us at seven o'clock tomorrow in front of the Post Office."

"Yes, suh. I'll be there."

As he climbed back in the pick-up, Pete remarked, "That was easier than getting' on at the car plant in Detroit. Prob'ly not as good a job, but they'll pay me cash, and I can work all around outside of town, 'n it won't be too easy for Mister George to know I'm here."

When the pick-up drove up in the yard, Daisy came out to greet them.

"Got me a job, Daisy! Sim and Mose Harrington put me where I could get me a job! Hooray!"

When Sim got back to the Harrington place he reported that Pete had found a job. Mose was not surprised. "That Pete Bates is a worker. I knowed it wouldn't take him long. Didn't know where he'd find it, but I figgered he'd find something!"

* * *

Pete got along fine with the work crew. The wagon picked them up at the Post Office each morning, then went by the ice house where they got 25 pounds of ice and some water for the wooden water keg that rode on the wagon with them. They were then ready to proceed to the place they would begin the day's work. Pete was strong, in the prime of his life, and was soon one of the steadfast members of the crew. The foreman, Josh Bridges, soon depending on Pete to keep things going, fell into the habit of drifting off to sleep in the shade of an overhanging tree to lengthen his lunch break.

A number of weeks later, the pole-setting crew was hard at work on Rogers Road a mile or so from town, when a Model "A" Ford came by. It passed the crew at a moderate speed down the middle of the dirt road. In a few minutes, the same Ford appeared again, this time from the other direction, from their front. The car drove slower this time, the driver peering intently at the workers as he passed. A third time the car passed them, and Pete looked up in curiosity at the unusual amount of traffic. He got a glimpse of the driver and instinctively turned his head away. It was Mister George!

"Uh-oh," he thought. "It was bound to happen sometime. Now it's done happened. What's goin' to happen next?"

Mister George continued on his way and did not reappear.

Two days later, as the crew continued its way out Rogers Road, the same Model "A" came along, passed them, and pulled over the side of the road. Mister George emerged from the car and sauntered back to the foreman.

"Mornin', Josh," he said pleasantly.

"Mornin'." was the reply.

"Josh, passing by your crew I notice you got with you a dangerous character."

"That so?" Josh responded.

"Yep. Ain't that boy there named Pete Bates?"

"That's what he said his name is."

"I thought I recognized him. He used to work at the gin several years ago. Weren't much help, but I let him stay on 'cause he was good about coming to work every day. Well, I come to find out he was stealing from me....cigarettes and chewing tobacco that I kept in the office for my customers. They kept disappearing. When I figured out it had to be him, I fired him for it, and would you believe it, my gin caught on fire that same evening and burnt to the ground! It was too much of a coincidence for it to not be Pete gettin' back at me for firing him. Uppity nigger. I talked to the sheriff about it, and he was about to arrest this black boy when we learned he had skipped town. Another sign he was guilty, if you ask me,.!"

Josh listened impassively to this recital, as did the entire crew. "Why are you telling me all this?" he asked.

"Why, I want you to fire the thievin' fire-settin' criminal," Mister George shot back.

Josh stood there, hands on hips, showing no emotion, no hint of his thoughts. "I don't reckon I'll do that," he finally said.

You mean you're goin' to keep this dangerous criminal working in the midst of these good men, who he'll lead into law-breaking along with him? That ain't being a responsible citizen, Josh!"

"Call it what you want to, George. Pete is a good worker. I ain't going to fire him for something he might have done several years ago.... Now, George, you've had your say. You'd better get along. We've got poles to set before sundown." He waved the men back into action.

"I ain't forgettin' this, Josh! And as for you, Black Boy, you'll hear from me soon!"

* * *

Pete arrived back home that afternoon, wearing a hangdog look. Daisy took one look at him, asked a silent question, and received a negative head shake in return. The family went through its normal suppertime conversation while each polished off a steaming bowl (or two) of white bean soup and cornbread.

"Pretty good rations, eh, chillun? 'Tween you and your daddy, we got money and we can eat a lot better now," Daisy beamed.

Soon the children left the table, the dishes were washed, and Daisy and her husband went outside for a chance to talk privately.

"What's wrong, Pete?" she asked. "I can tell it's something, by the expression on your face. Tell me!"

Pete spread his hands despondently. "I knowed it was gonna happen, sooner or later. It happened today."

"What happened today? Tell me!"

"Mister George. He saw me working and stopped to make sure. Then he told Mister Josh to fire me, said I am a dangerous criminal."

"What did Mister Josh say?"

"Said he didn't have no reason to fire me. Said I am a good worker. Told Mister George to get on his way, and let us work."

"What did Mister George say then?"

"He blew off some steam. Called Mister Josh a poor citizen. Called me "Black Boy", said he warn't through with me yet. Went off huffin' an' puffin'. Man, was I glad to see him go—but he'll be back, somehow, some way."

"What we gon' do, Pete?"

"Just keep on keepin' on, I reckon. I'll go to my job every day, and come straight home every evenin'. Mister Josh will keep an eye on things at work, and won't let Mister George run me off, or pick a fight, or anything. On the way to work, or coming home, I'll just have to be real careful. Colored folks ain't got much rights around here if a white man don't want him here."

"Lordy, I hope you'll be careful!"

"I'll be just as careful as I can, Daisy."

* * *

Two or three days went by, then early one morning the pole-setting crew had a visit from the sheriff. He parked his official vehicle on the side of the road, got out and approached Josh Bridges.

"Morning, Josh."

"Morning, Sheriff."

"You got a boy here on this crew by the name of Pete Bates?"

"Sure do."

"I'd like a word with him, if you can excuse him a minute."

"Sure." Josh turned to Pete. "Sheriff wants to talk to you, Pete.'

Pete slowly put down his shovel and followed the sheriff a few yards up the road, out of earshot of the others. When the Sheriff stopped and faced him, Pete snatched off his hat.

"What's your name, Boy"?

"Pete Bates, suh."

"Your wife named Daisy?"

"Yes, suh.

You live on Juniper Road?"

"Yes, suh."

"You used to work at the gin for George Sampson?"

"Yes, suh."

"Why did you quit?"

"Didn't quit, suh. He fired me."

"Why did he fire you?"

"We had a argument, suh."

"What about?"

Pete said nothing.

"Was you uppity to him?"

"Naw, suh."

"The gin burned that same night. Did you set fire to his gin?"

"No, siree! When he fired me I left that gin and ain't been back since!"

"You haven't been around here. Where you been?"

"Dee-troit, suh. Car factory."

"Why you come back here?"

"Riots up there, suh. Big trouble. And I miss my family."

"I want you to know I'm keeping my eye on you. George says you're a troublemaker and a criminal. If you are either one, I'm going to catch you and send you to jail, and then you'll really miss your family. You understand me?"

"Yes, suh."

"Then get on back to work."

* * *

When he got home that day, Pete told Daisy the sheriff had questioned him. "He wasn't ugly, Daisy. He just asked me some questions 'bout workin' for Mister George. Said Mister George told him I'm a troublemaker and a criminal. Sheriff said he be watching me from now on."

"Lordy me, Pete!" Mister George is gonna bring us some trouble, for sure! You think we ought to move somewhere else?"

"I don't think so, Daisy. We got a house here. It ain't much, I know, but it don't leak much. I got a job, all the chillun got jobs. They ain't much, but we got 'em, and we getting' enough to eat. If we move somewheres else, it'll be a long time before we be getting' along as well as this."

"Yeah, but, suppose the sheriff gets you…suppose the Klan gets you!"

All was quiet for the next few days. Pete went to work every day, and returned home as soon as Mister Josh dismissed the crew for the day.

* * *

A week later, the family had finished supper, shared the news of the day, and were settled down in their beds for the night. All of a sudden, the quiet of the evening was broken by the blowing of car horns and the shouts of men. Pete took a look outside, peeping through the hole in a window shade. He pulled his head back quickly and whispered urgently to his family, "Everybody stay in bed! Don't look out the window! Put your shoes on, and get dressed, but *stay in bed*!"

"What's out there, Pete?" Daisy asked in a quavering voice.

"Bunch of men in white sheets." He answered grimly.

"Oh, my God! It's the Klan!" she shrieked, setting the entire family to crying and screaming.

"Be quiet! Get your clothes on! We may have to run! But be quiet!"

A fusillade of shots rang out through the night. Those inside the shack whimpered in fear, Pete still whispering for quiet.

A voice, probably enhanced by a megaphone, shouted from the group outside. "Pete Bates! This is a warning. A courtesy call! The Klan is watching you! You are on our Watch List! You step out of line, one little bit, we'll be back—and it won't be no courtesy call! If you know what's good for you, Nigger, you'll step careful!!"

A few more shots rang out, and the cars sped away, the men whooping and hollering.

* * *

It was finally quiet inside the little shack, broken only by the sounds of moans and sniffles from the girls. "Ma! Daddy! What they goin' do to us?" they wailed. "We so scared! Were those real pistols? Did they burn a cross? Are they comin' back?"

"Hush, chillun! It ain't goin' do any good to carry on like this. Yo' daddy don't know, and I don't know what they are goin' to do,." Daisy hushed them. "What we're all goin' to do is get quiet, stay in our own bed, and try to get some sleep. It's early now, plenty of time to sleep before morning, and we all got plenty to do tomorrow."

Later, when the children had gone to sleep, she nudged Pete, who also was still awake, just listening for sounds from outside.

"Pete," she whispered. "you awake?"

"Um," he replied. Just lyin' here, listenin'."

"Hear anything?"

"Nope."

"Pete, what we goin' to do? I'm scared, just like those chillins."

"Daisy, I tell you the truth, I don't know anything to do but keep on keepin' on, just like I told you the other day."

"But, Pete, they'll see you, they can find you....they can get you!"

"Daisy, you know I got to work. We all got to work, to keep food on the table. Ain't no two ways about it. We just keep on working, tryin' to stay clean with the Klan and the sheriff, and pray to the Lord to help us stay outa their way."

* * *

On his next visit to his parents, Sim was apprised of the situation. He listened, understood the gravity of the predicament they were in, but had no suggestions for courses of action. He did agree with his father that the best way to cope was for each one to "keep his head down, and try not to attract attention." He said he would ask Mose Harrington's advice about dealing with the Klan.

Mose's advice: "Keep your head down."

* * *

They kept their heads down, and a number of weeks went by without incident.

Then, one Friday, just before the time when pay was distributed to the pole-setting crew—always in cash, because none of them had, or wanted, a bank account. One of the crew members suggested, "Why don't we all put twenty-five cents in the pot, and we can all go to the riverbank and get a jug of liquor from my friend who sells it down there? Then we can have a drink together before we go home?"

That sounded like a reasonable and inexpensive request to all, including Pete, who had not taken an alcoholic drink of any kind since he came home from Detroit. In two shakes of a lamb's tail the money was collected and the deal was made—and in three shakes of a lamb's tail, they found themselves on the riverbank, taking pulls from the jug that was being passed around.

That first session progressed harmlessly, and all the men arrived home safely. When the next payday rolled around the suggestion was again made that they gather at the riverbank, and again attendance was perfect. "Three times makes a habit," they say, and "habit soon becomes ritual". The group began to lengthen its stay at the gathering place, and that necessitated a fifty cent participation fee instead of twenty-five. The longer they stayed, the more they drank; and the more they drank, the more raucous they became, and the more wobbly they were when they finally got home.

After several of these longer, boozier affairs, Pete found Daisy waiting for him with fire in her eye when he arrived home.

"What time y'all get off this afternoon?"

Pete mumbled, "Four o'clock."

"It 'bout seven o'clock now. Where you been?"

"Down to the river."

"I can look in your eye, and smell your breath, and watch you stumble down the road, stagnatin' like a 'toxicant man and I can tell you been down there with that crowd, drinkin' likker—'stead of bringing home your pay like you used to do."

"Daisy, we ain't hurting nobody...."

"You hurting me, and you hurting our chillun if you don't bring your pay home to the family before something else gets it!"

"Daisy, I been under a strain, worryin' 'bout the Klan...."

"And what you doin' now is a good way for the Klan to get on you! Drinkin' likker and raisin' Hell like a common nigger! You ain't no help to me when you ack like this!"

"But, Daisy...." he pleaded....

"Don't you "but Daisy" me, she retorted sharply. "You think I'm mad now—You just pull this trick one more time and you'll find out what mad is! Now get out of my kitchen and go on to bed!"

For several weeks Pete was the perfect husband. He went to work, lunch bucket in hand, and he returned home promptly after the workday ended. Paydays came around, week by week, and on those days, too, he came straight home, without a hint of strong drink on his breath. Daisy was happy, and all was well.

* * *

The cold, gray, wet days of February passed, and March came in with its drying winds and an occasional sunny and warmer day. The atmosphere inside Truro High school underwent a similar transformation. Those students, like Wilson and Betsy, who were scheduled to graduate at the end of the school year, realized now that the end of their high school days was close at hand, and they were in high spirits.

"I can't believe it, Cowboy! I really never thought we would get out of high school. That's something that happens to older people, not kids like us! Even when Mother and Daddy took me to Concord College and signed me up to be a freshman next year—it didn't sink in that it could be so close. I'm excited, but I'm a little nervous, too."

"Yeah, I know. It does make you nervous, to think about leaving home, maybe for good. But you'll get along fine. Schoolwork never gave you any problems, and if you get homesick. Concord is not but three hours away. I don't think you'll get homesick, though. They tell me most girls have a wonderful time at college. You'll probably find some fraternity boys who will want to line up for a chance to date you," he said in a teasing way, while not relishing that idea from his point of view.

"Wilson, you never have said very much about your plans after we graduate. I'm sure you've been thinking about it. What do you think you'll do?"

"Tell you the truth, Betsy, I don't know any more right now than the last time we talked. Matt would probably let me stay on at the hardware store, and that's better than nothing; but I don't think there's much future in it for me. I'd really like to find some job that has a path for promotion. That's pretty hard to find in Truro.

I certainly am not going to college. No money. I could get a job in a mill, with no windows, and nothing but machines. I could maybe be an insurance salesman like Jim Lane. I've seen him with a leather purse on his belt and a big wallet in his back pocket that's attached to his belt. He hangs around the bank and the post office, hoping to collect "funeral insurance" premiums every week from those poor people who work in the mills.

I'm even thinking about joining the Army. I read in the paper that they want to increase the size of the Army because of the bad news out of Europe. The Germans are making their neighbors very nervous and the Italians aren't any better. The Japanese are really tearing up China. Seems to me like it would be good to go on in now and get ahead of the large numbers of men who would get drafted, if Congress sets up a Draft, like they're talking about."

He was walking her home from school, as they had done almost every day for four years. And, as had become their habit, they walked up on the front porch and stood close together, behind one of the supports that held up the porch roof. Thus, somewhat sheltered from view from the street, they exchanged a brief kiss.

"I love the way you smell, Betsy, so clean and fresh. And, you kiss good, too. I think you're the best kisser in the whole high school," he teased.

She rose to the bait. "What do you mean, you rascal! Have you been kissing other girls?"

"Only the ones who chased me down and wouldn't take 'no' for answer," he replied with a grin.

"Get out of here, you no-good cowboy! See if you ever get another kiss from me!" She opened the door and went inside, slamming it behind her, feigning displeasure.

Wilson, in love, stepped lightly down the brick steps, and continued his walk to work at the hardware store, a happy smile on his face.

* * *

Each evening, Mose Harrington, Dinah and Sim had their meal around the table in the kitchen. Mose asked Sim about his father, his job with the pole-setting crew, and his situation with Mister George.

"Has that old gin man been causing him any trouble?" He wanted to know.

"Not since those first times when he discovered Daddy was back in town. I told you about that. Josh Bridges and the sheriff took up for him, and Mister George has left him alone since then."

"What about the Klan? They been raising any Hell?"

"Not that Ma and Daddy have told me about. I think things are quiet right now. Hope they stay that way."

"Me, too." The old man pushed his chair back from the table and stood up. "I'm glad things are quiet. Your daddy is a good man. I'd hate to see him get tangled up with the Klan. They are bad medicine." Then, "I'm going to call it a day. Spring plowing has started, and I've got a lot of things to look after right now. Not as young as I used to be."

After Mose went to bed, Sim looked at his wife and said, "Well, Dinah, you've almost put in a full year of teaching school. Is it a long way from what you expected, or is it about what you thought?"

"About what I expected. The children are OK, though we had some bad days. Attendance is not good. Their parents don't think school is real important, 'cause they themselves had very little of it—and, of course, school is called off in cotton picking time, and chopping time. I guess prob'ly the hardest thing has been keeping them all busy. You know I have all ages, in one room, so each age has a different lessons from the others. And, if I don't keep 'em busy, they distract the others and disrupt the whole room. Keeps me on my toes."

"What are you thinkin' about doing this summer when school is out?"

"Guess I'll help Granddaddy with the garden, and put up as much of the produce as I can get in jars so we can eat better next winter. That way we can get away from a steady diet of turnips, beets, collards and sweet potatoes."

"Boy, I'll vote for that—if colored folks can get a vote in this house. Sho' can't vote in this county! You reckon they'll ever let us vote?"

"Lord, I hope so! But I'm 'fraid it won't be anytime soon.

"Well, one thing I vote for, right now, is for us to go to bed together. What do you say?"

"It's unanimous." She smiled and reached for his hand.

* * *

Thinking about it, Mary could not believe her good fortune. Like a bolt out of the blue, here she is, living in a huge Victorian house—the biggest on the street! It has bathrooms, with running water, and one of them is hers and Wilson's! The house has electric lights, too, which she never dreamed she'd have.

She had enjoyed her work at the Sanitary Café with Frank, six days a week. That is, she enjoyed it most of the time. Any waitress runs into an ornery, or drunk, customer from time to time. That's part of the territory, but she never really had any real trouble.

But she doesn't have to do even that, now that she is the housekeeper/companion for the sweetest little old lady in Truro. She and Mrs. Irene Stone have hit it off from the start, and both are enjoying having some female companionship for a change. There is a cleaning woman who comes in and does the heavy cleaning, so all Mary has to do is plan the meals, order the groceries and prepare them, and a little bit of laundry.

That leaves her plenty of time for sitting and rocking with Miss Irene.

The meals are happy times. Wilson and Tom are good friends, and there's a good bit of teasing back and forth between them. Miss Irene likes to reminisce about her younger days living in this very house with her husband, Judge Stone. She is quick to relate, too, what a handsome little boy Tom had been when he was small.

"But look at him now! What happened?" Wilson teased.

One of Mrs. Stone's reminiscences involved helping to save the trees in town. She said that when the streets in Truro were originally surveyed out and dedicated, a row of trees was planted down the center of each street, as well as along the shoulders. The beauty of the trees added a great deal to the charm of the town, and until the day of the automobile they did not present any problem to the traffic on the streets. However, when auto traffic increased, the Town Council decided to pave the streets and remove the trees that were in the center.

When the ladies of the town realized the town's streets would be swept clean of the majestic elms and oaks, a committee was hastily formed to attend the next Town Council meeting. Five or six ladies descended on the Council 'with fire in their eyes', chuckled Mrs. Stone to the little audience sitting around her table. "You should have seen those men start to back up when they realized how angry we were!"

She went on to say she was glad that had happened when she was younger. "I'm not up to that kind of thing now," she said, with a laugh.

Tom, too, was pleased with the way the household arrangements were working out. His mother seemed much more relaxed. She was satisfied with the way Mary ran the house, preparing the meals, and removing all the responsibility from her shoulders. She had been worried about having a high school boy in the house, but now was charmed with Wilson's sweetness with his mother and his courtesy to Mrs. Stone herself.

CHAPTER EIGHT

TROUBLE

It was some weeks later, and Daisy had had a bad day. It was the first really warm day of the spring, and she'd spent the day washing clothes in the big iron wash pot. That meant keeping a fire going around that pot, out in the sun, then stirring the clothes in the hot water with a paddle.. But that wasn't all. Next came bending over the rubbing board and scrubbing the clothes against its corrugations. Made her back hurt to even think about it, but it *really* made her back hurt to do it!

That evening, when Pete came home, she was cross as two sticks. Nothing seemed to please her. She fussed about this, and she fussed about that. She fussed about her children not helping her, she fussed about her back hurting, and she fussed about the heat. A couple of times Pete said the wrong thing and she jumped all over him, telling him off in no uncertain terms.

Pete went to bed bewildered at the outbursts from the normally sweet and loving Daisy. He thought about it a good bit during the night. When he awoke his bewilderment had turned to resentment, and he departed for his day's work in an angry mood which didn't improve as the day progressed.

It was Friday, and at the end of the workday the crew was transported back to town. The men were given their pay envelopes for the week. As Pete pocketed his envelope he heard some of the men talking about having a little drink down by the river.

"Hey, Pete! We're going down by the river for a little while. You want to come?"

Pete thought, "If I go on home like I been doin', that old woman will no doubt chew my butt, just like she did last night. She was really on my case, and I hadn't done nuthin'. Mean old woman—serve her right if I have a drink or two. She gives me a hard way to go!"

Aloud, he said, "Yeah. Think I'll go with you today."

The little group took up a collection, then stopped by the bootlegger's place for a jug, and proceeded on down to their favorite spot on the riverside.

* * *

Earlier that afternoon, two small boats powered by outboard motors were launched on the river from a landing that served the town of Truro. There were two men in each boat, intent on an afternoon of fishing and conversation. As was their custom, each boat carried a pint bottle of a high-powered liquid, purchased from a nearby bootlegger, possibly the same dealer frequented by Pete and his friends.

The fishermen made their way upstream to one of their favorite fishing spots, where they anchored and began to fish. The conversation was more active than the fishing.

"Hey, George, whatever happened to that boy that used to work for you at the gin? He still around?" one of the men inquired.

"He shore as Hell is," Mister George replied. "He skipped town for several years , then came back. I tried my damndest to get the sheriff to run him out of town after he got back. Sheriff wouldn't do nuthin'. Then I went to Josh Bridges—he's the foreman for the pole-setting crew, where Pete works. Tried to get him fired for being a dangerous criminal—you know, I think he's the sorry S. O. B. that set fire to my gin—but old Josh wouldn't listen, and he's still working there."

"Did you ever ask the Klan to pay him a visit? Seems like I remember something like that."

"Yeah. We rode out to his little shanty one night, shooting off pistols and raising Hell. It mighta scared him some, but not enough to make him leave town, 'cause he's still here. I sure would like to find some guy, or two, who might have seen him set fire to my gin. I'd love to pin it on that uppity nigger."

"Maybe we oughta go out there again and set fire to that shanty. It looks like it would burn real easy. Hell, I'd be glad to go with you and teach that Dee-troit car factory nigger not to burn down gins in our town, or even live here where decent folks are living peacefully together! And, George, if you'd rather do it another way, I'd be glad to testify that I seen Pete set fire to your gin."

As they fished and talked, they took little nips from their bottles, and soon all of them were enthusiastic about helping Mister George teach the uppity nigger a lesson.

* * *

The daylight began to fade, and the boats pulled anchor and drifted back toward the landing. They began to hear sounds from the riverbank where the members of the pole-setting crew were still enjoying the remainder of their jug. Attracted by the loud, raucous talk on the bank, the boats came closer. The revelers had built a small fire, and in the flickering firelight the fishermen were able to distinguish the identity of several.

"Hey, George, ain't that the boy we were just talking about? The one who burned down your gin?" asked Jake, sitting in the bow of George's boat.

"Damn if it ain't," said Mister George. Let's get out of this boat and go find the sheriff. He needs to know about these niggers that are drunk out of their gourds and raising Cain down here so decent people can't have a quiet night on the river!"

The four fishermen brought their boats to shore and hurried to the sheriff's office. They found him there, leaning back in his swivel chair, feet on his desk, lighting his after-supper cigar.

"Glad we found you, Sheriff," Mister George greeted the sleepy-eyed large man who had held the post of "high sheriff" for eight years.

"What's up, boys? Some of your cows out in the road, endangering passing motorists?"

"Naw, Sheriff. You know we ain't got no cows. This a serious matter."

"Well, tell me about it, then. Don't just stand there."

"We were down at the river, fishing, and were just coming in 'cause it was getting dark. When we got closer to the landing where we put our boats in, we heard the Godawfulest noise you ever heard. Bunch o' niggers down there, around a fire on the bank, talking loud and cussin', soundin' like they was fixin' to fight. It's plumb dangerous for law-abiding citizens to be exposed to behavior like that. Plumb dangerous! Can the law do something about that?"

"How many of 'em?"

"Looked like six or more, wouldn't you say, boys?"

I'll need one of you to sign a complaint—but tomorrow will be soon enough. You can drop by this office and sign it. I'll call two deputies in and we'll go round 'em up."

We'll be glad to help if you need us, Sheriff. We've got pistols in the car."

"I think me and my deputies can handle it. Thank you, though."

In half an hour the deputies arrived at the sheriff's office and received their instructions. The three law officers proceeded to the spot Mister George had described, then split up to surround the unsuspecting celebrants.

When all three were in place, the sheriff called out, "All right, you boys around the fire! You're under arrest! I've had a complaint about you disturbing the peace. I want you-all to come with me and my deputies back to my office, so we can get your names. Fall in over here where I am."

The crestfallen merrymakers began to shuffle over in the direction of the sheriff, except for one. Pete Bates all of a sudden realized he was going to be in trouble with Daisy as well as with the sheriff, so he bolted out of the firelight in an attempt to get back home without being arrested. He managed to elude the deputy who was guarding that sector and melted into the darkness of the trees. He slowed down his headlong pace in an attempt to make a noiseless flight.

Another ten steps, then ten more, and Pete was beginning to think his flight had been successful. Then he heard, "Hold it, Nigger! Don't move a muscle or I'll blow you to Kingdom Come for resisting arrest!" It was Jake, Mister George's fishing buddy.

The fishermen were self-appointed deputies, unrelenting in helping keep the colored community under tight control. They had quietly followed the sheriff and his deputies at a discreet distance, hoping to see and hear without being seen or heard.

They had formed a loose circle outside the lawmen's circle, thus were in perfect position to intercept Pete when he broke out of the inner circle. He almost walked into Jake, who was quietly standing beside a tree, his pistol in his hand.

Jake led Pete back to the main group, and the sheriff said, "Well, hello, Jake!. What are you doing out here in the woods with a pistol this hour of the night?"

"Looking for a little peace and quiet, Sheriff, and looking out for snakes and niggers trying to evade arrest. This one just ran right to me."

"I'm mighty glad you were here, then. Come on back to the office with us."

* * *

At the office, the sheriff took the names of all those arrested. He booked Pete for running from a law officer and put him in a cell, intending to release him the next morning. The others he allowed to go home but charged them with creating a disturbance.

Pete called to his buddy who lived closest to Juniper Road, and asked him to go by his house and tell Daisy where he was spending the night. She received the message and went to bed with a heavy heart.

* * *

The fishermen left the sheriff's office, jubilant. Another Negro had been harassed and put in jail for a trivial offense. This was their number one mission, and number one entertainment, so they'd had a good night.

All four piled into the pickup truck belonging to one of them, and drove off to a quiet, private spot near the boat landing where they could finish off the whiskey that remained in the bottles and discuss the events of the afternoon and evening. Congratulations and back-slapping, grins and whoops of exultation were the tone of the conversation that followed.

"Jake, you sure put yourself in the right place back yonder! Didn't you say he walked right up to you?"

"Yep, he'd have bumped into me if he hadn't bumped into my pistol first. He was one surprised boy when I spoke to him and poked him in the stomach with the barrel. He shore stopped cold then!"

After a few more comments, and frequent chuckles and laughter, one of them inquired, "And, George, is the one who's in the pokey now the same one that used to work for you?"

"Doggone right. That's Pete Bates—worked for me for more'n ten years, I reckon. Sum-bitch started the fire the same day I fired him. Shore would love to pin it on him."

"Well, can't we do that?" Jake queried. "I'd be glad to swear that I seen that boy throwing cigarettes into piles of cotton waste."

There were murmurs of approval from all the other members of the group. "Yeah. I'll be a witness!" "Me, too, Count me in!"

Mister George was impressed with his friends' willingness to take the stand and swear they had seen Pete start the fire. Nonetheless, he was alert enough to heed the warning signal that went off in his head.

"Wait a minute now. I 'preciate y'all being willing to do this, but we've got to get our stories straight so we don't go off half-cocked. Think about it, now. If you saw Pete light that fire, you had to be at the gin. What were you doing there? The lawyer, or the judge, or the sheriff is going to want to know."

Jake quickly said, "I was down there on business"

"If the lawyer says, 'Do you grow cotton?', "What do you say?"

Jake was stumped. He was not a farmer, and grew no cotton.

"Jake, you got to have a reason to be there if you ain't a farmer."

After a lengthy discussion, they agreed that two "witnesses" would be enough, and they selected Jake and Duncan as the two with the nimblest minds. Then followed an hour-long debate of suggestions, alternate suggestions and rejections. Eventually a strategy was agreed upon by the fishermen-turned conspirators.

They agreed to meet at the sheriff's office at ten o'clock the next morning.

As they pulled away in the pick-up truck, none of them happened to look in the rear-view mirror. If they had, they might have seen two figures emerge from the underbrush near here they had parked. The man carried a folded blanket over one arm. With the other arm he was assisting the woman who was tugging at her dress.

* * *

George did not sleep well that night. He was excited over the prospects of getting even with that uppity nigger and his no-good, trashy wife. They had been an irritant in the back of his mind for years, and it would give him great pleasure to pay them back!

By the time of "first light" he was fully awake. He had his oatmeal and coffee and was soon headed down town, bound for the sheriff's office. He arrived there about nine o'clock. Of course neither the sheriff nor the two witnesses had yet arrived, so George sat himself down in a rocking chair belonging to the furniture store across the street. He rocked and waited. About 9:30 he got up and walked a couple of times to the corner and back, trying to make the time pass a little faster.

Eventually Jake strolled up, picking his teeth, yawning, and scratching his capacious stomach. Duncan arrived around ten after ten, saying to his exasperated friend George that he had had a hard time going to sleep, and when he did, he just plain overslept.

The three men opened the door to the office/jail and walked inside. They found the sheriff seated at his desk, wearing spectacles as he read the morning paper from a nearby city.

"Morning, boys," he greeted, "did you come by to sign that complaint? I only need one of you."

"Mornin', Sheriff," George responded. "Yeah, we can take care of the complaint while we're here, but we got another matter to talk to you about."

"Okay. What's on your minds, besides your hats? Neighbor's cows get in your watermelon patch?" He grinned.

"Naw, Sheriff. You know we ain't got no watermelons, or cows. It's something else."

"Well, come on out with it, then. Can't you see I'm a busy man?"

"'Course you are, Sheriff. And what we've got to tell you will give you even more to do. Jake, why don't you tell the sheriff what you told me."

Jake cleared his throat several times before beginning. "Harrumph! Harrumph! Sheriff, we reported those boys that were raising so much Hell on the riverbank last night. I'm glad you got 'em, 'cause they were a danger to law-abiding people…Anyway, when you and your deppities brought 'em in here , in the light, I thought I recognized one of 'em. Then…. Sheriff, you know how it is when you see a colored person? You see 'em, but you don't look at their face, 'cause your mind tells you, 'That's just a nigger', and you never notice what they look like. And I've heard them say the same thing about white people."

"Go on, Jake, get on with it!" Mister George urged.

"I'm going on with it, George. Give me time!" Jake replied, unruffled.

He continued, "Well, when George was in the cotton gin business several years ago, me and Duncan, here, went out to the gin see him. We wanted to sell him a ticket to the catfish stew supper being put on by the Cypress Swamp True Gospel Baptist Church. George bought one, and we talked to him a little bit. He was kinda busy, cause it was quitting time and his hands were gathering up their lunch buckets and leaving for home. Well, Dunk and me, we walked around the gin yard, trying to find somebody else to sell a ticket to, when we saw this colored feller actin' strange. He was walkin' around the yard, lightin' one cigarette after another, takin' about two puffs on each one and then throwin' it down in a pile of cotton waste that the wind piled up. You know how the cotton waste settles into corners on a windy day, don't you, Sheriff? Every gin I've ever been around had waste cotton flyin' and lyin' everywhere.

Well, Dunk says to me, "Them cigarettes are dangerous around all this cotton. Could start a fire, easy!"

"Sheriff, when we were in this office last night and I saw that Bates feller, it came to me like a bolt of lightnin'—Bates is the spittin' image of the boy that was actin' so strange with those cigarettes!

Now, Sheriff, take a guess what day it was that we saw this happen. It was the very same day George's gin caught on fire and burned plumb to the ground. Since he was actin' so suspicious, Dunk and me think that nigger, Bates, started that terrible fire!"

The sheriff remained in his chair and listened impassively to Jake's recital. He asked a question or two of Jake. He then turned to Dunk and asked more questions. He asked George the exact date of the fire, and scribbled a note to himself to check with the church for the date of the catfish stew supper.

The sheriff said, "Well, boys, I 'preciate you bringing me this new information. I was just about to release Bates and let him go home this morning, but I guess I'll hold him a little longer and ask him some questions. If the facts in this story check out, and if Bates doesn't have proof of where he was that afternoon, we're liable to have an arson trial around here pretty soon. And you three will be called to testify. So—don't plan any trips to New York City or San Francisco without checkin' with me first!". He grinned.

"What about Rio de Janeerio, Sheriff?" asked George, laughing.

Sim and Dinah were coming to town to do their weekly shopping, and while they were on the way, Dinah suggested they stop by Daisy's house to see if she needed anything. They drove up in the yard and were greeted by the entire family. Everyone was talking at once, and Sim had to call for silence to allow one person to tell the news.

"Daddy didn't come home last night, Sim! He sent somebody by to tell us he is in jail!" said Gracie, the youngest, wringing her hands.

Dorothy chimed in, "The man said a bunch of them were arrested for disturbing the peace. The sheriff let all of them go 'cept Daddy, and he spent the night in jail."

"He ain't home yet," from Frank-o.

"What you think we ought to do, Sim? asked his mother. "That jail ain't no good place for a colored man to be."

Sim and Dinah exchanged looks. "Looks to me like you ought to ride into town with us, Ma, and we'll go by the jail and talk to the sheriff. That way we'll find out what's going on."

"We want to go, too!" chorused the other children.

"No siree." Said Sim firmly. "This ain't no party we're going to. You girls stay right here and clean up the house for Ma. Shad and Frank-o, ain't you supposed to be at work on Sat'day? What are you doing hanging around this house? Climb in the back of this pickup and we'll give you a ride into town, but you won't see the sheriff 'less you get arrested yourself!"

Daisy changed into a clean dress and climbed into the cab with Dinah and Sim. They were soon in Truro and dropped the two boys off at their places of employment. Then they drove to the sheriff's office/jailhouse and parked.

The three of them got out and timidly knocked on the wooden door which was closed against the cool outside air. A gruff voice shouted "Come!" and they entered. They stopped just inside, closed the door behind them, and stood silently.

"What do you want?" demanded the burly man sitting at the desk, his stomach straining at the buttons of his shirt, both at his waist and his wrists.

Sim spoke up, using his best vocabulary and clearest pronunciation "Sheriff, my name is Simeon Bates, and this is my wife and my mother. We are looking for my father, Pete Bates. We were told you might have him here."

"Yep, he's here. Been here all night," grumbled the sheriff.

"Can he go home with us now?" Daisy managed to croak out in her fear of the white lawman.

"No way," said the sheriff. "He has been accused of arson, and he'll stay right here in this jail until the trial."

"Arson…isn't that setting fire to something?"

"That's what it is all right."

"What do you think he set fire to?" asked Dinah. "We didn't hear about any fire."

"There are two witnesses who say they saw him setting fire to George Sampson's cotton gin," the sheriff responded.

"You mean that gin that burned years ago?" Sim wanted to know.

"That's right, Boy. That's the fire," the sheriff replied.

"But, Sheriff," Daisy spoke up. "Pete didn't start that fire. He was with me all that afternoon!"

The sheriff looked at her. "What's your name, woman?"

"Daisy Bates, sir."

"You his wife?"

She nodded.

"You can't give no alibi if you're his wife."

The Bates family looked at each other, perplexed, then Dinah asked, "Well, Sheriff if we can't take him home, can we talk to him here? Now?"

"No harm in that," the sheriff said wearily. "Come on back in the back."

He led them to the rear potion of the building. It was separated from the office area by a brick wall. In the middle of the wall was a door which opened onto a single room, the full width of the building. This room contained two large cells, enclosed by iron bars. Each cell had a locked door, and contained an iron cot, mattress and blanket, and a toilet that was not equipped with a seat or a cover for the tank. The floors were bare concrete. There was one window, outside the cell area, which admitted a little light and fresh air. The air was badly needed, for the area smelled strongly of sweat, urine and vomit, and less strongly of Lysol, which indicated that product had been applied, on occasion. The combination of powerful odors was penetrating and depressing.

In one cell a white man lay on a cot, snoring loudly and adding generously to the whiskey fumes that were already present in the air.

In the other cell was Pete Bates. He was standing dejectedly, head down, staring at the floor. He did not look up to see who had entered.

"Pete," Daisy said softly, reaching up to put her hand on his as he gripped the iron bars. "Pete."

"I hate for you to see me like this, Daisy," he said, still not raising his eyes from the floor. "The Man says he ain't goin' to let me out any time soon, neither. Said somethin' 'bout witnesses seein' me set fire to Mister George's cotton gin…" His head came up, and he looked wild-eyed at Daisy, "but you know I didn't set that fire! You was with me all that afternoon! Tell 'em, Daisy! Tell 'em you was with me!"

"Pete," she said, "I done told the sheriff we was together, and he said a wife couldn't testify."

He looked at her. "What we go' do, Daisy? What we go' do? A colored man's word against a white man's word don't amount to nothin' in this state!"

* * *

Pete said he was hungry, so they went back to the little house in the country. Daisy fixed him a good hot meal, and they all, including Dorothy and Gracie, went back to town and sat with him while he ate. Actually, they stood with him, because the sheriff was not about to think about providing seats for colored visitors! "No telling how many of them would pile in here if I gave them seats! And no telling how long they'd stay! It would be like Open House! Hell, no!"

After a long visit attempting to cheer up the prisoner, they departed for home, promising to come back the next day, which was Sunday. No one, as yet, had come up with any plan to help Pete in his predicament.

* * *

Following the week-end, on Monday, a downcast Sim entered Truro Hardware in the afternoon to get some files for sharpening his tools. Wilson came forward to wait on him, and, noticing his friend's glum demeanor, asked if any thing was wrong.

Sim shook his head slowly from side to side, "I can't believe how wrong things is. Wilson, we in a terrible mess. Old Job, in the Bible, you know, he put on sackcloth and ashes—I wish we could do that and it would help!

You know my daddy, Pete, came back from Dee-troit and was working and minding his own business, when two white men claimed they saw him set fire to Mister George's gin way back yonder when you 'n me was kids! After all that time! Can you believe that? Anyhow, they got him in jail, he can't get out, and they go' try him for arson! What chance does he have against a white jury?"

Wilson put his hand on Sim's shoulder. "That sure does seem like a long time to wait to identify somebody who committed a crime.. If they saw him do it, why didn't they tell somebody when it happened? This is a long time after."

Wilson thought about the situation all afternoon, and on his way home to High Street he stopped by the jail to see Pete.

"Hello, Pete," he began. "You prob'ly don't know me. My name is Wilson Jones. I'm a friend of your son Sim. He's a good friend. He came by the hardware store this afternoon and told me about your trouble, so I stopped by to tell you I'm sorry, and to see if I can bring you anything, or do anything to help."

Pete looked at him in surprise. He remembered that Sim had told him he had a white friend, but he never expected Sim's friend to go out of his way and visit him in jail, for God's sake! He warmed to Wilson immediately.

"Pleased to meetcha, Wilson," he said, bobbing his head in the accepted manner used when a colored man speaks to a white. "Thank ye very much. I don't know as I need anything right at the present—'-less'n you happen to know a good lawyer who'd work for free! I speck they go' take me to court, and I'll be like a fox terrier n the middle of a pack of wild boars!"

"Afraid I don't know too many lawyers, Pete," Wilson confessed." But I'll think on it, and see if I can come up with an idea. I'll try to drop by again tomorrow and see how you're doing."

"Thanks, Wilson."

* * *

On the way home from the jailhouse, Wilson "curved by" Betsy's house to say "Hello". It had become his habit to "curve by" two or three times a week on his way from the hardware store to High Street. They both looked forward to it.

Wilson stepped up on the porch and gave the front door his customary knock—"shave and a haircut, two bits." Betsy appeared at the door almost immediately, welcoming him with a warm smile. "Hey, Cowboy. I'm mighty glad to see you."

His wide grin indicated the feeling was mutual. He reached for her hand, gave it a squeeze, and led her over to the porch swing. "It's such a nice afternoon, let's sit out here and talk, instead of going inside."

Sometimes when they were together, their conversation was animated, both parties contributing somewhat equally, and that was fun. Sometimes, however, their mood was different, and they were content to sit amiably together, and just be together. This seemed to be one of those times, for she noticed that Wilson seemed preoccupied, was not really present with her.

"Something on your mind, Cowboy?" she asked.

"Yeah," he answered. "I've had some conversations this afternoon that bother me—make me sad, make me want to do something to help. You want to hear about it?"

"I sure do. Tell me."

With that, Wilson began to talk, and the words just poured out. He told her about his conversation with Sim in the store, and his decision to go see Pete in jail.

Oh, Wilson, that was so brave!" And then she said, "What was it like?"

"What was what like? Do you mean talking with Pete, or going to the jail?"

"I'm interested in Pete, but I've never been inside a jail before. I mean both."

When he described the jail and the conditions inside, her nose wrinkled in disgust and revulsion. "Unngh!" she shuddered. "Horrible!"

Then he described Pete's attitude about his situation, and his fear about a long prison term. "And," he concluded, "he's worried about not having any help in the courtroom. He's sure he'll be putty in the hands of those lawyers if he doesn't have a lawyer of his own to help him, and he 's got no money!"

Betsy took his hand in hers. "I know you want to help your friend," she said consolingly. "I do, too...but we have to remember we're still kids in school. What can we do?"

"Yeah, you're right," he said. "But I wish there was something..."

They sat there in the swing, silent. Wilson continued to push the swing gently with his foot. The chain creaked, the breeze rustled in the trees, and a mockingbird piped his song.

Suddenly, he snapped her fingers. He grabbed Betsy's shoulders with both hands and looked her in the eye, excited. "I've got it!" he said. "I've got it!"

* * *

After Wilson left Betsy's house he hurried on home. His mind was racing, his heart was beating wildly. He was both excited and worried. "How should I approach this?" he wondered.

When he arrived at High Street, his mother was just ready to put supper on the table. He washed his hands and helped with the final preparations, then they all sat down. As usual, Tom sat beside Miss Irene, and Mary and Wilson sat facing them. They joined hands, bowed their heads, and Tom said Grace. The dishes were passed around so each person could serve his plate, and they began to eat. There was not much conversation for a few minutes while the pangs of hunger were being assuaged. Later, the news of the day was discussed, along with happenings in the lives of the individuals at the table.

After a while, Tom cleared his throat and observed that Wilson was unusually quiet. "Did you and Betsy have a fight?" he inquired.

"No,", Wilson replied, "but we did have a serious conversation."

Mary, ever vigilant in guarding and protecting her teen-age son, pricked up her ears.

"What kind of serious conversation?" she asked.

"It goes right along with what Tom prayed in the Grace," he said. "Make us mindful of the needs of others."

Mary's alertness slipped back a peg. "Oh, good," she thought. "My boy has had a sweet thought. He is so wonderful!"

Wilson continued. "Two things happened to me today that I haven't run into before. First, during the afternoon at the store, my friend Sim—you might remember Sim, Miss Irene, he helped us move into this house."

She nodded.

"Sim told me his father, Pete Bates, has been arrested, is facing charges of arson of Mister George Sampson's cotton gin almost five years ago. Sim was all cut up about it. So after I got off work I went to the jail to see him. Told him I am sorry, offered to help. He said he didn't need any help right now, except legal help. He's sure he'll go to the pen if he doesn't have a lawyer on his side."

His mother interrupted, "Wilson! You went to the jail by yourself? You're just a high school boy! You've got no business being seen at a jail! It could ruin your reputation!"

"Yes'm. Maybe so. But I wasn't worried about that this afternoon…and I'm not too worried about it now. What I am worried about is Pete Bates going to trial on false charges, he says— and not being defended by somebody who is trained to defend an innocent person! And I'm worried about my friend Sim, too—and Daisy and her other children!"

There was utter silence around the table.

"Well! You did have an interesting afternoon!" was Tom's cautious response.

"Wilson, you be careful who sees you going in that jailhouse," his mother said.

Miss Irene chimed in with "I'll bet you are upset, Wilson. Good for you! A good citizen fights injustice wherever he finds it. My late husband would applaud you, and help you."

* * *

After supper was over, and the dishes were done, everyone went to his own room, and the house quieted down. Tom knocked at his mother's door, and she bade him enter.

"Hello, Son," she said. "Come on in."

"Mother, I'd like to talk with you about Wilson's comments at supper."

"Wonderful. I was hoping you would."

"He wasn't looking at me, but he was speaking directly to me. He said that Pete, (is that his name?) needed a trained attorney to defend him against "unjust" charges. Who knows if they're unjust? Who said so, other than the defendant?"

"I suppose the only one who would be likely to know, aside from the defendant, would be the defendant's lawyer."

"Mother, I'm not blaming Wilson for trying to put this in my lap. He's a good kid. Means well, and I applaud his desire to help the poor and oppressed. But he doesn't realize what would happen to the man who dared defend a Negro in a case brought by George Sampson, the kingpin of the local Klan. His law practice would vanish quicker than fried chicken at a church supper!"

"You're absolutely right, Tom. The danger is very real. It could ruin you to take this case. Especially volunteering to take it *pro bono*. You might have to leave here and practice law in a city that never heard of Truro, or the Ku Klux Klan— or justice to your fellow man."

"Well, Mother, you actually think I should defend Pete Bates?"

"I don't know, Tom. And I won't, or can't, tell you what to do. What I do know is that your father, Judge Thomas G. Stone, made his mark in this county, and surrounding counties, by his defense of a black man who was unable to talk plainly. He was accused of being impertinent and making suggestive remarks to the wife of the minister of the Piney Woods Tabernacle Church. Your father was twenty-seven, it was long before he was a judge, and he did not have a practice that supported us (without the help of my father), but he thought it was the right thing to do, so he did it!"

"I've heard a lot of stories about Dad, but that's a new one."

"Maybe the situation never arose to bring it to mind. But it's a true story," she said.

"I'll think about it tonight, and maybe tomorrow I'll drop by the jail and chat with Pete Bates, and the sheriff, too. Thanks for your input, Mother."

"Don't let me influence you too much, Tom. It's your law practice, your life, and your decision. Good night, Son."

* * *

The next morning when he left the house to go to his office, Tom walked to the sheriff's office and went inside. He found the sheriff sitting at his desk, reading the morning paper.

"Morning, Sheriff," greeted Tom.

"Morning, Counselor," the sheriff replied. "Will you have a seat?"

"Don't mind if I do," said Tom, pulling up a chair to face the sheriff.

"What can I do for you this morning?" inquired the sheriff.

"Well, Sheriff, I have a passing acquaintance with a man named Pete Bates, and I understand you have him registered here in your hotel."

The sheriff nodded assent.

"Can you share any details of the circumstances that brought him to you? Why is he here?"

"Bates and some of his buddies were having a party down on the riverbank, and the party got so noisy that a group of fishermen stopped fishing and came over to the office complaining about "disturbing the peace". I rounded up a couple of my deputies and we went down there and brought 'em all back here."

"I see. And the whole crew is in jail here now?"

"Naw. I let 'em all go home that night after a good lecture about "next time".

"But you said Pete is still here, two days later. Why is that?"

"A couple of those fishermen recognized Pete when they saw him in the bright light of this office that night. Said he is the same guy they saw throwing lighted cigarettes into the cotton waste at George Sampson's gin the night it burned. The next day they signed a complaint."

"Who were the fishermen who signed the Disturbing the Peace complaint?"

"Let's see. I've got it right here. It was Jake Bottoms and Duncan Pate that signed the complaint, and George Sampson was with 'em."

"I see. Tell me, Sheriff, I've been sitting here trying to remember when that gin burned. Do you have that information?"

"I'm planning on looking that up today. Don't rightly remember, but it was several years ago, seems to me."

"I see. Well, thanks, Sheriff for letting me know what's going on. Do you mind if I go back and speak to old Pete Bates for a minute?"

"No, Counselor, you go right ahead. I'll be right here, if you need me."

Tom walked into the jail portion of the building and found Pete sitting on the side of his bunk, his face in his hands, looking at the floor. He looked up when he heard footsteps.

"Howdy, Pete. My name is Tom Stone. I know your boy, Sim. His friend Wilson asked me to come by and check on you. Are they treating you all right?"

"Well, Mister, they keeping me here, which don't suit me none. I'd a whole lot rather be livin' at home, where I can help support my family."

"I certainly can understand that. Look here, Pete, Wilson said you need a lawyer to help you with your case in court. I am a lawyer—and I don't know if I can help you or not—but would you let me ask you some questions? Whatever you say will just be between us."

"Yessir, Mister. You can ask me, and I'll tell you the truth."

"First of all, did you set fire to the gin?"

"Naw suh!"

"Did you see anybody else start the fire?"

"Naw suh!"

"Why are these men swearing they saw you do it?"

"Mister George been mad with me for a long time."

"Why?"

You have to ask Daisy—my wife."

"Where can I find Daisy and talk to her?"

"She'll be at our house, out on Juniper Road."

"Is that farther out than where Wilson used to live?"

"Yessuh. The next house."

"Okay. I'll go and talk with her then, if you don't mind."

"Naw suh, I sho' don't mind. Thank ye, suh."

Tom left the jail and walked back to High Street. He telephoned Virginia from there to tell her he would be busy for another hour before coming to the office. He then got into his car and drove out Juniper Road. He passed the empty tenant house where Wilson and Mary had lived. "Funny how little time it takes for an empty house to look forlorn," he thought.

In a minute or two he could see Pete and Daisy's house, complete with its mismatched siding, metal signs covering the gaps and holes, and crooked chimney. "Picturesque," he thought wryly, and then was ashamed of the thought. He had seen worse living conditions in the country round about Truro. "Picturesque" and "interesting", yes— but definitely not "comfortable".

He drove into the yard, got out of the car, and approached the house. Before he could climb onto the porch to knock at the door, Daisy was on the porch with a wary look on her face. Seldom did a white man come to her house and walk to the door. Usually they sat in the car and blew the horn several times, announcing the presence of an important visitor, and demanding her presence at the car.

"Afternoon," "he said pleasantly. Are you Daisy, Pete's wife?"

"Yessuh, I sho' am," she replied.

"My name is Tom Stone. I'm a lawyer here in Truro. I know your son Sim. His friend Wilson is a friend of mine, and Wilson asked me to look in on your husband at the jail.

"Yessuh?" she said uncertainly.

"I saw Pete a little while ago, and talked to him about his trouble, his case. I don't know yet if I can, but I'm thinking about asking to be his lawyer."

"That sho' would be good, I think."

They sat down on two ramshackle chairs on the porch, and he began to ask her questions about her family, trying to put her at ease. She soon warmed up and enjoyed telling him about her children and husband, smiling and beaming all the while.

When Tom changed the focus of his question to George Sampson, her smile vanished and her expression became grim and glowering. It was obvious that Mister George was not her favorite friend.

"Pete worked at that gin just about every day of his life, and he loved it. Mister George treated him decent, and the pay was regular and pretty good. Mister George was nice to me, too, Smiled and spoke like he was glad to see me. Up 'til that day," she said, frowning in recollection.

"What day, Daisy? What happened that day?"

"I don't know as I should tell you," she said hesitatingly. "This is colored women's burden, and if you say I tol' you, it might bring me trouble."

"Daisy, I'm here trying to get you out of trouble, get Pete out of trouble, not get you in trouble. If you tell me about "that day" with Mister George, it might make it easier for me to get you out of trouble."

"Well... One Friday," she said. "I know it was Friday 'cause it was payday, 'n I walked into town to meet Pete 'n get a little bit of money. When I got to the gin Pete was still workin', so I just stood around, waitin'.

Mister George, he saw me an' invited me to wait in the office. "Pete will be finished in just a little while.," he said. Direckly, Mister George came into the office, too, wandered around, picking up one thing, then puttin' it down. He looked out the window that looks out over the gin yard, fooled with the shade... I could tell he was lookin' at me the whole time. Made me feel plumb uneasy. That was after my last baby came, but befo' I got so fat."

"You know," he said, "I always like to see a good-sized colored woman. That means somebody is takin' good care of her."

"I didn't say nothin," Then he said, "Your husband is lucky to have a wife as good lookin' as you. Very lucky."

"He moved closer to me. I moved away. He kep' comin'. He reached out and grabbed me around the waist with one of his hands.. His other hand covered my breast. I said, "Mister George, don't do that! It ain't right!'"

"I was scared!"

He said, "Hush your mouth, woman! And he forced his hand between my legs. I was plumb scared then! An' I hollered, 'Stop, Mister George! Stop! Help me, somebody!"

Just about that time my husband came into the office to check out and go home for the day. When he saw us his eyes bugged out like I never saw. '"What's going on here,?' he asked, not believin' his eyes.

"Get out of here. Finish your work!" Mister George said.

"I finished my work. What are you doing with my wife? Take your hands off her!"

"Boy, if you want to keep your job here, get out of this office!"

"I'll take my wife with me, or I'll whip your g—d—ass!"

That's it! You're fired, Nigger! Get off this property! Right now! And take your black slut with you!"

The recollection of that awful day left her wide-eyed, breast heaving with emotion. "An' after he treated me like he did, and was caught while doin' it, he was embarrassed! He's <u>still</u> embarrassed! He ain't ashamed because he done wrong! He's ashamed because he got caught with his hands "on a colored woman! An' he's a Klansman! An' he can't forgive Pete for knowin' it! An' he can't forgive me for being part of it!"

A moment later, she said, "And he called me a black slut….. Mister, I'm colored. I'm black. But I ain't no slut!"

Tom sat and listened. He was stirred. He had a lump in his throat and what felt like a boulder was lodged in the pit of his stomach. "I'm sorry, Daisy, for the way he treated you. Do you think 'that day' is the reason he and his friends brought these charges against Pete?"

"Yessuh! I sho' do! They didn't see Pete start that fire, 'cause Pete didn't start no fire! I know, 'cause he was with me!"

"Well, Daisy. What happened next?"

"Well, Mister, Pete didn't have no job. He made the rounds. He tried farmers, mills, railroads, yard work. Tines was hard. It was easy for them to say they didn't need no help, 'cause most of 'em didn't. But none of 'em was gonna hire a man the Klan didn't want hired, an' I promise you Mister George had put out the bad word on Pete!

He finally had to go Nawth to Dee-troit to find a job. He worked in a car factory, and didn't come home 'til this year."

* * *

Tom remained on the porch with Daisy for another half hour. When he left, he assured her that he would defend Pete against the arson charges, if he could. He did not specify what factors would enter into his decision. but in his mind were his mother, advice from old Sam Bedenbaugh, the long-retired friend and associate of his father. Lastly, he wanted to find out which judge would be appointed to hear the case.

He drove directly to his office and conferred with Virginia to become aware of any calls or messages that had come in while he was out of the office. Finding none that required immediate attention, he telephoned Mr. Bedenbaugh, who lived in the neighboring town of Chester. The call was answered after the first ring. "Poor old fellow," Tom thought. "Bored to death. Sitting by the phone, willing it to bring him something interesting to think about."

"Sam Bedenbaugh speaking."

"Hello, Mr. Sam. This is Tom Stone. How are you today?"

"Pretty good, thank ye. Since you called me Mr. Sam, you must be Tom Stone, junior—not my dear old friend, the Judge. You need to make yourself clear, boy."

"You're mighty right, Mr. Sam. This is not your old friend Judge Stone calling from the grave! 'Between you and him there is a great gulf fixed,' the Bible says."

"Hell, son, I know that. You didn't call to give me a Bible lesson, so you must have called to get a lesson in the law. It ain't the first time a Stone has done that. Your highly respected father used to use me as a law library all the time, when he was stumped. I was gratified that he realized what a marvelous legal mind I have—or, had. Not too much of it, or memory, is left, now."

"I think you're rating yourself too low, Mr. Sam. You've forgotten more law than we young fellows are supposed to know."

"That's what I'm telling, boy. I've forgotten it."

"Excuse that unfortunate phrasing, Sam. Even so, would you be willing to listen to my problem situation? I'm hoping you can give me some advice about how to handle it."

"Fire away, son. I've been hoping for something to think about other than old age, since I retired. Thinkin' is all I can do about most things, like women, and drinkin'."

Tom proceeded to outline the Bates family for the old lawyer, his knowledge of them gained through Wilson and Sim. He reminded him about the fire at the gin. He related Pete's journey to Detroit to find work, the involvement of the Ku Klux Klan and the charges of arson.

"I really sympathize with this Negro family, Mr. Sam, and believe in them. Apparently, through no fault of theirs, they've been caught between the Devil, played by the Klan, and the deep blue sea....My question to you is, do I dare to come up against the Klan in a court case I'm not sure I can win?"

"First question—what kind of fee will you get?"

"None. That is spelled Z-E-R-O.

"I was afraid of that. Next question. Can you get him off?"

I'm not sure. It depends on the validity of the alibi, which depends on whether I can get Daisy on the stand to tell her story, and who might have witnessed them together after the time the fire would have been set....'

"Dubious. You're trying to fill an inside straight, depending on too many cards falling your way. Bad poker, boy. Look at the odds. Bad lawyering, too."

Okay, bad odds. Right now, anyway. Aside from that, what do you think about challenging the Klan in a case they want to win?"

"But can they win it? Do they have the evidence? Do they have credible witnesses? If you choose the jury properly, can the Klan prove your man set the fire? Beyond a reasonable doubt?"

"No sir, I don't think they can."

"Think about it this way, Son. It may turn out that you lack enough positive evidence to *win* the case. The prosecution probably will present trumped up charges that won't hold water for a jury, and so they can *lose* the case. And, you are the son of the late respected Judge Thomas Stone, who set social injustice back fifty years with his sterling defense of that inarticulate young colored man unjustly accused of suggestive fornication. Think about it! Suggestive fornication, for God's sake!"

"You think I should go ahead, Mr. Sam?"

Hell, yeah, boy! It'll be the first juicy case since your old daddy whipped 'em thirty years ago! Give 'em hell! If you want me to sit with you in the courtroom, I'll be glad to do it. That'll improve the good looks of our team as well as the I. Q. Might even scare the diapers off that young prosecutor who thinks he's so wise. Heh! Heh! Heh!

Smiling, Tom hung up the phone, bade Virginia good-night and went home.

* * *

Tom found his mother in her favorite rocking chair, quietly knitting. She usually had some handwork in progress; sometimes it was needle embroidery, sometime crocheting or knitting. She was so accustomed to the handwork that she could carry on a conversation without missing a click with her needles.

She greeted Tom, gave him a cheek to kiss, and invited him to sit down. "How was your day, Son?"

"Very interesting, Mother. You remember last night Wilson told us about Pete Bates being in jail, unjustly accused, and he made an impassioned plea for 'some lawyer' to come to the rescue?"

"Yes, I remember it well."

"And later, I came to you, reluctant to do what Wilson urged. I asked for your advice, and you gave it. You told me about my father defending a similar case involving a handicapped Negro man, early in his legal career. At great risk to his future, you said.

Well, I spent the day looking into this case. Went to the jail first thing this morning. Interviewed the sheriff, found him fairly even-handed. He allowed me to interview the prisoner, Pete Bates. Do you know that he is the father of Wilson's friend, Sim, who helped them move into this house? Anyhow, I found Pete believable and most probably a decent man.

After that interview, I drove out to the Bates' house on Juniper Road. Mother, if you've ever seen anything like that house, you saw it in the funny papers. Like in Li'l Abner, or in the editorial cartoon! But it is not comical when you think of a man and his wife and five children living in those four rooms.

At the house, I spoke with Pete's wife, Sim's mother, a youthful, very fat woman whose name is Daisy. She was very forthcoming, and I learned a great deal about the situation at the gin, and at home. At this point, I write them down as admirable people.

If I am their defense counsel, I will need to look for an alibi for Pete, while attacking the credibility of the witnesses. At this point, I don't have the answers to the unknowns in either of those issues, but they can probably be found.

After hearing this recital, Mother, do you still think I should stick out my legal neck and volunteer to defend this case?"

"All I can say is you are certainly passionate about it, and any defendant who has a passionate lawyer is a fortunate man. I know you are a capable attorney, because your father's friend Sam Bedenbaugh has told me so on numerous occasions. If you take this case, Pete Bates will be very fortunate, and in my opinion, will possibly go free. In addition, and this is no small matter, you will fit the hero's mold that Wilson Jones firmly believes you deserve. He idolizes you, Tom.

CHAPTER NINE

"SEE YOU IN COURT"

As soon as Wilson came home from the hardware store, Tom took him aside and told him he had decided to request to be the attorney who would defend Pete Bates. Wilson listened to what he had to say, then, eyes shining and his mouth spread wide in a big grin, he clapped his hands together several times, as if applauding.

"Oh, Tom! I knew you'd do it! And yet, at the same time I was afraid you wouldn't, and Pete would get sent to that awful penitentiary for something he didn't do—they say it's not too nice in there. I know you will get him set free—I just know it! Thank you, Tom, thank you!"

"Now, wait a minute, Wilson. This case is not won yet. It's not even begun. I don't know anything about the defendant (except that he's your friend's father)—I don't know anything about the witnesses or how to attack their testimony, I don't know who the judge will be, and the jury has not been chosen. We're a long way from a verdict, Wilson."

"That may be, Tom, but I'm dern sure you can do it....Hey, Tom, if you don't have any plans for tonight, could I borrow your car and ride out to the sand hills and tell Sim and Dinah?"

"Go ahead. I'm hoping to go to bed early."

* * *

The next morning Tom went straight to the jail and asked the sheriff to allow him to see Pete Bates. When he entered the cell area he was struck by the combination of unpleasant odors. Unwashed bodies, urine, vomit—but maybe the penetrating harshness of Lysol was the most objectionable, he decided.

When the door opened for him, Pete arose from the cot where he had been sitting. He bobbed hid head in greeting, but said nothing.

"Morning, Pete. I'm Tom Stone. I was here yesterday, remember?"

"Yessuh, I remember. Good mornin' to you, too."

"Pete, when I left here yesterday I rode out and had a nice visit with your wife, Daisy. She's real worried about you being in jail and facing trial."

"Yessuh, I'm worried, myself."

"I've been thinking a lot about your situation, and I want to ask you one more time—did you set fire to that gin?"

"Naw suh! Just like I told you yestiddy, I did not set no fire to that gin."

"I believe you, Pete. I think you're innocent, Daisy thinks you're innocent, and you say you're innocent. I would like to be your lawyer and help you explain to the jury that you're innocent, so they'll set you free. Can I be your lawyer?"

"Lawd, Boss, you sho' can! Bless yo' heart!" Then he added, "But you need to know, right off, I ain't got no money to pay you. I can do some work in your yard, on Sat'days, 'til I get you paid off. Lawd, yes! Thank ye, Lawd, for answering my prayers. Boss man, you can be my lawyer and help me get back to work n' help my family!"

* * *

When Tom left the jail, he went to his office where he checked in with the faithful Virginia. She reported that there no messages or pending appointments. This was not unusual for a struggling law practice in a small agricultural town in the depressed South. Tom decided to place a telephone call to the magistrate.

He picked up the earpiece and tapped on the cradle that held it. A voice came on the line, "Central", she said.

"Emmy, please connect me with Ben Teal at the magistrate's office," he requested.

"Is that you, Tom?" she asked.

"Sure, Emmy, it's me."

"Well, I was looking out the window, and I just saw Ben go into the Sanitary Café for his morning cup of coffee."

"Was he by himself?"

"No, he was with the sheriff and somebody I didn't recognize."

"Don't believe I'll join them. How long does he usually drink coffee?

"Sometimes as much as an hour, if the conversation is good, and the lies are really flowing."

"Thank you, Emmy. I'll try him again in an hour," said Tom, and he started work on the morning crossword.

An hour later he tried again, and this time the magistrate was in his office. "Morning, Ben. This is Tom Stone."

"Hello, Tom. How are you?"

"Pretty good for a country lawyer, I guess. Hey, Ben, I understand you have an arson complaint. Is that right?"

"Yep, I just heard about it. How'd you find out so quick?"

"I'm going to be representing Pete Bates, the fellow who is accused. Can you tell me when the hearing will be?"

"Man! You must have been holding the matchbox for him, to find out about this case so quick! Talk about ambulance chasing! Don't take offense, Tom. I'm just jokin' you. To answer your question, though, let's see, today is Tuesday—I think we'll have the hearing on Friday. Does that suit your schedule?"

"Sure, Ben. That's fine. And, in the off chance there's enough evidence to send the case to grand jury, I'll be defending the accused in criminal court."

"I understand. You've got to do what's best for your client, to earn that big fee." He .chuckled. "You are getting a big fee, aren't you?"

"Don't I always? Thanks, Ben. See you in court. 'Bye."

* * *

Emmy called her boyfriend. "You'll never guess what I just heard...."

The news spread like wildfire along the sidewalks and in the shops and offices of Truro.

"Hey—I just heard—some witnesses have come forward who say they saw fire being set to George Sampson's gin, way back yonder; when was it, anyhow? 1934?...."

"The sheriff's got the boy in jail, waiting for the magistrate's court.....No, I don't know who he is, but I'll tell you this one thing. He's in a whole peck of trouble if he burned down George's gin!....Yeah, George is the power in the Klan, and if that boy set fire to George's gin, he might as well have spit in his face!"

And so the talk went....

Tom drove over to Chester to call on Sam Bedenbaugh. Mr. Bedenbaugh had a small fire burning in a fireplace grate in his living room, and he was sitting close to its warmth.

"Come on in, Tom," he greeted his young friend. "Pull up your chair. These old bones of mine are slow to warm up in the morning, even if it is past the Tenth of May. My old daddy—rest his soul!—would never let us boys go barefooted or take off our long underwear until after the Tenth of May. Did your daddy have the same rule? Old Gen'ral "Stonewall" Jackson died on that day back in the War of Northern Aggression, and it's been a benchmark around here ever since. Heck, they even let us out of school in the Old Days to march to the cemetery on the Tenth of May. Confederate Memorial Day, speeches and ev'rything!

Well, to get back to the fire—and I ain't goinn' to get too far from this one—the Tenth of May is 'way too early for my old bones. Tenth of June might suit me better.

Well, Tom. Come on! Don't just sit there with a bemused expression on your young face! 'Course I'm old, and 'course I rattle on about matters that are not germane to your case, but, Hellfire, boy, if you don't go ahead and talk to me about the case, how can I give you the benefit of my fifty years' experience at the bar of justice? Talk to me!"

"Mr. Sam, I apologize for not being more forthcoming. I came over here to share my meager knowledge of the situation in the Pete Bates case up to this point, and I'll get right to the heart of the matter. As I told you before, Pete is charged with arson, based on a complaint signed by Jake Bottoms and Duncan Pate. These two claim to have witnessed Pete setting the fire by throwing lighted cigarettes into a pile of cotton waste in the gin yard. Both the witnesses are friends and fishing buddies of George Sampson, the gin owner. I've asked a few questions around town, and am led to believe that all three men are big Klan members."

"Does our client have an alibi for his whereabouts at the time in question?"

"Only that he was with his wife."

"That's not much help. We need an alibi that will stand up in court."

"Yep. There's another angle, too. Pete's wife, Daisy, tells me George Sampson had his hands all over her, and was in the process of assaulting her against her will, when Pete walked into the gin office where this was going on, A terrible argument ensued, and the upshot of it was that Pete was fired on the spot. This was the same day the gin burned. Daisy says George is still furious, because Pete knows that George was sexually after a colored woman—Pete's wife—and George is <u>the</u> Big Dog in the local Klan."

"Well, let's keep in mind that we might want to put—Daisy?—on the stand. What's the potential down side to that?"

"In talking to me at her house, she was a forthright, unequivocal witness. I don't know how she'd stand up under cross-examination. Of course, we never know how people will stand up under "cross", when the other side is trying to pick holes in their story."

"Maybe you should arrange a session with Daisy, and pretend to be the prosecutor, to give her a sample of the questions she'll get, and to see how she handles it."

"Good idea, I'll try that."

"We probably need to spend some time checking on the two witnesses who say they saw Pete set the fire. How reliable are they? Ever been in court before? Do they have a connection to George Sampson, other than fishing, or the Klan? And how about the long years between the fire and their identifying Pete Bates as the culprit? But, Tom, above all, just like in real estate where LOCATION! is the key, what we need is ALIBI, ALIBI, ALIBI!"

"Anything else you can think of, Mister Sam?"

"Hellfire, boy! That's the most work I've done in a month! Let me rest 'til your next visit!"

* * *

Tom drove back to Truro. He needed to investigate the two witnesses. Were they familiar enough with Pete at the time of the fire to have recognized him, if they saw him tossing lighted cigarettes into waste cotton?

He also needed to research any insurance payoff to George Sampson that might have occurred.

And he absolutely had to nail down what Pete and Daisy did with their time and whereabouts, after Pete was fired from his job.

None of this had to be accomplished before the magistrate's hearing, but the more he learned, the better he could digest the testimony of the "witnesses".

* * *

The yellow DeSoto did a quick U-turn, and pulled up to the curb in front of the Sanitary Café, just at the stroke of four o'clock. Five minutes later, the Café door opened, and a feminine figure flounced across the sidewalk, entered the open front door of the car, and sat in the front seat beside the driver. She pulled the door closed, and the automobile roared away down the street.

"Gosh, Jim," she said breathlessly, "you sure do make a strong escape—no, that's not the word—is it "exit"?"

"Might be, Baby," he answered. "I just want to get away from all those old biddies who watch the street from their second-story windows—like Emmy, the phone operator. I want to get out of town so I can put my hand on that pretty knee that is covered by your skirt…"

She promptly slid the hem of her skirt up above the knee. "Be careful now, Jim, don't forget to drive this beautiful car. We don't want to end up in the ditch!"

A few minutes later she said, "Did you hear the big news in town this morning? About the arson trial?"

"Sure did. I don't miss much gossip. I hang around the Post Office, after all. You know, Bonnie, last week when we were down at the river having some private time on my blanket, we might have overheard the beginnings of that case. Those ol' boys were hatchin' up a plan to bring charges against a Pete somebody—and they were makin' it up as they went along!"

"Do you know who they are, or who he is?"

"I pretty well know who they are. Recognized some voices that night. And on the street today they were named as George Sampson, Jake Bottoms and Dunk Pate. Don't know, for sure, who the 'nig' is, but I'll prob'ly find out tomorrow. I feel kinda sorry for the poor devil. Those three boys are all Klan people, and they're gangin' up on him."

He looked at his watch, new and gold-colored and fancy. "Got to go now, Baby. I need to meet a payroll at Signet Knitting, so I can get the premiums and my commission. It's a lot easier to get in the current week. Collecting on those back weeks can be a booger. You're working late tomorrow? What time should I pick you up? I'm hungry for some more of our 'private time'."

* * *

Wilson was full of conflicting emotions. On the one hand, he was exultant about being two weeks away from the end of high school. No more "same old, same old!" But, at the same time, he was not certain what he should do with the rest of his life. He knew he couldn't go to college. That was a fact. So what could he do? Opportunities around Truro were few, and limited in their scope. And while he could probably live free at the big house on High Street, just as he'd been doing, there weren't many jobs that had any future, unless you happened to be in the family of a business owner, and there was no way he could qualify for that. It was beginning to look like the Army was his best option. He resolved to talk to the recruiter at the Post Office the next week.

Tom Stone spent time at the jail. The sheriff allowed him to bring a chair and a little table into the back room. He positioned this furniture just outside Pete's cell, so Pete could sit on his cot or pace the floor while Tom interviewed him. The conversations were far-ranging, as the defense counsel strove to learn everything he could about the prisoner's prior life. They talked about Pete's life at home with Daisy and the children, his experiences all those years at the gin, his relationship with Mister George.

Tom also devoted lots of time trying to discover how Pete and Daisy spent the hours of late afternoon and early evening after the argument at the gin office. He was desperately searching for anything that could become an alibi for Pete's whereabouts in the hours before the fire. Nothing that emerged from those conversations held any promise of denying Pete's ability to set the fire.

Having come to an impasse with Pete, Tom turned his attention to Daisy. He drove out to her house, and they sat together for hours on end while he questioned her about the same subjects he had discussed with Pete. Again, he gained not a glimmer of hope.

Next he decided to interview the two of them together, in the hope that something one said would trigger an unspoken thought in the other.

“Now, think, folks,” he began. “After Pete got fired from the gin, where did you go and who did you see when you left there?”

‘Don’t know,” said Pete. “I was too mad to notice who we saw.”

“Pete, think about it,” said his wife. “We went to the FCX to get a new water bucket. Remember you said it was cheaper there than at the hardware store?”

“Yeah, we did!” exclaimed Pete in admiration of his wife’s memory.

Who else did you see there? What time of day was it?”

“Musta been about 5:30,” Daisy replied. “Didn’t see nobody else, ‘cause we were the only ones in there.”

“Where did you go next?” the lawyer repeated.

“The grocery store.” Daisy continued. “Needed some corn meal and ‘lasses.”

“See anybody there?”

“Nope.”

“What then?”

“We walked home. Out Juniper Road, trying to get home before dark.”

“See anybody on the way?”

“Come to think of it, we did see Miz Mary Jones in front of her house. She waved to us and asked about the chillun.”

"What time was that?"

"Musta been about seven o'clock, 'cause it was about 'first dark'."

"See anybody else?"

"Can't think of anybody, 'cept our chillun when we got home."

Discouraged by the lack of information, Tom called the meeting to a close. As he was driving Daisy home from the jail, he promised to give her a ride to town for the magistrate's hearing, two days away. He reminded to bring a fresh set of clothing for Pete to wear, and a razor.

Thinking about the case during the next twenty-four hours, he was thankful that it was to be only a preliminary hearing and not a trial. "Maybe I'll learn something helpful from the prosecution's testimony," he thought. "I sure don't know enough to ask questions now!"

* * *

Friday, the day of the hearing, was a bright, clear day. It was one of those idyllic May days. Every tree was wearing its bright new green foliage, flouncing it around in the gentle breeze like a young girl in a new full skirt. The daffodils were finished, but dogwood remained, and the grass was growing for all it was worth. The air smelled clean from a recent rain, and the pollen had been washed away by the same shower.

Spring!

Not so wonderful for Pete and Daisy, or for their five children. The five had either skipped school or asked off from work so they could be present at the hearing. They had never witnessed anything like a hearing, or a trial, nor did they know anything of the workings of the law. It was "white man's law", anyway, wasn't it?

They were nervous, and rightfully so.

Wilson was not present. He had asked Tom's advice, and had been advised to go on to school. "Nothing's really going to happen today," he was assured.

Tom and Sam Bedenbaugh, dressed in their courtroom attire of dark suits, white shirts and ties, were waiting in the magistrate's courtroom when Pete Bates was led in by a deputy sheriff and told to take his seat.. Pete was newly shaved, and dressed in clean jeans and a fresh shirt. Tom gave him an encouraging nod of greeting, though they had conversed earlier in the morning.

Tom twisted in his chair and craned his head around to see who else was present in the small courtroom. He saw George Sampson and two other men, whom he supposed were to be the witnesses. He saw the usual five or six men who loitered around town and managed to be present at most court functions. He also saw Matt Stokes from the hardware store who was, he conjectured, acting as the eyes and ears of Wilson. There was also a youngish-looking couple sitting in the back row who looked somewhat familiar, but he couldn't quite place them.

After a few minutes, a door opened, and Ben Teal, the magistrate, entered and took his seat behind the bench. He looked around for a few seconds, cleared his throat and declared, "This hearing will be in order! We will hear evidence in the complaint against"—here he paused and looked at the papers in front of him—"against Pete Bates that he caused a fire which destroyed George Sampson's cotton gin back in October, 1934. I call to the stand Mr. Jake Bottoms."

Jake got to his feet and walked to the front, faced the magistrate.

"Do you promise to tell the truth, the whole truth, so help you God?"

"I do, Judge," Jake replied.

"Just stand right there, Jake, and tell the court what you saw on the day of that fire at Sampson's Gin back in 1934."

"Well, Judge, Duncan Pate and me were at the gin trying to sell tickets to the catfish stew supper our church was feedin' that evenin'. We sold one to George Sampson, and were walking around the gin yard looking for other suspects, I mean prospects, when we saw a colored fellow acting mighty suspicious, so we stopped to watch…"

"What was he doin', Jake?" the judge asked.

"He was walkin' around the yard, fast and furious, lighting cigarettes, taking three or four puffs from 'em, and throwin' 'em down—seemed like he was tryin' to throw 'em into piles of cotton waste that the wind was pushing into corners— it was awful windy that day. I said to Dunk, 'That's awful dangerous. He could start a fire, doin' that!"

"Anything else to add to your testimony before this court, Jake?"

"No, Judge. That's about it."

The judge turned toward the other witness. "Is that the way you saw it, Dunk?"

"That's just the way I saw it, Judge," replied Dunk, who didn't bother to rise from his seat.

The judge turned his gaze on Tom, sitting in the front row. "Mr. Stone, are you representing Bates, here?"

"Yes, Judge, I am."

"Do you have any questions of either witness?"

"No, sir. Not at this time."

"Then it is the finding of this hearing that the accused who is charged with arson, shall go before the Grand Jury. Which Jury shall determine whether the facts as presented by these witnesses constitute sufficient evidence to find a "true bill" and hold –another look downward at his papers—Pete Bates for the next session of the Court of Common Pleas. This hearing is adjourned."

* * *

The deputy rose, hauled Pete to his feet, and began to lead him out of the courtroom to return to his cell. Tom quickly reached out to him and said, "Don't be afraid. It's what I expected, and it's a long way from over. I'll see you later."

To Daisy and her children, who were in tears, he said, "Let's go over to my office where we can talk in private. Everything is OK."

When the Bates family gathered in Tom's office and all were seated, Tom introduced them to Sam Bedenbaugh. "This gentleman was my father's best friend. They worked together on many cases. He has offered to help me with Pete's case. I know he will lead me in the right way, and between us we'll be able to free this innocent man and return him home to you," he said confidently.

"But, Mr. Stone," Shad said impatiently, "why did you let that Jake guy tell lies about our daddy and say he set fire to that gin? Why didn't you ask him questions and make the Judge see he was lyin'? Why didn't you put Ma on the stand? She'd'a told 'em off!"

Tom answered him calmly. "Because, Shad, I didn't want them to know what kind of questions I'm going to ask. I want to save those questions for when we go before the real judge and jury."

Sam Bedenbaugh interjected, "That's what you call 'strategy'. You don't want the other side to know where you're heading. Tom did just right. He learned what the other side is presenting, but they didn't learn anything about our line of questioning. They will, when the time comes."

Tom said, "I don't want you to be discouraged. We're in jail, but we're not in a hole we can't get out of. When we get before a jury we'll ask the tough questions, and you'll see what will happen. Don't get discouraged. We have not lost."

The Bates family thanked him, trooped out of the office. The girls climbed into Sim's pickup. The boys made their way to their jobs, trying to finish out a day so they could ask for time off for the next day in court.

* * *

Tom and his senior advisor sat in the office after the Bates family had left. "How did we do today, Sam?" he asked.

"I think you did all that was possible without giving away any plans," he responded. "The magistrate was not going to throw the case out—he is in tight with the complainants. Hellfire! He may be a member of the Klan himself, who knows?

"The older man changed the subject. "How are you coming with that alibi?"

"Not worth a dern," Tom replied,

"We need it," Sam warned.

"We'll think of something."

* * *

Early that afternoon Tom received a message from the Clerk of Court. "Congratulations. You won't have to wait 'forever and a day' to defend your arson case. Grand Jury is scheduled for Thursday of next week, and Judge Hilliard Anthony Wayne will preside over the opening of Common Pleas Court the following

Monday, June 8, 1939. You will get a copy of the list of potential jurors on Friday, June 5, 1939."

* * *

Graduation ceremonies at Truro High School were scheduled for the first weekend in June, culminating on Saturday, June 6. Excitement reigned supreme at the Jordan household on Kershaw Street. Betsy's mother was all agog over Betsy being a finalist in contention for a high award at Commencement, "Best All-round Senior Girl". In contemplation of Betsy seizing that prize, her mother suggested Betsy take a trip to the hairdresser's for a permanent wave. Betsy could not believe her ears, for never had such an offer crossed her mother's lips before. More excitement!

Wilson, though holding the esteem of many of his classmates, was not expecting to receive any high honor at Commencement. He would graduate with solid grades which qualified him for his diploma, and he would be thrilled to have completed this portion of his life. Not planning to attend college, his formal education would most likely be over after Saturday. Okay, so be it! He was happy with his life, and thrilled for Betsy's prospects at graduation and beyond.

* * *

On Thursday, June 4, the Grand Jury met to hear the evidence in the pending arson case. According to state law, the only individuals who could be present when the Jury sat were the prosecutor and one or more witnesses. The defendant could not be present, nor could his lawyer. The prosecutor, at the invitation of the Grand Jury foreman, would then relate the evidence against the accused. Members of the Grand Jury could question the witnesses to clear up any points that were unclear to them. At the conclusion of the hearing, the Grand Jury would vote to determine whether the evidence merited sending the case to Common Pleas Court for trial.

* * *

The members of the Grand Jury filed into the room and took their seats. The foreman nodded to the prosecutor, Robert B. Daniels. "You may present the evidence, Mr. Daniels," he said.

The prosecutor called Jake Bottoms to the stand where he was sworn in. He led Jake in roundabout fashion through the entire story. Jake began with the fishing expedition, the noise on the riverbank, the trip to fetch the sheriff, and the arrest of the revelers for "disturbing the peace".

One of the jurors interrupted. "What does all this trivial stuff have to do with arson, Mr. Daniels?" he asked.

"If you'll just be patient a minute longer, I'll show you," promised the prosecutor.

He then led the witness through the second part of Jake's story, about recognizing Pete in the bright light of the sheriff's office and thus mentally connecting him to the gin fire of 1934.

"Now, gentlemen of the jury, I have another witness who has come forward to testify about the same sequence of events. After hearing his testimony, the witnesses will be glad to answer any questions you may have about either witness' story."

Daniels then called Duncan Pate to the stand, where he was sworn in. Pate was led through the same account, reporting in almost identical language what Jake had said ten minutes before.

"Now, gentlemen of the jury, both these witnesses are still sworn. They will be glad to answer any questions, clear up any points. Fire away."

"Well, I have a question," one member of the jury said. I'll ask Jake Bottoms. 'cause he said it first. Jake, the fire at the gin was 1934. That right?"

"That's right," Jake replied.

"This 'event' on the riverbank was two weeks ago. That right?"

"That's right," Jake answered.

"That's pretty much five years, ain't it?"

"Almost five years," Jake said.

"Jake, how come you wait so long to put the finger on this nig—fellow?" another juror broke in.

Jake answered with vigor. "Look, you boys grew up around here just like I did. You know how it is—you see a nigger, you don't bother to look at his face, 'cause you know you don't know him, and he's just a –he's just a colored fellow."

There was silence in the room.

Any further questions of these two witnesses from the Grand Jury?" asked the foreman.

No questions were raised.

"Then" said the foreman, "we will excuse all who are not members of this Grand Jury so we can debate the merits of the evidence in the case. You are excused."

Thirty minutes later a message arrived at Tom's office.. "The Grand Jury has found a "true bill", and the case will be on the docket beginning, Monday, June 8."

* * *

Tom and his his elderly associate were sitting in Tom's office, discussing the lack of any information on which they could build an alibi. Virginia could sense their frustration and offered to make fresh pot of coffee.

"Great!" said Sam Bedenbaugh, "Make it strong and hot, Virginia." To Tom, he said, "You got any brandy?"

"I was going to save it for a victory celebration, but we can have a sample now, if you like."

"God, I'd love it—but I've got to drive those ten miles back to Chester, and my driving's not too good, even when I'm cold sober."

"Let's wait for victory, then, and that day I promise to drive you home".

When Virginia brought in the coffee, she said, "Oh, Tom, just a while ago, a man called and asked for an appointment for 9 AM tomorrow morning. Said it was important."

"Good, good! Hope it's not another *pro bono* case. Who is the man?

"He didn't give his name. He said, though, that he was pretty sure you'd be interested in what he has to say."

"Well, we'll wait and see." Turning to Sam, he asked, "Do you want to come over tomorrow afternoon so we can look at the jury list together?"

"I sure do. Three o'clock soon enough? I ought to be bright eyed and bushy tailed by then."

"I thought you woke up that way every day."

* * *

When Tom arrived home for supper he found Wilson waiting for him, eager to hear the results of the Grand Jury session, which Tom related. Wilson was again disappointed that Pete was still in the jailhouse, but seemed more reconciled to waiting for final closure at Court of Common Pleas the following week. He was dressed in his "Sunday best", preparing to take Betsy to a movie at the local theatre.

"I'm not going anywhere tonight," Tom declared. "Do you want to use my car?"

"Boy! Do I!" Wilson's eyes were shining in anticipation of being alone in the car with Betsy after the movie. "That could be a lot more fun than the film," he thought.

During the evening she asked him again about his talks with the Army Recruiter. "I've had several interviews," he said, "and Mama went with me to one of them. She had some questions she wanted answers to, so she got it, 'direct from the horse's mouth'."

"Have you definitely decided to enlist?" she wanted to know.

"Pretty much," he replied. "The radio and the papers are more and more talking about the bad news from Europe. Germany just walked right in and took over Czechoslovakia and Austria, you know. Congress is bound to start a Draft soon. If I sign up this month, they'll want me to report in July, and I'll go to some camp for Basic Training, and after that I'll get to come home on furlough, before being ordered to some other post for my permanent assignment."

"Gosh! Suppose they send to some way-off place like California? I sure would miss you if you went a long ways off," she said wistfully.

"Well, you're planning to go to Concord College for four years," he retorted. "I'll miss you, too, whether I'm in Truro or Arizona."

"Arizona?" she gasped, thinking it the end of the world. "Oh, Wilson! I wish we could turn the clock back a little bit, stay in high school a little longer, and not have to face so many changes!" She impulsively threw her arms around his neck and held him tightly.

"Now, now, Betsy…calm down…" He pulled her even closer to him. "Regardless of where we are, I'll still love you, and want to be with you, and we'll get together. You'll see." And he gave her a long, tender kiss.

She pulled away to look in his eyes. "Love? Did you say love? We've never used that word before!"

"I've thought it plenty of times," he said. "Maybe we're old enough, now, to say it. I love you, Betsy."

"And I love you."

He was right. The ride home *was* better than the film.

* * *

Daisy was despondent. She knew it was her responsibility to come up with some kind of alibi for Pete, to prove that he couldn't have set the fire. She had spent days trying to remember who might have seen them that afternoon—who could testify in court that Pete was in such-and-such a place, at such-and-such a time, so it was not possible for him to set the fire. But, she was not able to come up with a face or a name or a location that would prove anything! "I'd be glad to lie," she thought, "but they'd find me out, 'cause I can't even think of a good lie!"

* * *

Out in the sand hills, Mose Harrington questioned Sim. "What happened today?"

"We don't know for sure, 'cause Mr. Tom Stone was not allowed in the jury room. Of course, he didn't ask any questions in that magistrate's court. In the end, though, the Grand Jury said the case will go to trial on Monday. My poor Daddy!"

Dinah patted his arm sympathetically.

Mose ventured, "Don't sell Tom Stone short. I knew his old daddy pretty well. A straight shooter. He took a case no other lawyer would touch with a ten-foot pole. A colored boy who couldn't talk plain was accused by a white preacher's wife of propositioning her! When he was just a young lawyer, starting out, Tom Stone's daddy took the case. And, believe it or not, he got that colored boy a 'not guilty' ruling! Young Tom might be a chip off the old block. We've got to hope he is, anyway!"

* * *

On Friday morning Tom Stone and Virginia were in the office when, promptly at nine o'clock, the door opened and a young man walked in.

"Good morning, sir," Virginia greeted him

"Good morning to you," he replied. "My name is Lane. I have an appointment with Mr. Stone."

"Yes, sir. Please take a seat. I'll see if Mr. Stone is ready for you."

In a minute she returned. "Yes, Mr. Lane. Please come in. Mr. Stone will see you now."

She led the way into the inner office. "Mr. Stone, this is Mr. Lane. He telephoned yesterday, asking for an appointment."

"Yes, Mr. Lane. Please have a chair. Would you care for coffee? Virginia makes the best."

"Yes. That would be nice. Sugar and milk, please."

After she brought the coffee and closed the door, the two men talked for ninety minutes before Jim Lane made his exit.

* * *

Sam Bedenbaugh arrived at Tom's office slightly before three, and was promptly ushered into the inner office by Virginia.

"Coffee, Mr. Sam?" she asked.

"Yes, ma'am. Black." Turning to Tom, he asked, "Did we get the jury list?"

"Sure did. They brought it over late this morning. Forty-five names, and I'm familiar with a number of them."

"That's a help. Thanks, Virginia." He accepted the coffee she had brought in. "That smells mighty good."

"Will you need me for anything, Tom? she inquired.

"Not right now, but we'll probably need some help in about an hour, so don't go far."

After she had gone out and closed the door, Tom, with a self-satisfied grin, said, "I had an interesting morning, Sam."

"I'm glad to hear it. Did an alibi for Pete and Daisy walk in the door, or something?"

"Not exactly. But it might be as good as an alibi. Let me tell you about it." Then Tom proceeded to relate what he had learned from Mr. Lane.

After he concluded, Sam exclaimed, "Well! That is interesting! Have you decided how you're going to use it?"

"What would you think about his being the first defense witness, or maybe the second, after we encourage Daisy to tell her experience with George Sampson in the office?"

"Do you think we ought to use Daisy's story? What would it accomplish, other than embarrassing George and making him even more vengeful toward the couple?"

"You may be right. We'll hold that in abeyance. Do you have any other thoughts?"

"I guess you're planning to kick holes in the testimony of those two so-called witnesses?"

'I plan to point out the inconsistencies in their stories, yes."

"That's my only suggestion at this point. What say we look at the jury list and decide who we want, and who we don't."

They immediately agreed they did not want any member of the Ku Klux Klan on the jury, as they would be predisposed to believe the whites' testimony and disbelieve any testimony from the colored. They also agreed to avoid any who might be friends or associates of George Sampson. After discussing each name on the list, they called Virginia back into the office, and asked her if she knew any of the names that were unfamiliar to the two men. After her input there still remained four names that none of the three of them had any reading on, Tom assigned himself the job of discovering their identities and characteristics on the next day, which was Saturday.

"I guess that winds up this session, Sam. Sure do appreciate your willingness to help. I'll see you in court on Monday."

* * *

Tom arose early Saturday morning, realizing he had a full day of activities before him. He spent a couple of hours after breakfast, calling some friends inquire about the potential jurors that he did not know. He discovered that one of the four would be very satisfactory to his side of the case, being an educated person with a reputation for good judgment. Two of the others were less desirable, but could be acceptable if 'push came to shove'. The fourth was completely unacceptable and Tom resolved to strike him. All of the people on the list, of course, were both white and male, as the law provided.

* * *

Graduation exercises were scheduled at the high school auditorium for 11 AM. Tom drove his mother and Wilson's mother to the school. Both were dressed as if for church, but without hats. The three arrived early in an effort to get seats near the front. As they filed into their seats, they found themselves directly behind the Jordans, Betsy's parents. The mothers of the soon-to-be graduates smiled their congratulations to each other, and Tom shook hands with John Jordan.

The auditorium was soon filled, and precisely at eleven o'clock the music teacher, seated at the grand piano, struck the opening notes of "Land of Hope and Glory'. The graduates began their solemn procession, keeping rigorously to the slow, measured tread they had practiced. Into the auditorium and up onto the stage they marched, each coming to a halt in front of the chair he was to occupy. Their expressions were serious, their faces scrubbed and hair carefully in place. The girls were wearing white dresses, and the boys wore white shirts and ties.

As the program progressed, there were a number of speeches. Most were delivered with great solemnity, and all seemed to be too lengthy. The captive audience sat through it, waiting for the presentation of awards and diplomas.

Finally, Professor Scott announced that the next part of the proceedings would be the presentation of awards. Sitting behind her, Mary Jones could see the tension increase in Alice Jordan's neck and shoulders as she waited, hoping to hear Betsy's name. When the announcement came, the award for Best All-round Senior Girl was won by Jane Muldrow. Betsy's mother's shoulders slumped in disappointment, but she turned a brave smile to her husband and patted his hand. Betsy's good friend, Dot Hubbard won the DAR Good Citizenship award.

As the diplomas were presented, the graduates received a smattering of applause from the audience. When Wilson received his, one wag in the rear called out" 'Cowboy", and several tittered and clapped.

The facial expressions of the graduates were totally different as they recessed out of the assembly. Exultation and broad grins, along with an occasional tear, replaced the solemn faces they had worn as they entered.

As soon as they could, the audience exited the auditorium and families found their special graduate on the lawn outside. Hugs and handshakes were liberally exchanged, and big smiles were everywhere. Mary Jones' eyes were glistening with tears of pride as she surveyed her son, the first high school graduate in her family. "Such a fine boy," she thought. "How did I ever get so lucky?"

The Joneses and the Stones walked over to speak to Betsy's family. They overheard Betsy consoling her mother. "But, Mother, she really deserved it. She was on the Student Council, and the basketball team and made good grades and all of that. I'm happy for her. Happy for me, too, because I've graduated. I've graduated!"

* * *

After attending services at his church Sunday morning, and having dinner with his mother and the two Joneses, Tom returned to his office. He spent the afternoon making lists of potential jurors, organizing his notes and formulating questions to be asked of probable witnesses. He could feel the tension and excitement build within his being, as it always did in the hours before a court contest.

* * *

At 9:30 Monday morning Tom and Sam Bedenbaugh walked into the county courtroom. The Clerk of Court was in charge at the moment, as the jurors who had been summoned reported their presence to that official. Ten o'clock arrived and the Judge entered the room.

Hilliard Anthony Wayne was a veteran jurist who had spent ten years on the bench. He had the reputation of being even-handed, a fair man, a strict interpreter of the law who treated opposing sides without favoritism. Lawyers felt comfortable in his court, believing they would be treated equally under the eyes of the law.

The judge asked the Clerk of Court, "Are all jury panel members present?"

"No, sir. Two are absent without authorization."

"Issue bench warrants and have the sheriff bring them in. In the meantime, have the opposing lawyers exercise their rights to select and strike," the judge ordered.

The Clerk of Court had the entire jury panel rise and raise their right hands. He then administered the Oath to them, requiring that they answer questions truthfully.

The Clerk called a single name. The individual named stood and acknowledged his identity. The prosecutor asked his education and profession.

"We accept him," the prosecutor said quickly.

Tom and Sam exchanged looks. They both knew the man was a crony of George Sampson. "Strike," was Tom's only comment. The man was excused from the case.

One by one, names were called. The prosecution accepted a number of the men, and Tom did not demur. However, after the sixth name called was accepted by the prosecution, Tom asked him, "Are you now, or have you ever been, a member of the Ku Klux Klan?"

A gasp went up from the audience, closely followed by a buzz of disbelief. The Klan is a secret society, and members do not normally profess their affiliation in public. As the object of the question hesitated and the prosecutor rose to object, the judge beckoned to both lawyers to approach the bench.

The prosecutor said, "Your Honor, I object. We all know that the Klan exists and has existed for more than fifty years. It is a secret society. Members should not be required to declare whether they are, or are not, members."

The judge lookd at Tom. "Mr. Stone, what is your purpose in asking this question?"

"Your honor, as you can see, my client, the defendant, is a colored man. In a previous hearing of this case, he has been accused by two white men of setting fire to a cotton gin owned by another white man. As a member of the court I am sworn to defend my client from injustice, which includes verdicts from juries which are improperly constituted. I appeal to your Honor's knowledge of the influence of the Klan in today's Southern society. I appeal to Your Honor's knowledge of the law and his sense of fairness, not to allow a colored man accused of a crime against a white man's property to have his guilt or innocence determined by a jury composed of Klan members."

Judge Wayne nodded, the two lawyers returned to their seats. The judge announced, Defense counsel's question is allowed." To the prospective juror, "You will answer the question. Remember you are under oath."

The juror replied, "Yes, I am a member."

Tom said, "Strike."

This process continued through the next hour, the prosecution and the defense sparring as each attempted to obtain a jury that would be the most favorable to his point of view. Three other Klansmen were struck by the defense. Finally, just before noon, the opposing sides had agreed on "twelve good men and true", and the jury was completed.

"It being the noon hour," the judge intoned, "this court is recessed until 2:30, at which time we will begin the actual trial."

* * *

During the lunch break, the news that the arson trial would begin in the afternoon spread over Truro like wildfire. Few of the citizens knew Pete Bates at all, nor were they concerned about him very much. Almost everyone knew George Sampson, and there were varying degrees of support for his loss. He was not admired in all quarters.

What excited their interest, however, was the fact that Tom Stone, the attractive and universally liked son of the revered Judge Stone was defending a colored man against the "Klan Ring", a name ascribed to the invisible power and influence that seemed to protect Klansmen in the eyes of the law.

When the court re-opened at 2:30, the public seating was nearly full. Wilson had arranged for the afternoon off, and his mother was there beside him. Josh Bridges, the boss of the pole-setting crew, was there also, as well as a number of other citizens who were interested some of the aspects of the case. The Colored Section of the courtroom was already nearly filled to capacity with the Bates family, including Dinah's grandfather, Mose Harrington.

Just before 2:30, a side door opened, and a deputy sheriff led in Pete Bates, dressed in the same clean jeans and shirt he had worn to the magistrate's hearing, and again freshly shaved. The two men took their seats beside Tom Stone and Sam Bedenbaugh. They were no sooner seated than the door behind the tall raised bench opened, the Bailiff called out, "All rise!", and Judge Hilliard Anthony Wayne entered the courtroom and took his seat behind the bench. His black robe and grave demeanor added to the solemnity of the occasion.

The Bailiff announced the case to be heard, and Judge Wayne nodded to the prosecutor, "You may proceed with your opening statement, Mr. Daniels."

Robert B. Daniels, dressed in a rumpled gray striped seersucker suit and black string tie, rose and faced the jury. "Members of the jury," he began in his most mellifluous courtroom voice, "You are assembled here today to fulfill one of the most hallowed rights and privileges of citizenship, that of defending the rule of law against those who would ignore that law and shape events to suit themselves, without regard for the rights or property of others. By serving on this jury you continue the rule of justice in our fair land, just as your fathers did before you.

We will today try the case of the deliberate setting afire of a cotton gin, a fire set by a former trusted employee of the gin who had just been terminated by the owner. The fire resulted in the complete destruction of the gin, and at the same time, the destruction of the means of livelihood the owner, one of our most respected and beloved citizens.

The prosecution will show, through the testimony of eyewitnesses, that the defendant did, maliciously and with full intent, set the fire, and did then disappear from the vicinity for several years in order to escape detection."

The prosecutor resumed his seat, and the judge turned to Tom and said, "Mr. Stone, do you wish to make a statement?"

Tom rose, said "Thank you, your honor, I do indeed."

Then, addressing the twelve men seated in the jury box, he said, "Gentlemen of the jury, you are indeed playing an ancient and important role. By serving on this jury you do, indeed, defend the rule of law. That involves, in addition to finding the guilt of a lawbreaker and bringing him to justice—it also involves an equally important function—that of defending an innocent man against charges brought against him falsely. Please keep in your mind, as we proceed, the possibility that testimony given under oath may not be entirely correct, whether intentionally or unintentionally given. I will attempt to point out inconsistencies as we go along. I believe Mr. Bedenbaugh and I will be able to show you that our client is as innocent of this crime as you yourselves are."

As Tom took his seat, Judge Wayne said to Mr, Daniels, "You may call your first witness."

Mr. Daniels said, "The prosecution calls Jake Bottoms'.

Bottoms approached the bench, was sworn and seated, and Mr. Daniels said, "State your name and address."

"Jake Bottoms. I live two miles east of Truro on Lynch's Road."

"Thank you, Mr. Bottoms. Where were you on the afternoon of October 24, 1934?"

Jake cleared his throat. "Harrumph! Well, sir," he said, "All my life I've been a faithful member of the Cypress Swamp True Gospel Baptist Church. My church was putting on a catfish stew supper that night to finish paying for our big bell that calls people to church. Bein' a faithful member, like I said, I was out tryin' to sell tickets to the supper. Duncan Pate was with me, and we went to George Sampson's cotton gin to see if he wanted one, and he did. We thanked him in the name of the Lord, and then went outside his office to see if we could sell any more tickets."

Jake paused to catch his breath and wipe his brow with the wadded-up handkerchief he carried in his pocket. Daniels gave him a nod to continue, and he began again. "Well, sir, we no sooner got outside and started walking around the yard than we seen a strange sight."

"What was that, Mr. Bottoms? Tell us what you saw."

"Well, sir, Dunk and me saw a colored feller walking around the gin yard, back and forth, walkin' in circles, like. He was puffin' 'fast and furious' on one cigarette after another. He'd take three or four puffs, then throw that cigarette down and right away light another one. He'd take three or four puffs on that one then throw it down, too. Strange…

I said to Dunk, 'Look at that nig—colored feller. Ain't that strange?' And, quick as a flash, Dunk says to me, 'Not only strange, but dangerous. Ain't he throwin' those burnin' cigarettes into the cotton waste the wind is pilin' up in those corners?' And sure enough, he was throwin' those cigarettes right into the cotton waste!"

"What happened then?"

"Well, we didn't see anybody to sell tickets to, so we went downtown to try to sell some to help the church—you know the one I mean. But—you know what? That very night was the night George Sampson's gin burned down, plumb to the ground!"

"A terrible loss," Daniels sympathized. "But there's more to tour story, isn't there? Something that happened just last month?"

"Oh, yeah. You mean what happened down at the river?" Receiving an encouraging nod, he launched forth again into his tale. "A few weeks ago some of us were fishin' in the river just outside Truro. It was getting' on towards dark, so we were headin' back to the boat landing. Then the quiet of that nice evenin' was disturbed by the loud noises comin' from a bunch of nig-, I mean colored fellers who were partyin' on the bank—raisin' all manner of Hell, if you want to know the truth. It was so loud it was frigtenin', and we decided we ought to notify the sheriff about the danger to innocent people."

"And did you do that?"

"Yessiree, we did. The sheriff gathered up some deppities, went down to the river, and they gathered up those boist'rous colored fellers and booked them for disturbing the peace."

"What happened next?"

"Well, sir, me and the other boys who had complained were down at the sheriff's office when he booked 'em. In the bright light of that office, all of a sudden I realized that one of those fellers was the very same boy Dunk and me had seen lightin' cigarettes at the gin the day of the fire! So, we told the sheriff about it, and he booked him, that feller right there," pointing to Pete Banks, "for suspicion of arson, or some'p'n like that."

Daniels turned to the defense table, "Do you have any questions of this witness, Mr. Stone?"

Tom rose from his chair and approached the witness stand. "Yes, Mr. Daniels, I have a question or two." Turning to the witness, he asked, "Do you often go fishing with George Sampson, Mr. Bottoms?"

"Yeah. We go a lot. Coupla times a week if the weather is nice."

"And you play cards together, too. Isn't that right?"

"A sly grin spread across Jake's face. "That's what we do when the weather ain't good." He chuckled to himself at his witticism.

"You consider George Sampson a good friend, do you?

"Oh, yeah. We're pretty tight."

"Now, Jake, let's go back a little ways in your testimony. You testified that you saw a 'colored feller' walkin' around fast and furious, puffing on one cigarette after another, and throwing the lighted cigarettes into piles cotton waste. Isn't that what you said?"

"That's pretty near exactly what I said."

"And then you said that you and your companion, Duncan Pate, talked about how dangerous that kind of behavior was. You agreed that throwing lighted cigarettes into cotton waste could cause a fire, and you said the wind was blowing that day. Isn't that right?"

"That's what I said. And the gin burned down that very night! And that boy caused it!"

"Well, now, Jake, let's think for a minute about the responsibility of a citizen. If a person sees a mad dog on a rampage, foam coming out of his mouth, and that dog is approaching a playground filled with schoolchildren, doesn't a good citizen call out a warning, and help get the children to safety?"

"Sure he does. Everybody knows that."

If a person sees a couple of robbers going into a bank with their guns drawn, doesn't a good citizen call the police?"

"'Course he does. Everybody knows that."

"Let's say a person sees someone who looks like he's trying to set fire to a cotton gin that belongs to a good friend like George Sampson. Wouldn't a good citizen and a good friend tell George Sampson of this suspicious behavior—or would he just go on down town and try to sell more tickets to the catfish stew supper at the church?"

Jake Bottoms' face was a study. He opened his mouth to speak, then closed it again. His face turned red, then pale. He said nothing.

"Oh, and one other thing. Did you see any signs of fire caused by the cigarette? Or even smoke?"

"No."

"No further questions of this witness," Tom said as he returned to his seat.

The Prosecutor said, "The prosecution calls Duncan Pate to the stand."

Duncan rose from his seat. He self-consciously walked to the front of the room where he was sworn, and took his seat in the witness chair. His cheeks were shaved, his hair slicked down with something from the barber shop where he had purchased a fresh haircut the afternoon before. Even a day later, the aroma of the shaving lotion and the hair dressing filled the room. He wore a yellow shirt, a bright blue tie, and an expression that said "Look at me! I never took so much trouble with my appearance before, but don't I look good!"

The prosecutor wasted very little time complimenting Dunk on his appearance. "State your name and address," he commanded.

"Duncan Pate is my name," he said, "and I live right down Lynch's Road from Jake Bottoms."

"What is your occupation, Mr. Pate?"

"I run a few cows. I help other people tend their cattle and hogs— castrate, that kind of thing, and then I help them butcher and preserve the meat, Do a little barbecuing, too. Keeps me as busy as I want to be," he said expansively.

"Mr. Pate, we're interested in hearing about your activities on the afternoon of October 24, 1934. Can you fill us in on the details of that afternoon?"

"Yessir, I remember it like it was yesterday. Me'n Jake went up to the gin in the late afternoon. Truro didn't have but one gin, so you know which one I mean. Jake had some catfish stew tickets he wanted to sell for his church. You need to understand that anytime we had tickets to sell, George Sampson would buy 'em—real buddies, we were. So, me'n Jake went up there to sell tickets, and, sure enough, George bought one—like he always did. You could depend on it!"

"Did you notice anything unusual going on at the gin while you were there?", Daniels asked.

"Nope. The hands were getting paid, because it was Friday. They picked up their envelopes and left as soon as they could. Might have been one or two family members hanging around to make sure the man didn't spend it all before he got home. You know how they are, don't you, Mister?"

"Tell us what happened next."

"Well, it was just like Jake said. There was a colored feller actin' strange—lightin' cigarettes and throwin' 'em down before he smoked 'em. Not smart, at all.

"What did you think, when you saw that?"

"Just like I told you—it ain't too smart, to light one cigarette and throw it down before it's used up and then light another one, and do the same thing over and over! It just ain't smart! Typical of nig— You know who I mean!"

"What do you think he was trying to do?"

"Who knows what those people are tryin' to do? They can't think much, like we can. He coulda been dyin' for a cigarette—he coulda been sick of cigarettes—Hell, he could even have been trying to start a fire with those cigarettes, I don't know!"

Then he remembered his instructions.

"But he was prob'ly tryin' to start a fire to burn the gin down, don't you think?" he asked the prosecutor.

Mr. Daniels, glad to find a way to end the testimony of this witness who was obviously enjoying his day on the stand, hurriedly said, "We'll have to let the jury decide that."

Daniels then turned to Tom and again asked, "Do you have any questions of this witness?"

"Yes, sir. We do, Tom replied. He approached the witness stand, feigned a casual attitude by leaning against the judge's bench, hips slung to one side. In a non-threatening conversational tone, he said, "Dunk, you and Jake have testified that you visited George Sampson often.

Dunk nodded his head.

"You played cards up there."

Dunk nodded. "You counted on George to buy a meal ticket whenever you were selling."

"And he did, too!" Dunk asserted.

"You went up to the gin pretty often, George being your good friend, so that you probably got familiar with his hired help; I mean the ones who worked there over a period of time."

Dunk nodded.

That feller seated over there next to my partner, Mr. Bedenbaugh. Do you recognize him?"

"Sure. That's Pete Bates. He worked for George a long time. I know him."

"Well, Dunk. When you testified about seeing a 'colored feller' acting strange, and suspicious, why didn't you identify him as 'Pete Bates' instead of 'a colored feller'? How come, Dunk? Somebody told me he worked there for ten years."

Dunk had no answer. Dunk's mouth fell open, but no sound came out. He was speechless, trying to grasp an answer.

"Dunk, if you thought lighting cigarettes and throwing them into a pile of cotton waste could start a fire, why in the world didn't you warn your buddy George of the danger? How come?"

No answer.

"By the way, Dunk, did you see any spark, or flame or smoke coming from those cigarettes he was, as you say, using to burn down the gin?"

No answer.

And since you knew the long-time employee at the gin so well, why did it take five years and a 'bright light' to identify the suspect' as Pete Bates?"

Again, no answer.

The defense counsel turned to the judge. "No further questions, your honor."

Daniels then faced the judge and said, "The prosecution rests its case."

Judge Wayne addressed Tom and Sam Bedenbaugh. "Does the defense wish to call any witnesses?"

"Yes, your Honor, we do," Tom declared. The defense calls James G. Lane."

There was a hum of puzzlement in the audience as Jim Lane strode up the center aisle, through the gate, and stood facing the bench. He was dressed in a neatly ironed, well-worn shirt, blue cotton trousers, also neatly ironed, and shined black shoes, a picture of a hard-working young man who intends to be on the rise.

He was sworn by the Clerk and took his seat. Tom walked to face him, being careful to give the jury an unimpeded look at this well-groomed young man who was about to testify for the defense.

Please state your name and address." he asked.

"James G. Lane. I am an account executive for Liberty Life Insurance Company. I live in an apartment in the Southland Inn on Second Street, here in Truro."

"Mr. Lane, do you know the defendant?"

"No, I do not."

"Do you have any information about this case?"

"Yes. That is the reason I came to your office Friday morning of last week. I had attended the magistrate's hearing, the day before, and was disturbed by the testimony offered by the same two witnesses we have heard today."

What disturbed you?"

"I had heard it before."

How could you have heard it before?"

Lane grinned, an easy smile that had no hint of embarrassment as he recounted his story. "I have a girlfriend, Mr. Stone. We see each other a couple of times a week. There's not very much to do in Truro—ride around, or go to a roadhouse for a snack or a meal. Sometimes my friend and I drive down to a spot on the river and park the car. We have found a quiet little clearing in the woods by the bank where we can hear the water and spread a blanket in complete privacy. It's nice."

"What does that have to do with this case?"

"We were there in our private place a week or two ago. The evening didn't turn out to be peaceful at all."

"How do you mean?"

"There was a group having a few drinks not far from us. They got a little loud, and began to argue. It was beginning to be uncomfortable for us, but eventually the sheriff and his deputies arrived and took them away."

"So you and your girlfriend packed up and went home?"

"No, we stayed right there and enjoyed our private time, finally. Then about an hour later when we were ready to get back in the car and call it a night, some more visitors drove up in a pickup truck and began having a meeting.

"What kind of a meeting, Mr. Lane?"

"They were planning how best to pin the blame of the fire at the gin on some colored man, named Pete. They argued over how to go about it, how to get their stories straight. We could hear every word."

"Do you know who these men were?"

"Sure I do. I've lived in Truro all my life. I recognized their voices, and knew right away who was doing the talking."

"Can you tell the court who you overheard doing this plotting?"

"Sure. The same two people who testified earlier, Jake Bottoms and Dunk Pate."

"Were they the only ones there?"

"No. There were four. George Sampson seemed to be the leader, and I don't know who the fourth one was."

"This is the same George Sampson who was the owner of the gin that burned to the ground?"

"Yes"

The courtroom was buzzing with talk and whispers as the audience heard the unexpected testimony. Judge Wayne rapped his gavel to restore order.

Tom continued. "Mr. Lane, you have said that your girlfriend was with you and heard the men as they talked. Is she present here today, and is she willing to take the stand and back up your story?"

"Yes sir, she is here, sitting in the rear. Her name is Bonnie Clark."

Tom turned to Mr. Daniels. "I have no further questions of Mr. Lane. Would you like to cross-examine?"

The obviously unsettled prosecutor shook his head. "I will defer until later," he said.

"The defense calls Bonnie Clark," Tom announced.

There was a stir in the courtroom as Bonnie swayed her way to the front, in much the same way she had promenaded to the kitchen at the Sanitary Café. Aware that every eye was on her, she made the most of her moment, hips gyrating from side to side, one arm swinging lazily, the other hand resting on her hip.

Wilson and Mary Jones exchanged amazed looks. "That's Bonnie, from the Café!," Mary whispered. He nodded excitedly and quickly turned his attention back to the front, where Bonnie was being sworn.

"Please tell us your name and address," Tom asked.

"Bonnie Clark," she replied demurely. I live at 43 Evergreen Street in Truro."

"Miss Clark, do you know the preceding witness, Mr. James Lane?"

"Oh, yes, I certainly do!" she said with emphasis.

"Were you and Mr. Lane at the riverbank on the night of the events he described?"

"Yes, sir," she replied, smiling at the memory.

Did the events of that evening unfold in the same way Mr. Lane related them to the court?"

"Oh, yes, sir," she said smiling again.

"And did you overhear these three men plotting, if you would use that word, to put the blame for the gin fire on a colored man? What did they say?"

"One of 'em said he'd be glad to testify he saw the man light the fire—and the other one said he would, too! Then they got in a discussion about who would say what. I thought they'd never get it straight so we could go home." She leaned conspiratorially toward the judge and whispered to him, "Them boys ain't too bright, if you ask me!"

Tom then said, "Any questions, Mr. Prosecutor?"

Daniels, obviously stunned by the turn of events, shook his head.

"The defense rests, your honor," said Tom, who took his seat, receiving a congratulatory 'pat on the back' from Sam Bedenbaugh.

"Mr. Daniels, you may sum up," said Judge Wayne.

Daniels rose from his chair, faced the jury, and began. "Gentlemen of the jury, you have heard the testimony of two witnesses who saw the defendant, Pete Bates, acting in a suspicious manner while throwing lighted cigarettes into combustible material. This action took place almost immediately after he had been fired from his long-time job by the gin owner. Surely this was an attempt on the part of the defendant to 'get even' with his former employer. The fact that no alibi was offered for the defendant that could account for his whereabouts and actions in the time frame following his firing and the start of the fire is a further indication that he is the arsonist who started a terrible fire and then skipped town. You should have no trouble finding Pete Bates 'guilty as charged. Thank you."

"Your turn, Mr. Stone," said the judge.

As Tom stood and faced the jury box, he received an encouraging pat and a whispered "Give 'em hell, Son!" from Sam Bedenbaugh.

"Gentlemen of the jury," he began, "we have seen and heard some unusual testimony here today. We have heard two so-called witnesses testify that they saw Pete Bates acting in a 'curious way', throwing lighted cigarettes into cotton waste. They said nothing about seeing a spark, or fire, or smoke as a result of this observed action. They said they thought the action was 'strange', 'curious', 'dangerous', but neither one found their close friend, George Sampson and reported that Pete Bates was arousing their suspicions. Instead, they thought it was curious, talked about it being dangerous, and went back to town to sell catfish stew tickets! Poor George! He doesn't need more friends like that!

Then, the defense brings in two witnesses who testify that they overheard these same two witnesses for the prosecution plotting with their friend, George Sampson to pin the guilt for the gin fire on Pete Bates. Both Jake Bottoms and Dunk Pate said they would be glad to testify, five years after the fact, that they had seen Pete Bates set the gin on fire by throwing lighted cigarettes into cotton waste.

The testimony of the witnesses for the defense completely contradicts that of Jake and Dunk, in fact it makes their testimony untrue! Remember, they were overheard plotting the details of their yarn which was offered here today as evidence!

Gentlemen, in view of the flimsy and false evidence presented by the prosecution I urge you to find Pete Bates 'not guilty', and return him to the bosom of his family."

The jury received its instructions from Judge Wayne and filed into the jury room.

* * *

One hour later, the jury returned to the courtroom with a verdict of "Not Guilty".

The bailiff called out "All rise", and the judge made his exit. As soon as his door closed, hubbub turned to pandemonium as Daisy and her children made a dash for Pete, crying in relief and practically bulldogging him to the floor in their exuberance,

Tom and Sam Bedenbaugh stood in place, shaking hands with each other, silly grins on their faces. "I knew you could do it, boy!, said the older man, his pride in his friend's son showing in every line in his face.

Wilson made his way to the back of the courtroom, where he found Jim Lane and Bonnie. "Jim," said Wilson, "how lucky that you and Bonnie overheard those people plotting—and how great of you to come forward and testify! Your testimony made all the difference!"

"Well, Wilson, I really hate to see a group of people gang up on somebody. It happened to me once or twice, and it's no fun. I've learned a little bit about being fair since our high school days, Wilson."

"Jim, did you know that Pete Bates is Sim's daddy? That's Sim, right over there."

"No, I didn't know, but I'm glad I was able to help Sim and his family. He was always fair to me, even when I picked on him that summer with Elijah."

Wilson then turned his attention to Bonnie. "Hi, Bonnie. My mama's on her way back here to speak to you. We haven't seen you in a long time. You look mighty pretty."

"Thanks, Wilson. Jim has a lot to do with how I look," and she smiled at her boyfriend.

Mary came up then, and gave Bonnie a big hug. "Thank you both for your testimony," she said.

The Joneses excused themselves and broke away to go back up front and congratulate the Bates family and the lawyers. Mary gave Daisy a hug, and they cried together, tears of relief and joy.

Wilson greeted the ex-prisoner, Pete, and said, "Welcome to the outside. I'm glad you can see the light of day and know you don't have to go back in that place."

"You mighty right, Wilson. I think I owe you a bunch. They tell me you the one who got Mr. Tom on my case."

"If I helped. I'm glad I could. Sim would have done the same for me."

Josh Bridges pushed his way through the crowd. "I'm saving your place on the crew, Pete. Why don't you take two days off and come to work Thursday."

"You mean I still got a job? Thank ye, Mr. Josh!"

Sim and Dinah smiled their thanks to Wilson as the family was leaving the courthouse.

Tom Stone and Sam Bedenbaugh, the victorious lawyers, walked arm in arm across the street to Tom's office, where they found Virginia wreathed in smiles. "I'd offer you two champions a fresh cup of coffee, but I seem to remember some talk about brandy. So, being an efficient secretary, I've brought out the brandy, and two glasses!"

"In addition to being an efficient secretary, Virginia, you are absolutely beautiful when you smile like that and have a bottle of brandy in your hand," Sam beamed. "Tom, don't you have a third glass in this establishment so the beautiful Virginia can join us?"

"I'll bet we do. Where do we keep them, beautiful Virginia?"

"If you boys keep this up, all the flattery will go to my head—along with the brandy! Here's a third glass."

They toasted each other and went over the details of the case, roaring with glee in recalling the expressions on the faces of the two witnesses when Jim Lane cut their stories to ribbons.

"And Daniels just shook his head in disbelief when his case evaporated before his very eyes!"

"You want another brandy, Sam?"

"Sure, if there's some left."

Tom decided to 'pass', since he had promised to drive Sam back to Chester.

After some more self-congratulation and laughter, the two happy lawyers climbed into Tom's car and drove off to Chester, after giving Virginia the rest of the day "off".

* * *

Wilson and his mother walked straight to High Street. Irene Stone had been sitting there all alone since lunch, and they wanted to tell her of the great victory as soon as they could. They walked into her sitting room wearing broad smiles, and as she saw them her face lighted up, and she said, "You don't have to tell me! I can see it in your faces. We won!"

"That's right, Irene! We won! Your wonderful son tore their case to shreds. They were so badly beaten that Tom asked the jury for a ruling of Not Guilty, and it didn't take the jury long to agree!

Wilson broke in. "Tom is driving Mr. Sam home to Chester, and I guess he'll be home before too much longer. They were two happy lawyers!"

Irene Stone spoke directly to Wilson. "Son, I'm very proud of Tom's skill in his profession, and I'm proud of the way he treats people. But, Wilson Jones, I'm really proud of you and your concern for Sim and Pete and their family. I believe that if it had not been for you, speaking up to Tom, none of this would have happened, and Pete would be on his way to the penitentiary! That's the way I see it, and I say 'thank you' to you, so your mother can hear it."

Mary's heart gave one or two extra beats at hearing this praise for her son.

* * *

Daisy and Pete rode home in Sim's pickup with their entire family. The jubilant boys and girls were grinning all over themselves, holding on to each other and the sides of the truck to keep from falling off.

"You chillun be careful! You're old enough to know to hang on," Daisy cautioned. When they reached home, everyone found a seat in the yard. It was a beautiful early June day. No mosquitoes, yet, to speak of, and the humidity had not reached the fever pitch it would attain in a few weeks.

"Man, I can't believe we are all sittin' here grinnin', and Daddy is out of that jail, and doesn't have to go back!" chortled Frank-o. "Things really looked bad this morning in court when those white men started lyin' about what happened."

"What I find hard to believe is that Jim Lane is the fellow that wiped out their story—and a couple of years ago he was on my back all that summer we were using axes at the State Park. It was 'nigger' this, and 'nigger' that—Wilson and I saw him every day that summer, and I don't believe he ever called me 'colored' the whole summer! 'Nigger'!" he snorted.

"Maybe he got educated when he got out of school and started selling insurance to colored people," Pete suggested. "Maybe learned some manners, too. And speakin' of manners, don't y'all let me forget to go by Mr. Tom's big old house Sat'day morning to see what work he wants me to do. When he offered to take my case, I told him I'd work for him on Sat'days 'til I paid off his bill."

Back on High Street, after their supper, Wilson and Tom chatted happily about the day in court, and they each gave the other credit for setting Pete free. Tom was exhilarated by the victory, but as soon as the excitement wore off, his energy went with it. The tension of the case had taken its toll. He realized he was exhausted, and he soon found his way to bed.

Wilson, however, picked up the phone and called Betsy. "Hello?" she answered when she picked up.

"Hi, Betsy, it's me."

Oh, Hi."

We won the case today. Sim's daddy was ruled "not guilty", and he's a free man. Out of jail, home with his family."

"Why, Wilson, that is just wonderful! I want to hear all about it!"

"Well, I called to see if I can come over this evening and see you, and tell you about it..."

"Well... actually, this is not a good time. There's someone here now, for the evening. Can we make it some other time?"

"Sure. I guess so...Why don't I give you a call tomorrow?"

"That'll be good. I'll listen for your call."

"Thanks. I'll call tomorrow afternoon. Good night."

He put down the telephone and thought, "What in the world? Has college started already?"

His feelings were bruised, to say the least.

The next morning after breakfast he sat down with his mother to talk seriously about enlisting. The day was Tuesday, and Tuesday was the day the Army Recruiter would be at the Truro Post Office.

"Mama, I think I might as well go on and sign up. There's not anything for me to do in Truro that has any future in it, and the sooner I get started, the sooner I get on the road to opportunity for advancement. According to the Recruiter, the Army offers lots of career paths, but you were there with me, you heard all that."

"Yes, Son, I heard all that, and I'm sure what he told you is correct. I just want to make sure you realize you'll be signing up for three whole years. After you sign, you can't change your mind, and you have to go wherever they send you. You understand that?"

"Yes, ma'am, I understand that."

"I'll hate to see you leave. You're all I have, and we've been mighty close....but if this is really what you want to do, I won't stand in your way. You're eighteen years old now, and a man. If the Army wants you, and you want the Army, that's a good match. Do I have to sign anything so you can enlist?"

"No'm. The Recruiter says if I'm eighteen I can do it on my own.

"Well, go on down to the Post Office, then, and get it done. I'm very proud of you, Wils!"

Wilson entered the Post Office lobby and found the Recruiting Sergeant sitting at his desk, waiting for someone to talk to.

"Well, Sergeant! Today's the day!"

"Morning, Jones. Do you mean today is the day you're going to enlist?"

"That's what I mean!"

"Well, congratulations! Have a chair and let's get started!

Wilson and the recruiter spent an hour together, talking, asking questions, filling out forms. Wilson learned that he would receive notification, by mail, that his enlistment was accepted, pending the results of his mental and physical examinations. Both these tests would be administered at Camp Jackson in Columbia after he reported for duty. A bus ticket to Columbia would be sent him by the Army, and he would be met at the Columbia bus depot by Army personnel.

"Jones, you have made a wise decision. By enlisting now, you will be in the front of a long line of thousands who will be coming into the Army in the next year. This will put you in excellent position for advancement. Again, congratulation!"

Feeling very heroic and wise, Wilson walked out of the Post Office and continued toward town. He entered Truro Hardware and waited to speak to Matt Sttokes when he was not busy with a customer.

"Morning, Wilson!" Matt greeted him. "Your trial turned out just the way you wanted it, I think, and right quickly, too!"

"Yep. Tom did a wonderful job with those two witnesses, and after 'James G Lane's' testimony, all they could do was slink away! The case was over!"

"I know you are pleased about that, and I am too. That Bates fellow is your friend's father, isn't he?"

"Sure is, and now he's out of jail, and already has his old job back. They are happy!"

"Hey, Wilson, you are a high school graduate now. How does it feel? What are your plans?"

"That's what I came by to talk to you about, Matt. I've been thinking, and looking around for a line of work that offers a future, and I've decided that kind of job doesn't exist around Truro, without education or family connection.

Matt nodded.

"So, I have decided to join the Army. It will undoubtedly be growing much larger, with the Draft, so I decided to sign up this morning and get ahead of the rush."

"You mean you enlisted—today?"

"Sure did. They'll have me report to Camp Jackson in a month."

"Well, sir! You're a man who can make up his mind and move along with a decision! You don't let any grass grow under your feet! Hey, Sam! Come listen to Wilson's news! This man has up and joined the Army!"

The three talked excitedly for several minutes, then Wilson said, seriously, "Matt, I expect you'll be looking for someone to take my place here. If you don't find him right away, I sure would like to work a few hours each week until I leave. Need a little money from time to time, you know."

"Sure, Wilson, why don't you come in Thursday and Friday afternoons, and all day Saturday."

"Thanks, Matt! I really appreciate how nice you've been to me!"

"You're a good worker, boy."

* * *

It was nearing the noon hour, so Wilson returned to High Street for dinner. 'Dinner' In the Carolinas in the Thirties was generally served in the middle of the day, and it was followed by a lighter meal, 'supper', in the evening. Of course, if members of the family were working, and not able to come home for a meal in the middle of the day, the order of the meals was reversed, and 'lunch' was the midday meal.

The two primary topics of conversation at the dinner table that day were yesterday's trial and Wilson's enlistment. Tom related how friends and acquaintances had stopped by the office to congratulate him on his victory. He also told of the two times he had been snubbed on the sidewalk by men who, undoubtedly, had been in sympathy with George, Jake and Dunk (and the Klan).

Wilson fielded questions from the Stones and his mother about his meeting with the recruiter and his expectation of receiving orders to report to Camp Jackson within a month.

"A month?" his mother reacted in disappointment. "So soon?"

"Yes'm. I want to get there and get started."

That's a good plan, Wilson," reassured Tom. "You'll be well ahead of the first draftees. You might even be selected to train them."

"Well, none of us knows much about the Army, yet. We'll just have to wait and see what happens," said Wilson, sounding wise beyond his years.

"And, there's some good news from the hardware store. Matt is going to look for someone to replace me, but he says I can work several hours a week until I leave. That will give me a little 'walking-around' money."

"That is so nice of Mr. Stokes. He has really been a good man for you to work for, and a good friend," Mary said.

"He knows a good man when he sees one," Irene Stone opined, loyally.

* * *

After helping his mother clear away the dinner dishes, Wilson picked up the phone and called Betsy. "Hello," he said, I'm wondering if you'd like to talk this afternoon. That is, if you're free." He was still feeling the rebuff of the night before, and couldn't help the 'dig' of 'if you're free'.

"Yes, I'm free. What time did you have in mind?"

"What about four o'clock?"

"That's great. I'll look for you."

At 3:30 he washed his face and hands, put on a fresh shirt and walked the several blocks to her house on Kershaw Street. He mounted the steps and gave the front door his jaunty 'shave and a haircut' knock.

She came promptly to the door and greeted him enthusiastically. "Hey, Wilson, come in! Or would you rather sit in the swing, like the old days, or maybe you'd rather walk, as you said?"

"Let's begin by walking, and maybe we'll graduate to the other things later."

Betsy called back toward the rear of the house. "Mother! We're going to take a little walk".

As they sauntered down the sidewalk, she said, "Wilson, I want you to tell me all about the trial. I think it's absolutely wonderful that Sim's daddy is free! I wanted to go to the courthouse and listen, but Mother wouldn't hear of it. Wish I'd been there."

"It was exciting. In the beginning it looked pretty bleak for Pete, that's Sim's father. But you'll never guess who showed up to testify,sand his testimony actually turned the tide and exposed the lies in the so-called witnesses' story right out in the open for all to see!"

"Who was it?"

"Our friend Jim Lane!"

"That awful boy? What did he know about it?"

Then Wilson went through the trial in detail, telling her what Jake and Dunk claimed to have seen, and then told her about Jim Lane and his girlfriend Bonnie being on a blanket in the vicinity of the river bank and being able to hear everything that went on.

"My Lord!" Betsy said. "If I'd been on a blanket at the river with a man, I'd have been mortified to get up in court and admit it, in front of all those people! My Lord, Miss Agnes!!"

"Well, she did, and he did, and thank Goodness for it. He told me afterward he hated to see people gang up against a person. Said it had happened to him a time or two, and it's rough. Said Sim had always been decent to him, though he admitted he had many times not been decent to Sim. Just goes to show, you never know!"

So Sim's daddy is free now?"

Free as a breeze. He goes back to his old job Thursday."

She changed the subject. "So what are you doing now, with no school and no trial?"

"I had a big morning, this morning. You remember I told you I've been thinking of enlisting, since I have no connections to get a good job, and no prospects of being able to go to college to be trained for a good job. I've been talking to the recruiter for several weeks. He comes to the Post Office each Tuesday. This morning I went there and signed up. I enlisted, and will report to Camp Jackson in about a month.

Her face fell. "You really did it! Already? I was hoping you wouldn't go through with it. What did your mother say?"

"She said if I am sure that's what I want to do she won't stand in my way. ' And whatever you put your hand to, do the best you can,' she said."

"Oh, wow," she said, in a hollow voice. When will I ever see you again, if you're in California or Arizona, or some far-distant place like that?"

"Well, I may stay in Columbia, or North Carolina or Georgia. And you're going off to Concord College for four years! I'm only enlisting for three!"

"Well, I wish you would wait at least until the end of summer vacation. I really don't want you to go at all, and certainly don't want you to go far away. Remember, two weeks ago we were talking about 'love'?"

"Sure I remember. That was some great conversation. I loved the evening. It was special, and I still feel the same way about you that I did then. That's why I wanted to see you last night, but you were tied up. Can I ask you, was it a date?"

Hesitantly, she replied, "Yes, it was a date my mother arranged for me. She wanted me to meet this boy from Chester who is to be a sophomore at Woolford next year. Woolford and Concord are located in the same town, you know."

"No, I didn't know that until you told me. I'm not 'up' on colleges... So your mother is getting you set up for next year, is she? Not even waiting until I get out of town?"

"That date was not something I wanted to do, Wilson. She made me do it."

They walked in silence back to Kershaw Street. When Betsy reached her front door, she turned to him, kissed him on the cheek, and said, "Please don't be angry with me, Wilson. She insisted on setting it up."

"I still love you, Betsy, but I have a bad case of hurt feelings." He turned away to return home, and she went inside.

Wilson walked back home, shaking his head. "Women!", he said, dumbfounded. "Last week we were talking about 'love'. Yesterday, she was entertaining somebody else at her house. Today, she's all out of joint over my decision to leave town and look for my Future in the Army!"

* * *

Over the next two weeks Wilson managed to see all the people he cared about, telling them of his decision to seek a career in the Army, and thanking them for their kindness to him over the years. He spent an evening with Sim, Dinah and Mose Harrington. He realized that he felt closer to Sim than anyone else, with the exception of his mother, and also excepting Betsy. He and Sim had been comrades in the woods with their axes, had drunk from the same dipper, had counseled each other in times of decision. They had no secrets from each other. They had a grand time reminiscing about their younger days.

He respected Mose Harrington as a man of honor and integrity, and Dinah as a sweet loving wife to Sim. He had grown very fond of her. "I hope, when the time comes for me to get married, I can do as well as you, Sim," he said in the presence of all three.

He also went by the Sanitary Café for a goodbye visit with Frank Zervos, the former employer of his mother. Frank had fed him on many occasions with choice bits of food. "You gotta good head on your shoulders, Wilson. Use it, and be careful! Here, if you're going home, take this piece of pound cake to your family!"

He encountered Jim Lane outside the Post Office one afternoon and they spent a good while in conversation. Again, he thanked Jim for his testimony that freed Pete Bates from jail. Jim dismissed that with a wave of his hand. "Don't say nuthin' more about that, Wilson," he said. "I used to be one way—my way—and thought everybody was against me. That was when we were in school. But I've grown up some, and I don't like to see people get the shaft! In my business, collecting insurance premiums, I've found it best to treat people fair, ''cause 'what goes around, comes around'.

"Did I ever tell you about the time I almost got beat up?" Wilson shook his head. Jim continued. "It happened a year or so ago. I had been fishing out at 'Old Man' Jackson's millpond. Had the best luck I've ever had in my fishing life. Later I was walking back home with maybe twenty nice fat br'im, each one about the size of your hand. Happy as I could be, walking along, whistling. Then, out of the bushes by the side of the road stepped three colored men, all of 'em bigger'n me. They greeted me, nice as you please, then asked me to hand over the fish. I said 'No'. They grinned like they were glad of what was going to happen. Then they kinda spread out a little and came closer, so I was more or less surrounded.

I figgered I was in for it, and was thinkin' about handin' the fish over, 'cause I knew if I didn't I'd get my butt kicked…when down the road behind them came another colored man, older. He saw what was happenin' and started hurryin' toward us. I figgered he was comin' to join 'em and the odds would be worse, but he called 'em off and sent 'em home. Guess he might have been their daddy. Whatever he was, he saved my skin from a bad whipping. That's why I'm not too comfortable when a group starts ganging up on somebody."

Jim continued. "So you're going in the Army? I just might think about doing that myself. This job is OK, but I'd hate to think about doing it the rest of my life."

In another week, Wilson's orders arrived, along with a bus ticket to Columbia for June 28th. He worked his last day at Truro Hardware, feeling very sentimental as he bid Matt and Sam good-bye.

On the afternoon of the 27th he telephoned Betsy to tell her he would be leaving the next day. "Wilson," she said, "I'm sorry I hurt you by dating that Woolford boy. Mother says I need friends who are 'fraternity men', and she set it up, but he wasn't all that cute. I would much rather have been with you. It's true I am disappointed to see you leave us, but that's your decision to make, and you've made it. I'll never forget our high school days and the good times we had. Please write to me, and I'll do the same."

She paused for a second, then asked, "Cowboy, what time does your Bus leave tomorrow?"

"8:30", he replied.

"Would it be all right if I walk down to the bus station to see you off?"

He hesitated for a split second, while his heart threw in an extra beat. The hesitation was just long enough for her to consider retrieving the question, but then he said, "Gosh, Betsy, do you want to do that? I thought—that is, I thought you—*Yes!* I'd love for you to see me off! Mama will be there, of course..."

"I figured she would be there, and, if you really don't mind, I'll be there, too."

Wilson spent the evening at home with his mother, and Tom and Irene Stone. They talked about all the things, and events, they'd shared since Wilson and his mother had moved to town in January, five short months before. When they went to bed Miss Irene was almost in tears. She had grown very fond of Wilson.

Tom bade him "Good Night", making an effort to hide the sentiment he was feeling for this young man who had entered his life four years before and had become such an integral part of the events that followed.

Wilson and Mary had a longer conversation in the privacy of her room. They talked about the early days, when Dave had been healthy and a vital part of the little family. They talked about his illness, and the trips to Columbia to see him. They talked about how, through hard work and co-operation, the two of them had been able to survive those hard years when they were alone on Juniper Road. They both wept, a little, or a lot, contemplating their closely shared life, and thinking ahead to the months of separation in the unknown future.

Wilson thought, and said, "We are so lucky, Mama, that I am leaving you in such a good situation, rather than in our little house out on Juniper Road. Here you have a job paying cash money, room and board; companionship with that sweet Miss Irene who cares a great deal about you, and also, you're in town instead of the being all alone on Juniper Road out in the country."

* * *

The next morning, they all rose early so Mary could fix Wilson a full breakfast, one that would 'stick to his ribs'; grits, scrambled eggs, breakfast bacon and toast. After the soon-to-be-soldier had demolished his repast, he told the Stones good-bye once again and he and Mary walked downtown to the bus station.

Betsy was already there, dressed in a fluttery cotton dress with a full skirt, her hair shining. She greeted Mary warmly, then turned to Wilson. "Wilson…" she began, then stopped. "Cowboy," she began again, I'm really going to miss you, and I want us to write, to stay in touch. Will you write me?"

"You bet I will, Betsy,' he replied, and made a move to kiss her. She met him halfway (at least) and they kissed emphatically.

"Bye, Wilson! Bye, Mrs. Jones!" Betsy said as she ran from the bus station toward her house, eyes streaming.

The Trailways bus rolled into the station. Wilson gave his mother a hug and a kiss. Carrying a small package containing a toothbrush, shaving equipment, his pocketknife, a pen and writing paper, he boarded the bus for Columbia and Camp Jackson.

Made in the USA